THE LIES BETWEEN US

THE DEVILS DUST
book four

M.N. FORGY

I dedicate this book to those who were underestimated,

and to those who fucked up and need

a second chance at making things right.

Love is raw, and hurts... but that's

how you know it's real... you feel.

Think twice about the people you think are of lesser value,

one could turn out to be

the most important person in your life one day.

1

Cherry

SIX YEARS BEFORE

MY HEAD IS SPINNING, AND MY BODY FEELS LIKE DEAD WEIGHT. I'm falling into everything, as if I were top-heavy, and can barely stand straight. I lick my lips, and they tingle with an unusual sensation. I giggle and trip on my heels, falling right into a dresser. My elbow crashes into it, but it doesn't hurt. Though I doubt I'll be saying the same thing in the morning.

"I am so fucked up," I slur. I drank way too much. I smoked too much. Drugs and liquor don't mix well. My brother Tyler threw a party for landing his first DJ gig and invited everyone he knew.

"How many have you had to drink?" I look behind me and see two Erics. *God, two of him is way better than one.* I blink my eyes rapidly, and he finally comes into focus along with the rest of the room. A bedroom. *How did I get in here?* His arms are so muscular from college football. He's played since high school; only before he was a bully to me. Always teasing me and calling me names. Now, he wants me, and has been flirting with me all night. He closes the gap between us and I stop giggling.

"You wanna fool around?" he whispers into my ear, his breath smelling of alcohol. I throw my head back and laugh.

"And why would I want to do that? You used—" I pause, trying to get my thoughts right. "You used to make fun of me in high school." I sway on my heels, the drugs and booze wreaking havoc on my balance. He tilts his head to the side, his long, blond hair falling to his chin.

"Did I now?" His voice comes out like silk, enveloping me in a warm cocoon.

"Freckled-face Lindsay Cole, has an ugly pie hole." I shake my head. Hearing the words leaving my lips sound just as ridiculous as they did back then.

He laughs and rubs at his chin. "Yeah, well, that was high school." He steps forward and grabs my hips. His touch shoots sparks through my body, and I mewl in response. Drunk Lindsay has no control of her sexual reactions, apparently.

"You were just a girl." He pulls his brows together. "You've really filled out nicely since then." He chuckles and tilts his head back, assessing me. "Are you still a girl, Lindsay, or has some lucky man made you into a woman?" My body sobers, and my legs clench beneath my little pink dress.

"Wh-what?" I stammer, my eyes widening. Eric smiles and pulls away from me. He kicks the door shut, the music from the party drowned out instantly.

"I am going to take that reply as you're still a virgin." He turns and pulls his shirt over his head, revealing all his muscled glory. I sway and lean over, trying to get my fucking eyes to focus on his lean torso.

"Oh, wow," I mutter. He steps forward and grasps my hips,

walking me backward until the backs of my knees hit the bed.

"I'm going to make you a woman tonight, Lindsay Cole," he whispers as my back presses into the mattress. I close my eyes and sigh.

Finally. Eric McCormick wants me. For some reason, I feel like everything I ever wanted to achieve as a naïve nineteen-year-old has just been accomplished.

◆◆◆

Eight Weeks Later

I cough and choke on my thick saliva over the toilet.

"Just puke already," I slur, trying to encourage my body to give in to the nausea. I've been sick for two weeks and cannot for the life of me shake this fucking flu. My brother Tyler hangs out at those stupid clubs; he probably gave me something.

I stand and wipe my mouth with the back of my hand, my mission to vomit failing for the fifth time this morning. *When I see Tyler, I'm going to chew him out and then demand he make me a grilled cheese sandwich with chicken noodle soup for getting me sick.*

I zombie-walk into the living room, my tongue filling my mouth like it's too big while my gag reflex is twitching with the urge to puke again. I close my eyes and swallow hard, trying to get a hold of myself. Slowly opening my eyes, I spot Tyler putting groceries away. I don't live here, but I visit often. I moved out of the house when I was young. I couldn't stand my father punching me in the face anymore so I said fuck it and bolted. I have learned to handle things on my own, and not expect others to do things for me. Tyler offered our old trailer to me once our dad moved out. He found some butch-looking woman who drove a Mac truck and ran off with her. Good

3

riddance. I took the trailer 'cause living in a shelter sucks, and I was done spending sweltering nights in my car. But, I hate that fucking trailer. It brings back too many memories.

"Damn, Lindsay, you look like shit," Tyler states, putting some cereal in a cupboard.

"I feel like shit," I groan, plopping on the couch. I can't stand this couch. The material feels like old yarn, and it's rough and itchy against my skin.

"How long have you been sick?" Tyler questions. I turn in my seat and look at him. His hair is dyed black, with some blue and red streaks through it. Piercings in his eye and nose shine with the sun coming through the blinds. He looks like a punk.

I shrug. "About two weeks."

Tyler shakes his head. "You got a fever?"

"Nah, no fever. Just tired and feel like throwing up. I can't shit, either." I lay my head down on the couch and yawn.

"You pregnant?"

My eyes snap open in panic. I sit up and look over the couch, leveling Tyler with a look of dread.

"You better go get a test. Then tell me the fucker you screwed so I can tear his nuts off."

"Fuck," I whisper, throwing my head into my hands.

"I got one in the bathroom. Go piss on it. Now!" Tyler points to his bedroom that holds a private bathroom. I tilt my head to the side and squint my eyes.

"Why do you have—"

"This chick I was fucking thought she was knocked up. I bought the whole damn shelf," he informs. I roll my eyes. That doesn't surprise me. Tyler is a player when it comes to girls.

I find the test under the sink and piss on it quickly. Setting it on the counter, I turn, waiting for it to show a plus or negative sign.

"What's it say?" Tyler mumbles from the other side of the

door.

"I can't look," I mutter, not sure if he even heard me. I can't look at it 'cause I know what it will say. It'll say I'm pregnant. Pregnant with Eric McCormick's child.

Tyler pushes into the bathroom. My back is still turned and I'm facing the tub, the test sitting on the sink behind me. I hear him sigh loudly, and with that exhale, my heart literally sinks into the pit of my stomach.

"You're pregnant."

"No," I whisper, tears filling my eyes. He grabs me and engulfs me in his arms. I sob 'cause I'm too young to be a mother. I cry because Eric McCormick would be a shittier dad than I would a mom.

"Shhh. It's okay. You can do this, Lindsay," my brother comforts. This is why I love him. Granted, growing up we did the typical brother and sister shenanigans—he'd destroy my Barbies, and I would annoy him and his friends. But we always had each other's back. My mother left when I was a baby; being a mother just wasn't her forte, I guess. Our father became a drunk when I was around the age of six and was non-existent unless he was out of beer, which was when he was at his worst. My presence alone angered him; I think I reminded him of my mother. Tyler stepped in front of my father a few times, when our dad would get rough with me. It granted Tyler a broken arm once.

"Tell me, whose is it?" Tyler pushes me an arm's length away and searches my face. I bite my bottom lip, tears sliding down my cheeks.

"Eric's," I mutter, looking down.

"Fucking seriously, Lindsay?" Tyler knows how much of a hard time Eric gave me in high school.

"What can I say, I like the challenge. Bad boys." I shrug.

"Goddamn boy is about right!" Tyler hollers. He turns and

5

shoves his hand through his hair angrily before lowering his head. "Do yourself a favor and stay away from the *bad boys*, Lindsay. They're nothing but assholes who will just hurt you in the end." I cross my arms as a barrier to protect myself. Seeing Tyler disappointed stings.

"You didn't use any," he pauses, still not looking at me, "protection or anything?"

Wow, this is very embarrassing.

"We were really drunk," I explain. Tyler winces, like I just gave him a mental image.

"Look." Tyler glances up at me with dark eyes. "Go find that piece of shit, and tell him. Maybe he'll step up." Tyler shrugs. I roll my eyes and scoff. "Do it, Lindsay," Tyler's voice comes out bitter.

I roll my eyes and grab the pregnancy test off the counter. How do I begin to tell a one-night stand that I'm pregnant?

◆ ◆ ◆

Standing on the porch of Eric's house, my body trembles with the amount of adrenaline surfing through my veins. Fear wracks my kneecaps, and my fingers clench the pregnancy stick in my hand. Eric lives in the same trailer park I grew up in as a kid, so basically he's my neighbor. His father built this two-story house at the end of the park and gave it to Eric just recently. Told him to watch over the trailer park while his father and stepmom traveled the world. He's my landlord, in short.

Sweat cascades down my spine as I lift my fist and knock on the door. It swings open, and I gasp.

"Er- Eric," I stammer. I can't seem to speak; the words are lodged in my throat. That night after Eric took my virginity, I passed out and woke up with dried blood streaking down my legs and him gone. He's given me the cold shoulder since. I figured it was a one-night stand and brushed it off. I was so fucked-up I could barely remember any of it anyway. Don't get me wrong, it sucked knowing my first time was a one-night stand and not some love-struck moment you see on TV. But look at where I grew up—shit like that doesn't happen here.

"What do you want?" he questions, his tone harsh. He leans against the doorframe, one arm resting above his head. He's not wearing a shirt, and that six-pack I thought he had weeks before is definitely not a six-pack. Gotta love the fairytale effect alcohol can give.

"I need to talk to you," I reply meekly. I look past him and see a bunch of his buddies eyeing me. Buddies who used to join in with him bullying me in high school. Insecurities shift in my head, and I swallow hard.

He looks over his shoulder then back to me with a crooked smile. He knows I'm uneasy and is getting off on it. Asshole.

"Just spit it out and get the fuck off my porch." His words shoot straight to my heart like cancer. My blood runs toxic and my lips curl. Total prick!

"I'm fucking pregnant!" I snap.

His eyes go wide, and his friends go quiet. Eric glances over his shoulder with a look of embarrassment, and walks out of the house, slamming the door.

"What the fuck do you mean? You weren't on the pill?" He strides up to me, his body way too close.

I hold my hands out and push him away from me.

"No, I wasn't on the fucking pill. I was a virgin, you dumb-ass." I throw the pee stick at him.

"I don't want anything to do with it - with you." He holds his hands up and walks backwards like the baby growing in my belly might jump out at any minute.

"I can get an abortion or something," I mutter, not really

thinking. My brain feels stuffed, like it's at max capacity and pushing against my skull. All of this is happening at once and I can't deal. I press the heel of my hand to my forehead trying to ease the pain, the racing thoughts.

"What? Jesus, Lindsay. I guess you can just put me first on a long list of those, huh? They'll know you by name in a couple years, I bet." He chuckles, his tone back to that bully in high school. My hands clench, and I want to rip his smug face off his head. I don't want to give the baby up, I'm just nervous and word vomited before I could really think about what I was saying. This baby has a piece of me, and I would never harm him or her.

"But it's probably for the best looking at who her mother is," Eric clips. My heart sinks, knowing he would want to cause harm to our child just because of me though.

"Yeah, know what? I'll keep it and get your ass for every fucking dime." I turn to walk down the stairs and he grabs my arm.

"You wouldn't dare." His face holds a deathly promise, but I don't falter. Eric's real mother left his dad when Eric was young, after she bled his father dry for years. Everyone around the trailer park heard the fights late at night. I knew saying I would take all of Eric's money would spark his wick of anger.

"Try me, ass-wipe," I grit. He digs his hold into my arm, and I whimper.

"You don't want to mess with me. I know people, Lindsay Cole," he threatens. I bring my knee up and slam it into his balls. He instantly lets go of my arm and drops to the porch. If I learned anything from my piece-of-shit father, it's that the balls are your best option when you want to get away.

"You don't want to mess with me. I don't need people to do my dirty work, Eric. I'll just fucking tear you to shreds myself." I step over him, a smirk of pride fitting my face.

"I'm not scared of you, freckled-face Lindsay Cole." His voice is laced with a screech from the amount of pain he's in. I walk down the steps and flip him the bird. "Then you're one stupid motherfucker!"

◆◆◆

10 Months Later

"Judge, Mr. McCormick is an unacceptable guardian for the child. He-"

"I'm going to cut you off right there, counselor. Looking at Ms. Cole's file here, I would have to beg to differ," Judge Calhoun interjects. I swallow the dry lump in my throat, my tongue sticking to the roof of my mouth. A nervous sweat breaks out on my forehead. Judge Calhoun is an older man; his hair is curly and mostly white, with a few specks of black sweeping through the back. He's wearing rimless glasses that sit on the bridge of his nose, and he has that 'don't give me shit' look down pat.

"Judge, i-if I m-may," my lawyer stammers, and I give him a sideways glance. I couldn't afford a lawyer, so I was handed this fucktard, who doesn't seem to know what the hell he's doing. I can't tell if he's trying to be bad at this, or if he just sucks outright.

"No, you may not," the judge cuts him off. He holds up a piece of paper, tilting his head back to look through his glasses. "Lindsay Cole, two counts of theft, illegal substances, assault," Judge Calhoun rambles onward, reading my record of all the unlawful incidents I've been pegged for over time. *How does he have that shit on me?* He sighs and swipes his glasses off his face, narrowing his eyes at me like I'm the Devil. "She has a rap sheet a mile long. As for the father, he's as clean as a whistle. I think I would be doing this child a favor taking the mother out of the picture." I gasp with dread and pull on my lawyer's arm. My ears ring, and I feel like I may faint.

"How does he know about those things? All of it happened when I was underage," I whisper in disbelief. "You have to do something!" My lawyer has a look of ignorance written on his face, like he's in above his head, and my mouth pops open. I'm dumbfounded at how stupid he is for a fucking lawyer.

I avert my eyes from my lawyer and glance at Eric across the way. He's sitting back in his chair, an arrogant smirk across his face as if he doesn't have a care in the world. He thinks he's going to win this, and by the way this is going, he just might. Gah! I just want to slam his face into that table. My fingernails dig into my chair with the unbearable urge to do it. He doesn't want Piper; he just wants her so I can't tarnish his name. He wants to prove a point his father couldn't prove with his mother. He wants to hurt me 'cause he knows he can. That is who he is, after all; he's a bully and he won't change. A little boy with a magnifying glass, and I'm the ant that was stupid enough to walk right in his line of sight.

The gavel slams, making me jump.

"I've made my decision. Lindsay Cole, you are denied guardianship over Piper Cole. Full custody is granted to Mr. Eric McCormick."

The air is sucked from my lungs. "No!" I wheeze, shooting up from my chair. I glare at Eric, who is smiling proudly. Stepping forward, I'm more than ready to give myself the treat of slamming his face into that table. My lawyer grabs my arms, stopping me. "You'll be held in contempt if you touch him," he warns.

"No. He can't get away with this!" I scream, pointing at Eric.

My eyes fill with tears as my heart is smothered with the inevitable feeling of being empty. I carried Piper for nine months, had her naturally all on my own. Then he showed up at the hospital, and that was when it all went wrong. He saw how happy she made me, and he knew he could take it away... and he just did. This is a game to him. A tug of war based on control and I just fell on my ass, letting the rope slide against my palms.

◆ ◆ ◆

The courtroom is empty, but I can't seem to get my ass out of the chair. Everything from the moment I saw Piper's ultrasound picture, to hearing her heartbeat, and hearing her first cry play in my head. I sob. *How did that judge know all that about me? I thought those things were hidden from your record when you turned eighteen. Why didn't my lawyer fight for me?* I narrow my eyes and bite my lip in confusion. I need to know. I demand to know. I stand on shaky legs and walk to where the judge sat. He slipped into a room just behind his stand. I've heard voices muffled through the door for the last thirty minutes, so I know he's still here. I close my eyes and blow out a slow breath. Maybe if he sees how determined I am, he'll have second thoughts on his ruling. I push the door open and open my eyes. The judge is standing behind his desk, my lawyer standing beside him, and Eric and his lawyer standing on the other side of the desk. Eric's lawyer is handing Judge Calhoun and my lawyer a big stack of cash. I blink a couple times. *Surely this isn't real.*

"You paid him off?" I whisper, looking at the group dumbfounded. *That's* why my lawyer didn't fight for me. *That's* why the judge was so uncaring of a daughter needing her mother. He was being paid by Eric and his lawyer. Anger fills my veins.

The judge sighs and snatches the cash from the lawyer.

"Sit, Ms. Cole," the judge demands.

"No!" I respond firmly.

"Sitting would be in your best interest," he insists, counting his money. My nostrils flare as I inhale a breath of rage. "What is it you want? Money? Your daughter on the weekends? What? What will it take for you not to have seen this?" The judge sets the stack of cash on the desk and pinches the bridge of his nose.

My face cracks as my lips tremble with humor before I laugh. I laugh so hard, the group of dishonest bastards look at me as if I've gone crazy. Maybe I have.

"Oh, God," I mutter, my laughter gone and my voice cracking with emotion. I run my hand through my hair and put the other on my hip. *How can this be? I just walked in on the father of my child paying off my lawyer and the judge handling our custody battle. How many times has this judge and team of lawyers been paid off? How many mothers have lost their kids? How many people lost unfair cases?*

My eyes snap to theirs, my blood running ice-cold to the point goosebumps race up my arms.

"You know what? No." My voice is deadly serious.

"No?" The judge tilts his head to the side, confused.

"No. I am taking this higher. I will get my daughter the right way, and you guys will burn for this. I'll bury all of you to your fucking necks." I point at every one of them as I back my way out of the door. "This isn't over, Eric," I promise then hightail it out of there.

◆ ◆ ◆

Two Days Later

I pay for my pack of gum and leave the gas station, heading back to my car. I had reported the judge and the lawyers, and was waiting on a return call to reclaim my case with someone from the courthouse. They said they'd call me back with the next step, but the sound of their voice made me unsure. *Maybe I should go back and demand to talk to someone else.* The hairs on my neck suddenly stand as I pop a piece of gum into my mouth. My gaze slowly trails up the street, trying to find what has my body in a sense of alarm, when a green raggedy truck creeps beside the gas station. Men stand in the back, holding large guns. My breath shallows, and people begin screaming.

Pop Pop Pop sounds in the night air. I'm frozen with fear.

"Get down!" a man yells, knocking me to the ground. I look up from under the strange guy who is laying over me and see the green truck come to a stop.

"Did you get her?" one of the guys in the cab of the truck questions.

Sirens sound from afar, and fire spreads from one of the gas pumps.

"It doesn't matter. We got company. We'll go to her trailer and wait for her there!" Hearing those words, I knew right then they were sent from the judge and lawyers, maybe even Eric. My heart goes cold, and my hope of having my daughter back evaporates into ash, along with the piece of my heart that just died. I can't go home. I can't go to the police. I'm fucked. I'm alone. All because I wanted the attention of Eric fucking McCormick. Now I have it, and it's the last fucking thing I want.

◆ ◆ ◆

The car is hot and acting as a barrier against the breeze. Well, what breeze there is in the middle of summer in LA. Pulling my hair away from my sweaty face, I fan myself with my hand. I managed to get one guy to stop yesterday, so hopefully I can get another person to stop today. I have been living out of my car for two days now. I haven't contacted my brother, because I don't want whoever is trying to kill me to link us and put Tyler in danger. If they haven't already. Every day, I stop on the side of the road miles away from my old stomping ground and act as if my car is broken down. I've been conning men, women, anyone who stops. It's not something I'm proud of, but what choice do I have? I'm running and I'm desperate. I step out of the car, the back of my legs streaming with a steady sweat from the heat. Popping the hood of the car, I lean against the hot metal that makes up the front bumper. My eyes prick with tears that this is what it's come to. I lean my head back and close my eyes against the hot summer sun.

"God, give me a sign that you're up there and can see the pain I'm in," I whisper to myself. My family was never big on religion, but when you get desperate, when you reach the point nobody on Earth is going to help you, you pray that there *is* a higher power, something that can pull you from the dark pit you're in. You hope with all your might that things will get better; otherwise, why the hell are we even here?

A loud rumble speeds down the off ramp. I jump where I stand when I notice a motorcycle suddenly stop next to my car.

"Looks like you're having some car trouble." The man smirks, swinging his leg over his black bike. My mouth goes as dry from the heat wafting from the pavement. I can't reply because I'm dumbstruck. He is sexy. Fucking deliciously rugged and good enough to eat, in fact. He has short hair that's brown but with a tone of copper streaking through it when the sun shines on it just right. He has tattoos across his arms and a piercing in his lip that makes my panties instantly wet. He's wearing a leather vest and torn blue jeans. He looks so strong, and oozes bad guy. Staring at him, my body comes alive with a warmth I haven't felt since that night I got drunk with Eric. Only this warmth is much more intense.

"You okay?" he asks, the words falling from his mouth roughly. His shoulders are built, making his arms hang from his sides with a distance, his strides long and masculine. He looks massive, and delicious. I blink and open my lips to speak.

"Um, yeah. Yeah, I'm n-not sure what's wrong w-with it," I stutter on my words, trying to wake myself from eye-fucking him and wave my hand toward the car. It's a beat-up station wagon that has seen better days. With the hood up and the constant smoke rolling out from under it, it's easy to pull off that my car has broken down.

He bends over the car, eyeing the engine, and I take the opportunity to check him out. My eyes sweep down his muscled back; his tattooed biceps are built and stretching the sleeves on the white shirt he's wearing under his leather vest. His ass looks fit and hard. The way it appears in those jeans should be illegal.

He fiddles with caps and oil sticks under the hood, trying to figure out the problem, and I keep checking his hard body out, imagining what it would be like having it over me. *Yeah, 'cause the last time that happened it went so well.* I close my eyes and shake my head at myself, but I can't help but open them again and look back at his body. When my gaze catches his wallet, I'm reminded what I'm really after. Money. Food. Gas. I walk around him and trail my hand along his back seductively. His head slowly turns, eyeing my hand that caresses his shoulder. That's the key, getting him to focus on this hand instead of where I'm about to put my other hand.

"Yeah, I'm not sure what's wrong with it," I lie, trying to distract him. He looks at me from the corner of his eyes and smirks before sliding his tongue along his bottom lip. The way his tongue flicks his lip ring, I almost forget to swipe his wallet. Almost. I slide my finger along the top of the billfold and gently pull it loose at the same time I slip my hand off his back.

I shove the wallet down my shorts quickly as he continues to look at the engine. "I'll try and start it again," I offer. Side-stepping him, I crawl behind the wheel and start it with ease.

"Yup. I think it just got too hot or something." I shrug. He gives me a confused look and runs his hands through his hair.

"Yeah, I guess so," he replies softly.

"See you around." I give a little wave and watch him climb on his bike. He looks over his shoulder and pins me with a stare I'll never forget. A stare that says a thousand things. Like he doesn't want to go, that he wants to say something else. I don't want him to leave either, but I am in no position to be with anyone, no matter how fucking hot he is. I tear my eyes from his first and look at the seat beside me.

After he leaves, I open his wallet, reading his name, address, weight. All of it.

"Phillip DeLuca." I taste his name running off my lips as I trace my finger over his picture. He's so handsome. He's the kind of guy most people would be afraid of, but not me. I want to get to know him. Lost in a daydream, my car door is yanked open.

"Where the fuck is it, bitch?"

"What?" I shriek as I'm pulled out of the car and slammed forward onto the hot hood. "I don't have anything!" I scream, trying to pull free. He shoves me back down on the hood. His hand tangled in my hair.

"Don't think about moving," he spits, his tone harsh. I roll my eyes and continue leaning over the hood. My heart slams against my chest in pure panic, and my hands shake. He pulls away and leans in to the car. Within seconds, he finds his wallet. *Shit.*

He peers at me with a fierce energy in his eyes. The intensity has me pulling off the hood, scared out of my mind.

"You have some balls," he mutters, shoving his wallet back

in his pocket. His tone is soft and tender suddenly. I turn my head and eye him angrily.

"Fuck you." I cross my arms and lean my hip against the car. My choice of words more confident than I'm feeling.

He steps up to me and grabs my hips hard with both hands. My skin burns, and my mouth parts with desire. His brown eyes find mine, and his hands yank my body closer to his. I feel like all the air is sucked from my lungs as I search his dark eyes. Placing my hands on his solid chest to steady myself, my palms buzz with excitement.

"You'd like that, wouldn't you?" He looks me up and down and leans in close. "You'd like it if I pushed you over the hood of this car and fucked you 'til your legs gave out." His words feather against my lips, he's so close. I hold my breath, willing my body to pull away, but I don't move. Just when I think he's going to kiss me, he grabs my hand and pulls it upward. I furrow my brows and watch as he pulls a pen from his back pocket, pulling the cap off with his teeth. He writes his number and the word 'Lip' on my hand.

"Call me. Don't make me come find you, Cherry."

"Cherry?" I ask out loud.

"Your swimsuit," he yells over his shoulder before starting his bike. I look down at my white shirt noticing my cherry bikini peeking out from the bust line. A smile creeps across my face. I know I shouldn't like him, but I kind of do. Driving past me, he winks and I swear I sigh like a damn fool.

2

Cherry

SITTING IN THE CAR, I WATCH THE MOON RISE HIGH IN THE SKY. It's still hot out, and my legs stick to the seat of the car. I can't sleep, and all I can think about is Piper. I know it's stupid, but I want to go get her from Eric. I hate for her to think that I've given up on her, that I didn't fight harder for her. Looking at the moon, I sigh heavily.

I remember as a little girl how bad I wanted to know if my mom ever wanted me. I wonder if Piper will feel like that. The thought saddens me.

"I can't give up. Not yet," I mumble, sitting up in the seat of the car. Starting the engine, I pull onto the highway. I'm going to get my daughter back, damn it. I want my daughter, and I'll get her one way or another.

I drive and drive until I make my way to the trailer park. The sun is nearly rising by the time I finally reach the shitty area. My hands begin to build a nervous sweat, and my stomach flutters with unease to the point I may puke as I get closer.

I can't believe what I'm doing. I'm stupid. I'm being reckless.

I blow out an unsteady breath and pull into the circle drive, but I still don't turn around. I'm determined to continue my journey, even if it kills me.

"You can do this. You can do this," I whisper to myself. I don't even know what this is. All I know is I want my daughter back. I guess if I have to put a label on it, I'm kidnapping my daughter. Opening the car door, it creaks loudly and I wince. I slowly close it, hoping it doesn't make as much noise, but it does. Thankfully, nobody comes out to investigate the noise.

Looking the house over, I notice only two lights on. One on the second story and another in the front of the house. My best bet would be to enter from the back. I tiptoe around the house and chills run up my back, so I rub up and down my arms trying to smooth them away. Climbing the steps, I test the door to find it's unlocked. I shake my head; Eric is so fucking stupid to leave his house unlocked in this neighborhood.

Slowly, I push the door open and hear a TV playing in the front room. The house is dark, and nobody seems to be moving around, so I quietly proceed into what looks like a kitchen. Crying sounds from upstairs, and my eyes prick with tears. Piper. I step to where the TV is playing and find Eric passed out in a chair, his hands down his pants. This is it, my time to take Piper. I turn quickly and make my way up the stairs to the crying. I pass pictures of little Eric and his family, and find the one bedroom that is lit up. There, in a small white crib, is Piper. She has little red curls and is bundled in a white blanket. I sob and step closer, just wanting to feel her small little body in my arms.

"I wouldn't." I freeze, panicking. I turn slowly, finding an older lady with silver curls and a long, off-white pajama gown. "Lindsay, right?" I don't answer, frozen scared. "I get it. I knew you would show up. I'd expect it from any mother who cares about her child." She shuffles past me, and I frown in confusion. Is she just going to give me Piper?

I follow her into the room as she scoops up my little girl.

"I'm Eric's grandma, and I'm taking care of Piper. No need to worry." She pats Piper to soothe her.

"It's not fair," I mutter. I should be taking care of Piper. I *want* to take care of her, yet Eric just passes her off to anyone who will do his dirty work. Anyone but me that is.

Eric's grandma scoffs at my remark. "Get real, honey; nothing in life is fair." I scowl. "I've raised my children, yet here I am raising yours."

I close my eyes and shake my head, not wanting to hear that.

"You need to leave." Her voice cuts me, the words searing through my heart. I should have known it wouldn't have been as easy as sneaking into Eric's house and taking Piper.

"No, I am not leaving without my daughter." I lift my chin in confidence. The lady narrows her wrinkled eyes.

"I don't think you understand. Eric wants you dead. That judge wants you dead. You are a dead woman as long as you are around this little girl. How much are you going to help her if you're dead?"

"I can't just leave her with him," I cry, tears filling my eyes.

She looks at Piper then to me. "You're not; you're leaving her with me. I have another six or seven good years in me before Eric checks me into a nursing home. That's when she'll really need a mother, and that is when you need to come back." She looks up at me. "When Eric thinks you're gone, when you can put your emotions to the side and really fight for what you want in life."

"No. I can't leave her," I sob. I step up to her and rub my finger along Piper's cheek. It's so soft and silky.

"I'm afraid you don't have a choice." Her hand sweeps

beside her, grabbing a rifle. My body freezes, and my eyes widen.

"If I let anything happen to Piper, Eric has threatened to end my life, honey. So as much as I want you to be reunited with your daughter, it ain't happening," she sneers.

I look at the rifle then her. "I ain't leaving without her," I reaffirm, tears in my eyes.

"ERIC!" she screams. My eyes widen, and my heart jump starts in fear. "You better run," she whispers, her tone eerie. I look at Piper one last time, and then her.

"Go, before he finds you and knows you're alive," she mutters. I purse my lips, and as much as I don't want to, I pull away from Piper. I run down the stairs and out of the house as fast as I can, passing a sleeping Eric on the way, nearly tripping on my feet as I head toward my car. I jump in and look at Eric's house one last time. I don't want to leave, but if I stay it could get me killed.

"I'll be back, baby girl." I sob, starting the car. "I'll be back one day," I mutter, tears falling down my cheeks. I pull out onto the road and gun it, driving as fast as I can back to where I belong. Nowhere, and out of Piper's life.

◆ ◆ ◆

I sit in the car two freeways over from where I ran into Phillip yesterday. I thought about calling him. I more than thought about it actually, but I just can't. Men and I, we don't mix. Obviously. I just need to figure my shit out right now and not be distracted by some dirty-talking, rugged-looking biker guy. No matter how sexy he is; it's best if I keep my drama to myself. Like Tyler said, I need to stay clear of bad boys, and looking at Phillip I can tell he is every bit of a bad boy. I need to focus on my next pickpocket; I need money. My seat vibrates, and the familiar thunder of a motorcycle sounds behind me. I look in the rearview mirror and find Phillip on his bike, staring right back at me in the mirror. A huge smile creeps across my face, and my toes curl in excitement. *How many ramps did he search for me?* He swings his leg off the bike, carrying something black in his hand. I frown, unsure what it is. I climb out of the car and that's when I see it—a helmet. It's small, so I know it's not for him. My face falls. *What is he planning on doing with that?*

"Pretty sure I said don't make me come find you," he growls, his tone coming off angry.

I cross my arms and pop my hip out. "Look, Phillip--"

"Lip," he interrupts.

"What?"

His left eyebrow lifts as he shoves a hand in his jeans pocket.

"My name is Lip," he reaffirms, his tone coming off strong and confident. I cock my head to the side and eye him from boot, built torso, to rugged face. He looks like a Lip.

"Okay, Lip," I continue. "I can't get involved right now. I'm just..." I shake my head, humiliated to say I'm living out of my car and poor. Looking at Lip, I'm sure he has no problem finding girls. He can definitely do better than me. "I'm not the girl for you. I have too much baggage right now, and I can't get involved. Not to mention I'm staying in my..." I look at my car, but decide against telling him I'm homeless. "I'm staying with my brother until I can find a place to live."

Lip cocks his head to the side, that tongue of his flicking his lip ring. My stomach flutters with lust. I want to bite that lip ring.

"The way I see it, you should really come with me then." I snap my head toward him, and my mouth falls open with shock. "And why don't you let me decide what woman is good enough for me, hmm?"

"What?" I mumble. He walks up to me and grabs my chin softly, lifting it so I have to look at his brown eyes. There is something about gazing into someone's eyes that makes you vulnerable. You see more than just the color of the iris—you see the color of their soul. The intensity of them has me taking a step back, and I draw in a sudden breath.

"If you're staying with your brother, then why are you out here picking strange men's pockets?" he whispers. I furrow my brows. "It's dangerous," he breathes.

"Not that it's any of your business, but..." I inhale, looking at my fingers while I think up an excuse. "It's just complicated," I exhale.

"Come with me, Cherry, just for the night." He shrugs. "If you don't like it, I'll bring you back to your car," he offers. "Come on, there's a party tonight. Don't make me show up alone," he flirts, a gorgeous smirk lifting the corner of his lips. *Fuck, those lips are amazing.* I tear my eyes from him and look at my feet.

"I'm sure you don't have trouble finding a date, Lip," I reply, sweeping my hair out of my face. I peer up from under my eyelashes, risking a look at him, and find his chest rising as he juts his chin out. He looks even sexier, and is making it that much harder to reject his offer. I shouldn't have looked.

"I don't have a problem finding dates, no." He laughs. "But there's something about you, something that has me searching six freeways trying to find you."

"Six?" I repeat meekly. He smiles a big grin and nods.

"Yeah, six."

Fuck me.

"Do you normally chase strange women along the freeway?" I tease, crossing my arms.

"Nah, just the ones who have a nice rack." He winks, his

tone not holding any humor. My face falls, my urge to tease him vanishes. For some reason, I want to look at my tits, to see what he's seeing, but I hold his hard stare.

He steps toward me, and I uncross my arms. "Come," he whispers. My eyes flick to his; hearing him say the simple word sounds so erotic. He grins like a Cheshire cat. *Oh, yeah, he knows what he's doing.*

He tucks my hair behind my ears, his finger skirting against my skin, and pushes the black helmet on my head. He smiles, and little wrinkles form around his eyes.

"What?" I smile in return, his energy contagious.

"You look fucking adorable," he whispers ever so softly, like he didn't mean to actually say it. His eyes flick to mine, as if he just realized what he said out loud. His smile fades into something hard, his eyes never leaving mine as he awaits my answer. After him putting the helmet on my head, I don't see him getting on his bike and riding off solo.

"All right, I'll go," I whisper back. My heart slams against my chest, telling me not to do this, not to give in. But the churning in my stomach and the throb between my legs have me climbing on the back of his massive bike with him moments later.

I wrap my arms around his solid body, and my nipples are flush with his back, suddenly aching with arousal. His vest is hot and smells of leather. The scent has me inhaling deeply; it's sexy and masculine. *Fuck, I'm in trouble. Why did I do this? Why in the hell did I climb on his bike?* I know nothing good can come of this. "Just one night," I mutter, trying to talk some reason into myself.

Lip shifts in front of me, resting his hand on my knee. "You okay?" he questions, his touch making my knee tingle. I nod, and the helmet that's suffocating my head shifts forward slightly. I lean back to adjust it when I notice his leather vest says 'Devil's Dust' across the back of it with a menacing-look-

24

ing skull right dead in the center. My eyes widen. *How did I not see that before?* He's a part of that gang the news is always talking about. They say they're dangerous criminals. I swallow the lump in my throat and blow out a scared breath. Maybe I should step off and tell him this isn't a good idea.

He gives my bare knee a tender squeeze. "Hold on, Cherry." *Shit, I can't get off now.* I close my eyes tightly and claw at the front of his shirt in fear of falling off. The bike starts, and everything on my body vibrates with such intensity my vision doubles. Lip doesn't even look behind him and just jets off onto the freeway. The wind blows in my face harshly, nearly taking my breath away. I look over Lip's neck and strong shoulders. *God, he is the sexiest man I've ever seen.* Lip darts left quickly, and I cling to him as a squeal sounds from my chest. I can't help the big smile that forms along my face as Lip chuckles at my reaction. I've never been on a bike before—never really gave it much thought, to be honest. But this, it's amazing. It's dangerous yet freeing, daring yet comforting.

I love it.

◆◆◆

"You want a drink?" Lip asks me. I wasn't scared of coming to the party before, but now that we're here, I'm freaking out. We aren't at a party; no, we're at the fucking club where his motorcycle gang hangs out.

"Yeah. A soda would be nice," I yell, looking all around me. There is smoke dancing up into the ceiling from all the cigars and cigarettes, the smell of booze and cheap perfume strong. There are girls giving me dirty looks, and I'm pretty sure a man is getting head against the wall in the corner. I dig my nails into my palms and follow Lip to the bar. I've been to parties, but nothing this brazen. Girls are wearing leather chaps with no panties, and most of the men are shirtless revealing tattoos and piercings.

"Lip, who's your friend?" I slowly turn my head toward the unfamiliar rough voice, finding a tall man with dark-colored hair and the greenest eyes I've ever seen. His eyebrows are knitted together, causing hard wrinkles to form on his forehead. His jaw is defined, cheeks strong. He's even more intimidating than Lip, if that's possible.

The man holds his hand out to shake. "I'm Bull." His tone is friendly, contradicting the hard stare that's chiseled into his face. I shake his hand and muster a smile, my eyes falling to his patch on his leather jacket reading 'president'. *He must be in charge.* His strong palm grips my hand, and his arms are bigger than anything I've seen before. I gently pull my hand away and shrink where I stand, nerves and fear creeping up my back.

"I'm--"

"This is Cherry," Lip answers for me. I sigh with relief that he took over the conversation.

"Cherry, huh? I like it." Bull smiles, nodding. Actually, he doesn't look so scary when he smiles.

"She's truly beautiful, Lip. Why don't you take her out back, get her away from all this noise and commotion?" Bull suggests. Silence falls between the two and Bull pins Lip with an unknowing stare. I turn my head, watching Lip return the hard look.

"Yeah, sure. That sounds like a good idea," Lip replies, his tone dry as he takes a sip of his beer. "Come on, Cherry."

Once we're out back and the music is drowned out, cool air sweeps the hair off my neck. I inhale a deep breath, filling my lungs with clean air. Lip lets go of my hand and steps a few feet in front of me. His shoulders are tense, and his body is rising with rapid breaths. He looks pissed.

"Um, are you okay?" I ask softly. He lowers his head and

runs his hand back and forth through his hair. My thighs clench from the sight of him. It's dark out here—the only light is from the street lamp from above, casting the meanest shadow over him—but it makes him that much more appealing to me. He looks damaged, broken like me.

Lip slowly raises his head and tilts his chin upward. He has a look in his eyes that is hungry, primal. I swallow the lump in my throat, and my lips part to allow my harsh breathing to escape. I want him, even though I know I shouldn't. I know the timing is wrong, and I know a man like him can't love a woman. But it's not stopping me from craving him.

"Fuck, you're sexy," he breathes heavily. His eyes tear into my soul, unlocking things I couldn't yet figure out. He steps forward and cups the back of my neck. "Do you know that?" Glancing up under my lashes at him, I shrug. I'd never call myself sexy, average at most. Growing up, I was nothing but bullied, told how I was a geek and ugly. After hearing it for so long, you start to believe it. His eyes narrow with confusion as he looks me over. "You have no clue how attractive you are," he mutters as if he can't believe it. I inhale a shaky breath through my nose, my gaze never leaving his. His gorgeous eyes burn a trail of desire along my skin as he looks me over. "You have the eyes of a saint, but the body of a fucking temptress, Cherry." My eyes go heavy and my body rushes with adrenaline, making me feel drunk. His eyes fall to my lips, and my chest constricts. I want to pull away and break this spell I'm under, but I don't move, don't do anything. "I don't know if I should kiss those sugar lips or bite them." My lips suddenly ache with the urge to be tasted by him, to see if he tastes as dangerous as he looks. My gaze trails from his dark eyes to his lips. *I bet he tastes like sex and sin.*

As if he read my mind, he slowly lowers his head toward me, as if he's scared I might pull away. I should turn my head away, but I don't want to. When he figures out I'm not going anywhere, his lips claim mine with a hard demand, his tongue seeking entry and tasting me with a sense of urgency. I moan into his mouth, expelling the hurt and distress I've kept hinged within for months. My fingers tangle into his hair as my legs try to climb him, wanting to become one with his strong build. Our mouths explore each other's, taking and offering in a dance of chaos. His calloused hands grab at my ass, his touch foreign and rough.

He tastes like beer and mint, a flavor that is toxic to my resistance. He breathes in my pain and fills me with a sense of hope. A hope that not all men are assholes, and maybe, just maybe Lip is different. He pulls away slowly, nipping on my bottom lip.

"You scared?" he questions, his words feathering against my swollen mouth. My lips still feeling like his are devouring them, fluttering with phantom kisses. I keep my eyes closed for a second longer, wanting to stay in this state of bliss.

I thought about lying to Lip and telling him I wasn't scared at all, but the way he's smirking, he already knows I'm nervous. Being around a bunch of dangerous bikers, criminals who were known killers around the area, is enough to make anyone sweat. But what really scares me is the way I want Lip so badly, the way my thoughts of realism succumb to his confidence and aura of safety. He grasps the nape of my neck and kisses my lips softly, holding his against mine a second longer than needed.

"I got you, Cherry," he whispers. I close my eyes and inhale his scent as I soak in his words. I don't know what they mean, but I don't fucking care. I was literally just kissed stupid seconds ago, and the way my body warms with knowing that I'm safe... I can barely breathe.

He grabs my hand, and we sit down against the brick of the building. Heat wafts off it from the sun bearing down on it all day.

"You got a man?" he asks, and I look down at the gravel and laugh.

"You ask *after* you kiss me senseless?" His lip curls into an arrogant smile. "No, no man. What about you? Any girlfriend or kids?" I question.

Lip scoffs. "No woman, and fuck no to kids." He leans his head back against the wall. I laugh at how his tone dipped at the last part, but my fingers dig into my palm with unease at the same time.

"I'm serious. I can't have kids. I would make a shitty dad. They're a deal-breaker for me." I nod, unsure what to say, and look up at the night sky.

"You don't have kids, do you?" I can feel him staring at the side of my head, but I don't take my eyes from the stars. I just keep looking into the dark abyss.

"Does it matter?" I whisper. "I'm alone now, and I will be for who knows how long." Lip doesn't reply, and I look over at him. His brow is lifted and his face is hard.

"Someone did a number on you, didn't they?" Lip looks me over, and I pull my gaze from his before I see that same kind of sympathetic expression cross his face.

"Someone taught me that if you want to live, you have to have patience." I exhale loudly, closing my eyes to fight the tears. Lip grabs my hand and stands, pulling me with him.

"Come on. Let's go get a drink or something."

I smile, relieved he isn't going to push any further about me having kids.

Lip

I WATCH CHERRY CLOSELY AS SHE SEARCHES THE CROWD IN THE club. She seems nervous, but more curious than anything. I take another pull on my beer and drape my arm across her shoulders, my fingertips nearly brushing the top of her tits. I sweep my eyes up her frame, landing on her chest. *Man, she's got a nice rack.* She is so small standing next to me; it makes me wonder how small she would feel under me naked.

I didn't know what to think when I pulled over on that freeway the other day, but I sure as hell wasn't guessing it'd be a girl like Cherry. She's a spitfire, though. Most chicks go weak in the knees when they're around me, or are so scared they walk on the other side of the street to avoid me. Being a part of the Devil's Dust definitely has its perks—lots of pussy, and respect from those that fear us. But Cherry? Let's just say she wasn't something I was expecting.

"You want a drink?" I whisper into her ear. She nods, but doesn't stop watching the crowd. It's nuts in here tonight. Girls are fast, drugs are flowing, and the booze is top-notch. Heading toward the cooler, a small busty brunette steps in front of me.

"Hey, Lip, you look good tonight," she flirts. Recognizing her voice, I realize it's Chasity. She is a common ho around here, but she has the pinkest, wettest pussy I've ever had. She ain't tight by no means, and she's fucking annoying as hell with the way she clings, but she gets the job done. She has on a white tube top, her nipples clear as day through them, and a skull belly button ring shining against her tanned skin.

"You wanna go somewhere quiet?" she purrs, caressing her hand up my stomach.

I look over my shoulder at Cherry and groan. *Fuck.*

I grab Chasity's wrist, shaking my head. "Not tonight, babe."

Her face instantly drops into a pout. She pops her hip out, her mouth falling open.

"'Cause of her?" she sneers, looking around me at Cherry. I follow her line of sight, and find Cherry smiling at a couple of guys trying to dance with some girls, who have clearly had too much to drink cause they are falling everywhere. Watching Cherry giggle, seeing her without her knowing I'm seeing her, she looks fucking adorable. Cute and adorable isn't something you see around here much. I trail my gaze back to a fuming Chasity.

"Yeah, 'cause of her," I state up front.

"That is so fucked up. You always want me." She shakes her head, her lips pursed. Her self-assuredness pisses me off.

"Nah, that's where you're wrong. You're just the closest pussy around when I need to get my rocks off. You're always open, if you get what I'm saying." Her mouth falls open with shock, and her nostrils flare. "If you think we have anything more than me fucking you, then you have less brains than I thought," I insult, pushing past her.

"You are a fucking prick!" she yells in anger as I head toward Bobby, who's sitting on the cooler.

I tap his shoulder, urging him up.

"Hey, man," Bobby greets. "Who's the hot chick you're with? I haven't seen her around here before. She like to double team?" Bobby laughs, referring to Cherry as a club whore. My lips form a tight line as my hands fist at my side. A strike of jealousy paining my chest, I rub at it with my fist, the feeling unfamiliar and unwelcomed.

"Back off," I respond, my tone dry. Bobby's face falls before turning into a big-ass smile.

"All right, I get it she's yours." He laughs. I stare off, not liking the fact that I'm more than intrigued by Cherry. "Where did you find her?" he continues. I glance over to where Cherry is standing and find Bull behind the bar, smoking and talking to Cherry. Bull grins and glances at me. I swallow hard and look back at the cooler.

"Her car was broken down. I stopped to help her and the little shit stole my wallet." I laugh at the last part, remembering her ass taking it.

"No shit?" Bobby laughs. I nod and grab two beers from the melting ice. "I like her already."

"Yeah, she's hard not to like," I mumble, mostly to myself. I choke the neck of the beer bottle, thinking about how much I really do like Cherry. I don't *want* to like her, though, because I don't want to feel jealous when another guy looks at her; I hardly know her. A piece of me hopes she has flaws as big as some of these other girls who throw themselves at me. It would help get myself in check, and my dick. I'm not the relationship type; it's in my blood to be terrible at caring for another person. As my father used to say, "Phillip DeLuca, you are a prodigy of my blood. A powerful DeLuca doesn't have a woman by his side. He has many."

"Well, you enjoy that. I'm going to go find some ass to tap." Bobby chuckles. I nod at him and head back over to Cherry. Getting closer, I see a guy who hangs around the club occasionally leaning against the bar, talking to her. My jaw clenches.

He reaches forward and grabs her waist, and Cherry's body tenses with fear. Her eyes are wide, her face stoic. I double my step and toss the beers on the bar. Grabbing the guy by the wrist, I snatch if off her.

"She's not available," I snap, my brows drawn together, the wrath of hate bursting through my limbs to unleash on this fucker. Cherry's head lifts, staring at me in disbelief.

"Dude, I saw her over here by herself, and she ain't got a property patch on. She looked like free pussy." He gives Cherry a salacious grin and she scoots closer to me, her hands fisting my shirt in unease. I step forward, my left hand pushing Cherry behind me. Guys around here can get territorial over unclaimed women. "I saw her first, cock-block!" the guy hollers.

I grit my teeth and lower my head. I'm about to put this punk in his place but Bull suddenly steps between us, blocking me.

"Okay, why don't we all just calm down," Bull advises. My nostrils flare with anger; I don't need Bull handling my affairs. The guy rubs at his chin, eyeing Bull before walking away. Bull lifts his brow in a gesture that I need to turn away and leave. I bite my lip ring and give him an understanding nod, even if I don't agree with his order. I'm a prospect, so I don't get to argue or dictate his ruling. Not yet anyway.

I turn my back and lower my mouth to Cherry's ear. "You all right?"

She nods and runs her hands up and down her arms. She's uncomfortable. I shouldn't have left her; I knew better.

"How about we take these beers to my room?" She bites her bottom lip, unsure. I spread my feet apart and lower myself to her eye level. "We don't have to do anything you don't want to do. It's just quieter in there," I explain. She purses her lips as if she's thinking about it.

"I don't think that's a good idea." She shakes her head, avoiding eye contact. I grab her chin, forcing her to look me in the eyes, and her body nearly sways into me. Her lips part, and her body shivers beneath my hold. She's affected by me, and her body reacting to my simplest touch is a turn-on like I've never experienced before. I feel like a preteen touching his first female, ready to blow my load in my jeans.

"Look at me, Cherry. I wouldn't do anything to hurt you," I reaffirm. She blinks her eyes rapidly, as if she's trying to blink away the sexual spell I put her under.

"Then you'll take me back to my car?" She glances up at me from under her thick lashes and my dick jumps. She looks so vulnerable, so innocent, and the best part is she's not even trying.

"Yeah." I chuckle.

"All right," she finally responds, her lips curling into a small smile. I smirk and take her by the hip. We weave through the crowd and head to the back of the hall where my room is. I was just appointed it a few days ago from Bull himself. I have a place about fifteen minutes from here, but having a room at the club is way more convenient at times.

I open the door and turn the light on, and she instantly starts looking around the room. The walls are layered with porn stars and models. Most of them were plastered on the walls before, but I might have added to the collection.

"Shit, I forgot the beer," I mutter, turning to leave, but then I stop. I place my arm above the doorframe and rest my forehead on my forearm. "You're not going to try and run off or anything, are you?"

She smiles and sits down on the bed. "No, not yet."

"Okay, good."

I shut the door behind me and head back into the noisy-ass club to grab our beers. As soon as I spot them on the bar, Bull sits down on one of the stools.

"You better get your ass in check, boy," Bull informs, a cigarette between his lips. He squints as the smoke trails into his face.

"Come again?"

"Your little incident with that boy. You about broke his jaw for getting a little grabby."

"Yeah, so what?" I shrug. It's who I am. I'm hotheaded and won't hesitate to put someone in check real fucking quick. I fire first and ask questions later.

"You should have seen the look on her face, Lip. You better bury that shit and quick, or you will fuck this up." He blows out a puff of smoke, and I grit my teeth at his tone.

"I agree," Shadow adds, sitting down beside Bull. Shadow is a prospect, too. He has dark hair and crazy blue eyes; when he looks at you just right, they are freaky as shit. He's always kissing up to Bull. It gets irritating sometimes, but I understand it. He and I are a lot alike. He grew up without a father, and my dad was a prick, so getting approval from Bull is something we both aim for.

"What the fuck do you know about women?" I sneer at Shadow. He doesn't fuck with many girls and hasn't been in anything serious since I've known him, but now he's giving me advice about landing a chick?

"That girl is pretty—hot, even. They don't want damaged men who can't control their temper." Shadow shakes his head and takes a sip of his beer. "Nah, they want romance, all that fairytale bullshit," he continues.

Bull nods, and stands. "See," he clips, pointing at Shadow.

"What were you talking about with her?" I raise a brow at Bull. His mouth turns into a sly grin.

"She was asking about you, what you did here and all." He shrugs, and I can't help but smirk. *She asked about me, well damn.* Knowing she was talking and asking about me makes me a little giddy, like a fucking teenager or some shit.

"Yeah, she likes you all right. But it's up to you if it remains like that." Bull slams his cigarette in an ashtray, and my brows dive inward with his remark.

I open a beer and take a big gulp. *How do I keep a girl like that from running off? Fuck, this just got a whole lot harder.* I'm not a gentle kind of guy. I beat my dad with a steel pipe the first time he put his hands on my mother, landing him in the hospital. When my brother Zeek would tease me growing up, I would get so angry I would black out. One time, I came to with my mother screaming and pulling me off Zeek. He was blue and unresponsive from me choking him. He was okay, but it just goes to show how screwed up I am. My father was proud, my mother prayed. I walk through mayhem with ease and leave a tide of crimson behind.

"Now you see why I don't fuck with anyone 'cept club hoes." Shadow laughs. I flip him the bird and walk back down the hall.

"Hope that pussy's worth it!" Shadow hollers, making the guys cheer in agreement behind me.

3

Cherry

MY FINGERS GRIP THE SIDE OF THE MATTRESS, AND MY LUNGS burn to keep up with my harsh breathing.

What am I doing in here? What the hell am I doing?

I shake my head and stand on shaky legs. *I need to get out of here.* Lip is hot, he's sexy, and I know exactly why he wants me in here. I'm attracted to him, and not sure I'm strong enough to resist him either. There were a lot of beautiful women eyeing him out there. One in particular who had her paws all over him. They seemed more than acquainted, which makes me think he's a player. There were a couple of guys who were with one chick one minute, and when I'd turn my head they were with another. I'd never seen anything like it before. They live so freely, so open.

I bet he goes through a different girl every night. I don't want to be a notch on his bedpost. I can't handle that right now. I'd better get out of here then.

I blow out a determined breath and stand. Looking at the

dirty posters that have half-naked women on them one last time, I step toward the door. My hand is nearly inches from the doorknob when it opens as Lip walks in. I retract my hand and draw in a sharp breath. He smiles and shuts the door behind him. He's so big, so rugged; he makes a flare burn in my chest and sizzle all the way down my abdomen and between my thighs. My eyes sweep up his tattooed arms, one bicep holding a woman praying, so vibrant and beautiful. His muscle flexes and my gaze continues to trail upward, finding a sexy smirk across his face. I blush; he just caught me checking him out.

"Thought you weren't going to take off on me?" He chuckles and I smile, my heart beating against my ribcage. I rest my hand on my hip, the other on my forehead.

"Lip, I can't. I can't be in here," I respond on an exhale, my body defying my mind. It's hard to think clearly with him standing in front of me.

"Why's that?" Lip tilts his head to the side, his eyes running along my body. Goosebumps lick up my spine with the way he assesses me. I tear my eyes away from him and try to gather my thoughts.

"Because I'm..." I cross my arms and look at the bed. "I'm-I'm not sleeping with you." I finally spit the words out, wincing from my word vomit. He'll surely want to take me back to my car now. Lip bites at his lip ring and sighs as he sets the beers down on the dresser next to him. I uncross my arms, and my body tenses with fear.

He stalks toward me, one hand grasping my hip while the other fits behind my neck. His touch makes my skin tingle. My eyes go heavy, making my rejection a weak statement. I want Lip, want him to ravish me, make me forget about my pain and drown in a sea of bliss and hard muscle instead. But opening my legs didn't get me anything but trouble before.

"Cherry, calm down," he breathes heavily. "We don't have to

do anything you don't want to do." My body sags with relief, and a sigh escapes my lips. His fingers press firmly into my neck, pulling me closer.

"But if you think I'm not thinking about that fine ass of yours pressing against me while I take you from behind," he nips my ear and my eyes roll in the back of my head, "then you're mistaken."

He pulls away from me, and I sway on my feet, my body lost in a tide of lust and sinful thoughts.

"What do you do for fun? Why are you picking pockets?" he questions. My eyes go wide with surprise, like he didn't just fuck me with his words. I feel like someone just poured a bucket of ice over me, waking me from my high.

He takes a big gulp of his beer and winks. He's teasing me, and I'm taking the bait. He's so cocky, so sure of himself. He strides toward me and crosses his arms behind my neck. I slide one hand up his back, and the other up his arm to his wrist. My fingers touch his watch and I smile. *Let's see how self-assured he is when I take his watch.*

"I pick pockets because I can't get a job," I lie. My chest burns with how easily it is to be dishonest. *Well, it's not entirely a lie, because I really can't get a job. So it's an omission, really.*

"Okay, and what do you do for fun?" he asks.

"I like taking pictures of things." I shrug. The passion started with a disposable camera, and it grew from there.

He slides his hands down my back and grabs me by the ass. My stomach clenches and my nipples perk against the material of my bra. Damn, to have his strong palms on me feels incredible. He puts Eric to shame. *Eric who?* I shake my head from my dirty thoughts and smack at his hands. He smiles wolfishly at my rejection and walks us backward 'til we fall onto the bed. He rolls his strong frame, putting him underneath me with my legs straddling his hips. *Yeah, this is not happening.* I press my palms against his hard chest and roll beside him.

"Pictures, huh? Of what?" He tilts his head up and grabs the pillow, stuffing it under his head. I think about that question for a second.

"Everything. But I like taking pictures of distressed things, usually. I like to manipulate them, bring them to life where most people wouldn't look for it in such a thing."

Lip's face softens. "Well, when you put it like that, it sounds incredible." I laugh at his reaction. Most people don't see beauty in things around them. They only see faults and mistakes, often looking past their potential.

"What do you do when you're not doing that?" he interrogates. I smirk and lift my hand, revealing his heavy silver watch.

"What the?" He brings his wrist up, finding it bare. "You sneaky little shit!" My cheeks flush and a smile splits my face. He's so sure of himself, but when I take something from him without him knowing, it unravels that ego of his. "You're good at that." He chuckles, swiping the watch from my hand, and I shrug.

"Where did you learn how to do that? I didn't even feel you take it off me," he questions, putting it back on his wrist.

"My dad taught me. I didn't live in the best part of town growing up, or have the best upbringing. Stealing food and belongings around the neighborhood to sell for money was something I was raised to do." I look up from fumbling with my hands and see Lip's eyes wide. My face goes stoic when I realize what I just fucking said. I close my eyes and curse myself. *I can't believe I just said all that to him.*

"Yeah, I know what you mean. We didn't struggle for food growing up, but my father was a piece of shit who took what he wanted. He made sure me and my brother learned that trait early on." My head jerks up, surprised he shared something personal, too. He brings his gaze from the ceiling to me and pulls me close. The music from the party blares with such intensity the walls shake.

I rest my chin on his chest and look at the door. This man who lies next to me, a man full of many dark secrets and an edge as sharp as a serrated knife, makes me feel oddly safe. Maybe it's because we're both tainted with the horrendous upbringing our parents bestowed upon us. We have both seen hell at its finest, felt the warmth of its flames from a young age. Maybe if we stick together, we can find Heaven on Earth.

My eyes droop as the song "Kiss From A Rose" by Seal plays loudly from inside the main area. As if Lip notices the song too, his eyes slowly trail to mine. We lie here in silence, our lips mouthing the lyrics to the song every so often.

"Show me your horns." Lip smirks.

"My what?"

"Your horns. I bet you look sexy as fuck rocking out." He breathes heavily. I narrow my eyes, unsure what he means. I twist my lips. It's a little childish he's asking me to show him devil horns, but I do it anyways. I point my index fingers toward my head and he throws his head back laughing. My heart jumps in my chest and my cheeks flush.

"Not those horns. They're more than visible," he teases, lowering my hands. He pulls one of my hands up, tucking my middle finger and ring finger in with my thumb, making my index finger and pinky point straight up. "See, devil horns. The rockers do it." He smiles.

"Oh, Devil horns," I whisper. My brother does this all the time when he's listening to AC/DC. I raise both my hands up with Devil horns, and stick my tongue out.

"Shit, you look hot." He growls. "A girl rocking out, there's nothing sexier. You just need a little bit of leather and you'd be a wet dream." He winks.

I laugh, my cheeks warming. Noticing my embarrassment, he pulls me closer, easing my humiliation. Lying here, the song "Don't Cry" by Guns N' Roses blares. Listening to the song, I don't fight back my yawn, exhaustion weighing heavy.

"Lip, I think it's time you take me back," I state sleepily.

"I've been drinking," he mutters. "Just stay here with me."

I lift off the bed, my heart pitter-pattering off rhythm. "Lip, that's not a good idea," I object. I can't stay here with him; I don't trust myself not to do something stupid. He's stupidly good-looking, and I'm having a hard time not seeking more than comfort from him as it is. As much as I want to open my cold heart to him, to just be free, I'm afraid Eric has ruined me to let that flag fly any longer. I don't trust anyone, and I surely shouldn't trust a biker who has women flocking to him.

He stands and pulls his shirt above his head and my mouth snaps shut, my thoughts of ... *what was I thinking about?* He drops his jeans to the floor and my eyes immediately dart to his boxers. I can see his length pressing against the material, and my body throbs at the thought of how big he might be. I look away. The lights turn off, and I feel hands grabbing at my shorts.

"Lip, I-I..." I stammer frantically, my body tensing. He shuffles my shorts down, ignoring the warning in my voice, his fingers tickling the skin along my legs as he pulls them off. "I cant, I'm—"

"Relax." He laughs, climbing into the bed beside me. I don't relax, though; my body is stiff from fear beyond belief. He brings the blanket up and wraps his arm around me, tucking me into his frame. He's not trying to fuck me; instead, he's tucking me into bed. My chest eases, and I exhale a ragged breath. I am shocked that he's in here with me, not having sex, when he could be with one of those girls having lots of sex. He's not what I expected at all. He's sweet, sexy, and the right amount of rough around the edges.

I feel the head of his dick pressing at the small of my back, and realize it's getting harder. He shifts and it pokes at my butt cheeks, and my body comes alive with desire, desperately wanting to just give in to temptation.

My breathing shallows, and my sex throbs with a dangerous craving of whatever Lip is offering. His cock presses into my back again, hard. *Is he poking me on purpose?* I look over my side at him and he sits up, snatching the pillow at the foot of the bed, and wedges it between us. I turn, getting comfy on my side of the bed.

"Night, Cherry," he whispers into the back of my head.

"Night, Lip," I reply into the dark.

I try to keep my eyes open, attempting to defy the sleep stinging my eyes, but I can feel them getting heavier. *No! I can wait till Lip falls asleep, wait till the party stops and find my way back to the freeway. Though we did ride a ways away from my car.* I shift and blink a few times, trying to wake myself up, but my body soon takes comfort in the warm, solid muscle pressed against my back and the soft mattress beneath me. I easily fall asleep.

◆ ◆ ◆

I wake to the warm sun shining on my face. Moaning, I stretch out along the bed and soft sheets. *Bed. I'm in a bed.* I sit up suddenly, remembering where I am. The Devil's Dust club. I look around and find Lip missing. Shit. I close my eyes, and smack myself in the forehead. *Why did I sleep in his bed last night? Why didn't I have him take me back to my car?*

Throwing the blankets off me, I search for my shorts and flip-flops. I hurry and put them on then open the door to sneak out. I smell eggs, and my belly growls; I haven't had a decent meal in days. I cross my arms and curiously walk down the hall. The place is cleaner than it was last night. You can't even tell there was a party here. I come into the main area and see Bull, Lip, and some other guys sitting around the bar.

Lip stands from his seat and walks up to me. He gently grabs my wrist and tugs me closer.

"You hungry?"

I look around him and find all the guys staring at me before quickly turning back to their meal.

"Yeah, kinda," I lie. I'm so fucking hungry it's taking everything I have not to rush over to one of their plates and shovel down their eggs.

"Take my spot. I'll get you a plate." He walks away, pushing through two double doors that I assume lead into a kitchen.

I slowly head to the stool Lip was sitting on and take a seat. Looking over, Bull smiles at me around a mouth full of food.

"You sleep good, darling?" Bull questions. His smile is so contagious and welcoming that I can't help but smile back. He doesn't seem nearly as intimidating in the sunlight.

"Yeah, I did," I respond.

"Good. Good to hear," he mutters.

Lip comes out and places a plate of eggs in front of me, and I instantly pick the fork up and start eating. Actually, I inhale them. Quickly.

"You want more?" Lip laughs, grabbing my plate. I glance up and see Bull eyeing me with a look of concern. I flick my eyes down to the clean plate and my cheeks warm with embarrassment. *Shit, I should have paced myself or something.*

"No, I'm good," I mutter. I hop down from the stool and look around the room, finding two half-naked girls eyeing me from a black leather couch in the corner.

I glare at them. The guys might be a little scary, but girls don't faze me. I've been known to bloody my knuckles a few times.

Lip grabs my hand and leads me back down the hall. My hand blazes with that familiar rush when he touches me. I close my eyes and gently pull it away before we reach his room. I need to get away from Lip. Far away. I am having a hard time telling him no to anything and need to put some distance between us before I regret it.

"I need to get back to my car before they tow it." I scrunch my lips to the side and give a half-nod.

"About that." Lip tucks his hands into his pockets. I shift my head sideways and lift an eyebrow. "I don't like you staying in that car all day by yourself." He shakes his head. "It's not safe."

I scowl. What does this guy think I'm going to do, sit in his room and play princess all day?

I purse my lips and give a curt nod. It's nice that he cares, but that's as far as that thought process needs to go.

"I'll be fine. I can stay at my brother's place," I state, looking off. He doesn't say anything, and tension rises. I finally look at him and notice his face is serious, lips in a firm line.

He flicks his brown eyes to mine. "Why don't you just stay here?" He shrugs.

My mouth pops open in shock. My pride rises, overcoming any attraction I might have for Lip.

"I don't need a man to take care of me," I snap. "Take me to my car. Now!"

Lip's head lowers with a loud exhale. He places his hands on his hips, and inhales slowly.

"You stay at your brother's, Cherry." He says it like an order, and it angers me. "Agree, or I'm not taking you back."

I growl in frustration. *Who the fuck does he think he is?*

"Yeah, fine. Okay, I will," I lie. There's no way I'm going to Tyler's; it's too dangerous.

Lip steps into the room, grabbing his keys.

"Let's ride," he mutters. His words come out masculine, and hard, but there is so much meaning behind them. Revving me just right, I nearly moan in response. Instead, I bite my inner cheek, nearly drawing blood. God, he's so rugged and alpha, it's hard not to be attracted to him. I follow him out of the club and toward his bike. He lowers the heavy black helmet on my head, his fingers adjusting the chin strap while his eyes search mine. He has that look again, the one that makes me feel vulnerable. It's as if he can see right down to my broken soul. It makes my chest tingle, and my toes curl into my foam flip-flops. He pulls his gaze from mine and throws his leg over his bike.

I climb on the back and wrap my arms around him, his fresh scent strong and refreshing first thing in the morning. The bike starts and the vibration rocks me. The sun is bearing down on my skin and the wind picks up, throwing my hair everywhere. I close my eyes and fly.

◆◆◆

I climb off the bike and hand Lip his helmet.

"Well, it's been fun." I laugh sheepishly, obviously terrible at this. Lip chuckles and takes the helmet.

"Yeah. It's been surprising; that's for sure."

"What's that mean?" I tilt my head to the side.

"I just..." Lip looks out at the traffic of the freeway. "I wasn't expecting someone as cool as you, is all."

I smile and give him a soft punch in the arm. "You're such a softie."

Lip's face goes serious, and he flexes his arm. "I'm not soft. Think you figured that out last night." He winks and I roll my eyes. *I knew he was poking me in the ass on purpose.*

"Okay, stud muffin, I'll see you around."

"Bet your ass you will." He starts the bike, and I head back to my car. My car that holds my broken dreams and heartache. Lip flies past me, the smell of exhaust the only thing of him left. I unlock the door and roll down the windows; it's hot as hell in the car. I plop down in the seat and blow a breath of air into my cheeks.

"Guess I'll pick a different freeway, see if I can pickpocket some clueless bastard." Another day, another wallet, or watch. I'm not sure where this will get me, but I'm also not looking at the bigger picture—just the here and now. Surviving, trying to live. If I'm dead, I'll never be able to save Piper.

❖ ❖ ❖

A loud knock wakes me and I jump from the front seat, my face stinging from the imprint of the shirt I used as a pillow on my face. The knocking sounds again and my head whips to the driver's side window, the laundromat sign that was on when I went to sleep is now turned off. I rub at my eyes and lower my head to look out the window. It's Lip. *Shit!* I roll the window down, a breeze of fresh air taking my breath away.

"So, where does your brother sleep?" Lip questions sarcastically. I roll my eyes and look out the front of the windshield. Lip darts his hand through the window and unlocks the door.

"How did you find me?" I ask, stepping out.

"Do you know how hot it is outside, not to mention in a fucking car with the windows rolled up?" I cross my arms, feeling like a scorned child. "You are a woman, and a sexy one at that. A guy sees you sleeping in there by yourself, you're putting yourself at risk!" he hollers, then pushes me to the side and leans into my car.

"What are you doing?" I try to look around him, but he's so broad, he takes up most of the front. He draws back out of the car, my purse and clothes in his hands.

"Enough of this shit. You're coming to live with me." He stomps past me and throws my things in his saddlebags.

"Lip!" I follow after him, my bare feet burning along the asphalt. "I'm not going with you. I'm fine. I-I don't even know you, Lip. Hell, you don't even know me. You can't just walk into my life and demand—"

"You're coming with me." His words are stern, contradicting his behavior and vibe the whole time I've known him. The intensity coming off him makes me nervous. He's obviously a control freak.

"And if I don't?" I ask, my voice shaky.

"You will if I have to put you on the bike myself." I cross my arms, my eyes burning with the urge to cry. Lip lets out a long sigh. He slowly steps up to me, both of his hands grabbing my elbows softly. "Let me take care of you-"

"I don't need you to take care of me," I interrupt. He lifts his hand and trails the pad of his finger along my jaw line and my skin tingles, my heart beating faster.

"No, but you want me to," he breathes heavily. My eyes flick to his, the depth of his brown eyes consuming me, devouring me, claiming me. "You're strong and can take care of yourself; I get that. But if something happened to you, I'd blame myself knowing I could have done something—"

"I don't need your sympathy, Lip. I can stay at—"

"Your brother's, right. I remember you saying something about that before," he sneers. "You're coming with me one way or another. I'll tow this damn car with you in it if I have to, so just agree and make this easier on both of us." I turn my head and look at the closed laundromat, my vision blurry, dizzy from dehydration. I do need help or this heat is going to kill me. He obviously isn't going to hurt me or he would have last night. Maybe a little reprieve from this heat will help me figure out a new plan.

"Trust me," he mutters, his voice rough. My eyes shoot to his, his words searing through my resolve. I want to walk away, but the energy coming from him, that magnetic pull I can't seem to escape, has me stilled. I'm like a butterfly attracted to a warm light, a light that shows the path of possibility. Hopefully, that light doesn't burn me in the end, and possibly turn me into ashes. I'm not sure I can take any more heartache.

"Okay," I whisper. "I'll follow you to your house." As soon as the words leave my mouth, a sharp pain stabs at my chest. I am going to get hurt in the end. I just know it. He obviously wants more, but I'll eventually have to tell him about my daughter and he'll want nothing to do with me. Then this fucking car and I will be alone again.

"I'll have one of the guys come get it, take it to the club, and see about getting some AC in it or something." He shrugs, walking back toward his bike.

I huff and follow him. I'm one who practices independence, but I'm not about to argue with air conditioning.

◆◆◆

Even with the sun down, the air is still warm as it swims through my hair. Lip coming on so hard is not something I'm used to. It doesn't help that he's sexy as fuck, and sweet to boot. He has this alpha thing going on when he thinks he knows what's best for me. Even though it's irritating, it's flattering that he cares so much.

Lip slows down as we turn into a suburban area, houses lining up and down the road. They aren't magnificent ones like those you might pass in some of the areas in LA, but they *are* nice compared to what I've lived in. He idles up to a light blue, one-story house with the porch light on.

He presses a button on a garage door opener and the door slowly lifts, loud and cranking with all its might. Inside there are shelves lined with tools, and what looks like a stripped motorcycle sitting on cylinder blocks in the center. Lip puts his feet on the ground and walks the bike and us into the garage, the door closing behind us. Climbing off the bike, I pull the helmet off my head, setting it on the seat.

"Well, this is home," Lip states. I smile and follow behind him as he opens a door leading into the house.

The house smells of clean laundry and looks smaller than the garage. I smirk; just like a guy, more garage than house.

There are little lights in the ceiling shining just enough on the hardwood floor as he leads me down a small corridor.

"That's the kitchen." Lip points to the right. The walls look to be a light brown, the cabinets white and matching the appliances. A small kitchen island with two barstools sits in the middle of the room.

The house curves to the left, and Lip leads me into a small living room. The walls are white and lined with paintings of older motorcycles in black and white. A large flat-screen sits on a small wooden entertainment center in front of a brown fluffy couch and chaise lounge.

"Bathroom." Lip points to a small room right in front of us. It's nothing special, just a tub and sink. "This is my room." He points to the left of the bathroom. I peer in and see a big bed with blue and gray blankets, plus clothes and beer cans on the floor.

"You can stay in this room." Lip gestures to the room sitting opposite of his, putting the bathroom between the two. I step into the room he appointed as mine and Lip turns on the light. A small, full-sized bed sits in the corner with a white comforter. A little white dresser resides in the opposite corner, and a red guitar is placed on the other side.

"You play?" I question.

Lip shrugs and leans against the doorframe.

"Eh, I try but I suck." He laughs, and I smile. Seeing Lip play rocker would be a sight.

Awkward silence fills the area between us.

"Well, it's late. You were sweating pretty hard when I found you, so you wanna shower and get some sleep?"

I run my hand over the fluffy white blanket sitting on the bed. I never had something so fluffy before. Growing up, I had an old quilt that used to be my mother's.

"That sounds great, actually."

"I'll go get your things then." Lip turns to leave and I fall on the bed with a deep sigh. It feels wrong to be here, in a guy's house I hardly know. But the cold air conditioning, the clean blankets, and company? It's amazing.

I head toward the bathroom and shut the door. My body is nearly vibrating with excitement to dive into a nice, cool shower. I catch myself in the mirror and gasp. There's a crease in my cheek from the shirt I was using as a pillow, my hair is sticking to my forehead from the sweat, and I have bags under my eyes. *Damn, I look a hot mess.*

I don't even let the water get to its full heat before stepping under the showerhead. The cool water cascades down my chest and between my legs, and I can't help but moan loudly. I grab the soap and squirt a shit load into my palm, and the smell of Lip invades the small tub. I close my eyes and inhale the tones of mint and spice before fingering it into my hair.

I shower till the water runs freezing cold. Climbing out, the bathroom door swings open and Lip crashes into me. I'm naked and wet and standing right before him, his arms full with a towel and what looks like a shirt. He lazily trails his eyes down my body and I swallow hard. I attempt to cross my legs and cover my chest when Lip suddenly drops the linens. We both lean forward at the same time to grab them and bump heads.

"Shit!" I wince. I grab a towel quickly and wrap it around myself as Lip turns his body, looking at the wall.

"Sorry, I thought you were still in the shower." His words come out rough and heavy with lust. "I threw your clothes in the wash. You can sleep in one of my shirts tonight."

"Thanks," I whisper, clutching the towel around me tighter.

His eyes sweep toward me, giving me a once-over before turning and leaving.

My heart races in my chest and my hands shake with adrenaline as I shut the door. I lean over the sink, my fingers gripping the counter until my knuckles turn white. I raise my head, finding my reflection in the mirror.

"Holy shit," I mutter.

I wait in the bathroom until the door to Lip's room shuts. Peeking out, all the lights are off in the house, so I tiptoe to my room and shut the door. I look down at a Bud Light shirt of Lip's that I'm wearing. It's big; I'm practically swimming in the thing. I toss my head backward, the back of it hitting the door behind me.

"What am I doing?" I mutter, thumping my head against the door with each syllable. I really shouldn't be here. Lip's face flashes in my mind, the look of hunger flaring in his eyes when he saw me naked. I draw in a large breath and shake the image from my head. An unexpected yawn leaves my mouth when I lift my head and eye the extremely welcoming bed.

"Mmm. Sleep," I mumble before I flip the lights off and drag my feet to the bed. Plopping into the sea of white cotton, I curl myself into the comforter and close my eyes. It's going to be one of those nights where I'm too tired to think about anything else besides sleep.

Good.

"Goodnight, Lip," I whisper into oblivion.

Lip

SITTING ON THE BED, I RUN MY HANDS THROUGH MY HAIR IN distress. *I have a chick in my fucking home. A chick I'm not banging, at that.* I close my eyes, the image of her naked and beaded with water from the shower flaring behind my eyelids. She's freckled. Little dustings of freckles scatter along her chest, perky tits and thighs. A growl rumbles up my throat as I think about it, my briefs becoming strained as my dick lifts at the thought of her pussy dusted with little freckles. Who knew I was attracted to that shit? Those long legs that peeked out from beneath her towel make me want to do things to her, images of them draped around my shoulders filling my mind as I wring my fingers together in frustration. I stand and cross my hands behind my head, releasing a long breath and trying to clear my mind of her sexy ass.

I've never not fucked a girl I've brought back to my place before. Hell, I've never chased a girl before. But she's different somehow, and clearly needs help. I knew she was lying about her brother, I fucking knew it. But coming across her at the laundromat was pure coincidence. I was there picking up a leather cut of a patched-in member who got spray paint on it. Life of a prospect, I suppose—I get the bitch work. But it will be worth it in the end, I know it.

When I saw Cherry's car sitting at the side of the building, I was pissed. I was saddened that she really didn't have any-body, and I was also furious. It's hotter than hell outside and she was locked up in that piece-of-shit car with the windows rolled up. I shake my head at the image of her sweating and nearly suffocating. Her grayish blue eyes do something to me. They make my chest anchor in the pit of my stomach, and my balls tighten at the same time. They are gorgeous yet hold so much sorrow and torment. You can tell just by looking at Cherry that she's been through something rough.

My gaze trails to the door. I wonder if she's asleep, or if she's up still. I know it's gotta be weird being in a strange guy's house. Opening the door, my heart beats off-rhythm against my chest. With each step toward her door, my mind runs with confusion on what the fuck I'm doing. It's quiet; maybe she's asleep. I gently place my ear to the door, but hear nothing.

"Night, Cherry," I whisper. I pull from the door and head back to my room, where I'll jerk off to a feisty little ginger that plagues my mind.

Cherry

A HAND TRAILS ALONG MY CHEEK, WAKING ME FROM MY SLEEP.

I moan and snuggle the covers into my chest. Deep laughter makes my eyes pop open with sudden awareness.

Looking up, I find a freshly showered Lip hovering over me. He's wearing a black shirt that's distressed to the point it looks white in some spots, and his leather vest over that. He smiles, and my eyes trail from his tattooed arms to his lips and up to his eyes.

"I got church this morning. There's plenty of food in the kitchen, so make whatever you want. I'll be back when I can," he informs.

"Church?" My eyes furrow in confusion. It's not Sunday.

Lip lifts his head and licks his bottom lip, like he's thinking.

"Umm. It's not the kind of church you're thinking of. The

club, they meet in this room sometimes called a chapel. We have our daily meetings in it. Prospects don't always attend them, but we're to be present in case there's something the patched-in members need from us," he explains.

"Hmm. So how do you become a patched-in member or whatever it is you called it," I ask, my voice husky from sleep.

"Gotta prove my worth, show 'em I've got what it takes." Lip looks off.

"Ah, okay." *Whatever that means.*

"See you in a bit." He grabs the covers and pulls them over my head playfully before leaving.

A half hour later, I finally pull my ass out of bed in search of some food. I find some cereal and settle with that. Walking around the place with a red bowl full of Lucky Charms, I survey my surroundings. It's definitely masculine. It could use some color, a touch of feminism for sure. I risk stepping out of the front door, just needing some sun on my face. A small breeze shifts Lip's shirt around my thighs. I glance downward, eyeing my bare legs. The bottoms of my feet are warm from the patio steps, and I wiggle them. I should probably get back inside before Lip gets a call that a half-naked chick eating cereal is standing at his front door.

Turning to head back inside, my eyes land on a cluster of purple tulips across the street at the neighbor's house. They're beautiful, with a splatter of white along the petals. I don't think I've ever seen tulips like that before.

I wash my bowl and spoon and before I know it, I've washed all the dirty dishes. I don't stop there, either: I wash the counters, pick up the dirty clothes, and take the trash out. I clean the whole house. It's the least I can do after Lip invited me to stay here.

Hours later, I plop down on his extremely comfortable couch and flip on the TV, exhausted. Pulling the pillows from behind me to get comfy, bright pink stands amongst the fabric. My eyes widen as I pull one of the pillows out and more pink panties fall into my lap. Screaming, I fall backward off the couch, my legs and arms going every which way.

Growling in frustration, I pull myself from the floor and stomp to the kitchen. I grab some tongs I just washed and head back to the lacy panties. This proves he can have any girl he wants, that he is indeed a playboy. And what girl forgets her damn panties? I reach my arm out as far as it will go and pluck the underwear up with the tongs. Keeping my hand outstretched, I head toward the trash to dispose of them.

Throwing them in the trash, I can't help but stare at them. As gross as it is, I find the playboy vibe hot.

"Jeez, get a grip, girl," I mutter to myself, slamming the lid of the trash back.

After searching the couch for more crusty panties—thankfully, I found none—I *watch Pretty In Pink, Riding in Cars With Boys,* and *Knocked Up* one right after the other. I cry during each movie, but after watching that last one, I can't help but sob uncontrollably. I miss my baby. I want my brother. I want someone to hold me and just let me cry it out, damn it!

I grew up strong and always pushing through the tough shit in my life. I just stepped over it and figured out what I needed to do next. I've never sat down and given myself the opportunity to feel bad for myself, and I sure as hell never depended on another to make me feel better. But I think that's starting to hit max capacity, and I'm beginning to crack. Lip is making me depend on him, and my wall of emotionless independence is tumbling. I'm tired of being that strong female; I'm just exhausted and beginning to feel nothing but numb.

The front door opens and I quickly wipe the snot from my nose and rub at my tears. *Shit. Shit.* Lip is home. I have the TV so loud I didn't even hear his motorcycle pull up.

Lip tosses his keys on the coffee table and stops. I can feel him eyeing me.

"You okay?" he questions, his tone soft.

"Um, yeah. Just a sad movie is all." I glance at the TV that is now showing *Don't Tell Mom The Babysitter's Dead*. Go figure.

Lip looks at the TV and then to me, his eyebrow arching.

"They should have told their mom," I mutter, turning away from his intense stare.

"The place looks great. You didn't have to do that, you know," he states, falling back into the couch. I pull my legs up Indian-style and shrug.

"It's the least I can do after you let me stay here for a while."

"I don't mind the company."

We sit in silence, watching the movie. Every now and then, I can feel his stare on my skin. I can't help but eventually glance at him and our eyes meet briefly, my stomach fluttering with little butterflies. My eyes catch a tattoo that looks like bolts in the shape of an X of some sort, the word 'PRIDE' written under it in cursive.

"What?" My eyes shoot to Lip, not realizing I was sitting here gawking at his impressive arms.

"What is that?" I question, running my finger along the ink. He looks down at my finger and smirks.

"It's a piston." My brows furrow. *What the hell is that?*

Registering the confusion on my face, Lip chuckles and explains. "It's a very important part of an engine. If it ain't got it, it ain't running."

I nod, looking back down at the tattoo when I realize my hand is still resting on his strong arm. I peer under my lashes at him. "And what does pride have to do with that?"

"If a man doesn't have pride, he ain't going anywhere," Lip replies, looking right at my mouth. A lump forms in my throat, and his eyes gleam with a gloss of desire.

I pull my hand away and clear my throat. Lip stretches out, running his hands down his jeans.

"You hungry?" Lip questions. I tear my eyes from the TV screen and nod eagerly, thankful for a distraction.

"Yeah, I could eat."

"Let me see what we got." He stands from the couch and my eyes sweep to his tight, jean-clad ass. The man *has* to work out with a body like that. I look down at my own, feeling incredibly insecure. I should tone up. I groan in frustration, feeling like a little girl sitting next to her crush. My heart is beating wildly, my palms are sweating, and I couldn't even tell you what the hell we just watched.

"Um, Cherry?" Lip chuckles my name. I turn in my seat, finding him carrying a cup with the purple and white flowers I put on the kitchen island. "Where did you get these?" He smiles, and I can't help but smile in return.

"Um, I may have plucked a few from your neighbor." I scrunch my face in confusion. I got them when I took the trash out.

"I thought they looked familiar." He shakes his head before returning them back to the kitchen. I hop up on my feet and follow him into the kitchen. He turns to face me and rests his hands on the counter behind him.

"She cleans, she decorates. Does she cook, too?" he teases. My lips purse and I look off.

"This place is so manly. It needed a female's touch." I cross my arms and look at the stove. "I don't know how to cook, though," I admit.

"Really?" He looks shocked. "What do you know how to cook?" I look up at the ceiling, trying to think.

"Um, I can put a pizza in the oven. Oh, those little dinners you put in the oven. Um--"

"Anything not in a box?" He tilts his head to the side and

chuckles. I bite my bottom lip, a little embarrassed, and shake my head.

"Well, you're in luck. I know how to cook everything." He pushes off the counter and opens the fridge. "My family is Italian, and we take food seriously," he informs.

"What are you doing?" I ask, stepping away from the fridge. He draws back with a carton of eggs.

"Do you know how to cook eggs?"

"I mean, I've tried, but they always stick to the pan and burn. Or I get the shell in them, or I burn myself," I ramble. Lip smirks.

"Eggs will be your best friend, rookie, because they're easy to cook. We'll start with those. My mom has a secret ingredient with her eggs; it makes them soft," Lip states, grabbing a pan and placing it on the stove. His arms bulge and flex as he moves things around. He looks so big in a kitchen, his tattooed arms, and scarred knuckles standing out among the light. He looks used and abused, and for some reason I can't comprehend, I crave to be the one to offer him a touch of softness, of care. The rose to his thorns.

"What is the ingredient?" I ask, poking my head over his shoulder as he digs into the cabinet. He slowly turns his head, his mouth nearly brushing my cheek, and my body instantly goes warm.

"If I told you," he pauses, his eyes searching my face, "my mother would kill me." I burst with laughter then step back and try to cover my mouth. He sweeps his hand through his hair and smirks. That sly smile he portrays has me squeezing my thighs together.

"I'm serious! My mom is a tough ole' bird." He laughs.

"I promise I won't tell anyone."

He pulls his hand from the cabinet, holding a can of baking powder.

"That?" I point at the can.

"Yep. Also you need this, since it helps with the sticking." He holds up a can of spray Pam, and my mouth falls open in a big 'O'. "This pan doesn't hurt either," he tells me, shuffling the pan on the stovetop.

"What is it?"

"A non-stick pan." I scrunch my lips to the side in a 'go fig-ure' gesture. We couldn't afford those fancy-ass pans growing up.

Lip sprays the skillet and grabs a bowl from the dish strainer. "Now, grab an egg."

I swallow the lump in my throat and remove a cold egg from the carton.

Lip raises a brow and gestures his hand toward the bowl. "Well, crack it."

I can do this. I can crack a simple egg. I bite my lip and slam the side of the egg along the edge of the bowl. The shell splinters, and pieces fall into the bowl along with the egg yolk.

"Shit! See, I told you I'm no good at this." I shake my head, trying to pry the small bits of shell out, my cheeks warm with embarrassment.

Lip walks behind me, his thighs against the backs of mine.

"Like this," he whispers into my ear.

My head gently falls backward as his words slide down my spine and buzz between my legs. My eyes go heavy with lust as I watch his hand rest on top of mine. He pushes my hand to grab an egg, and Lip gives a small amount of pressure on my fingers, gently tapping the egg along the side of the bowl and cracking it. His fingers lying on top of mine, we pull at the shell, prying it apart gently. The yolk gently plops into the bowl, no bits of shell in sight. My eyes skip from our hands to his eyes. He has that look, the one that sees right through me, to my soul. All the air is sucked from my lungs, and I can't breathe when he looks at me like that.

"Now, grab just a pinch of baking powder and flick it in," he mutters. My eyes fall to his lips closely and my mouth tingles, desperately wanting one of those earth-stopping kisses again.

"Okay," I mumble. Breaking eye contact, I flick in the powder.

"Now, scramble it in the bowl then pour it into the pan," he instructs. I do as he says, and I never burn myself. The spray Pam and pan worked wonders, because the egg never stuck. I take the egg and spoon it onto a plate, a smile on my face the whole time. I fucking cooked!

"Try some." Lip hands me a fork, and I stab at a piece and take a bite. My eyes go wide, and a moan leaves my mouth.

"Those are the best eggs I've ever made," I admit, stabbing at another piece and offering Lip a piece.

Smirking, he opens his mouth and takes a bite, slowly. My eyes watch his lips slide along the silver fork, his jaw flexing as he chews. A shiver runs down my back as I realize we just shared the same fork. I bite at my bottom lip, jealous the fork got to taste his sinful concoction.

Suddenly, Lip grabs the plate from my hands, placing it on the counter before he slams his mouth to mine. His hands palm my face and he kisses me harder. I close my eyes and return the kiss. The way his calloused hands feel on my face and the way he moves his mouth against mine has me falling apart. I wrap my arms around his neck, the fork still in my hand. His tongue slips between my lips and caresses along mine. He tastes amazing—sweet, yet spicy. I moan into his mouth, satisfied that my world of darkness has been shifted off its axis, even if it's just for a moment.

My lungs burn with the need to breathe, but I don't dare pull away. I want this, I need this, I crave this. The way Lip looks at me with such hunger, it's a turn-on I can't fight anymore. Strong palms trail down my sides and clasp along my butt cheeks, and I claw at his hard chest.

"Fuuuuuck," he mutters on a shaky breath. Hearing the struggle in his voice, I can't help but whimper. He pushes his hands up my shorts, trailing along the lace of my underwear, and I draw my head back and throw my leg around his waist. Everywhere he touches my skin tingles with a rush of excitement. His other hand skims up my leg and slowly up my thigh, and I can't help but rock myself against him, needing some kind of friction to ease the ache.

Lost in the frenzy of lust, I moan loudly, the pleasure of his skilled hands on my skin too much to contain anymore. His eyes go wide at the same time I open mine and we part. I gasp for air, my skin tingling everywhere from his wandering hands.

He drops his head and blows out a ragged breath, and I sway on my feet as I seek the counter for balance. It's as if north and south met in the middle. Every touch, every kiss I accept burns, melting the resolve I've built. Will we destroy one another, or make a new world with the pieces of each other?

"I'm going to shower," he whispers. I nod, not speaking. We need distance. *I* need distance. Lip looks me over once more and I nearly moan just by the starved glint in his eyes. As if he's just as affected, a low growl vibrates in his chest as he walks away.

◆◆◆

After my own shower, I head straight to my room, drop on the bed and look up at the ceiling, scorning myself. *Why can't I get some control of myself? Why can't I resist him?* My mind is emotionally confused, my body is sexually frustrated and my soul is dying piece by piece. I'm beyond broken and lonely. I roll over and huff, my eyes landing on the guitar in the corner of my room. It makes me think of my brother, of how much I miss him. My eyes burn with sadness, and a sob hiccups through my throat. Sorrow fills my chest, and tears start to fall in earnest. I miss Tyler, and I miss Piper. I want my family.

I clench the blankets and bury my face into the pillow. I want my daughter badly, but every time I get close to her, I'm nearly killed. I need to accept that I won't see Piper again, but a piece of me just won't allow myself to move forward, even if I know it's good for me. *Eric. Fucking. McCormick. Why did I have to be so stupid and stuck on high school bullshit?* I grab the pillow and shove it into my face again, screaming into it with rage. My knuckles burn from the death grip on the pillow, and my lungs gasp for air.

The door to the room creaks open, and the unmistakable shadow of Lip looms into the room. I wipe at my tears and open my mouth to explain my outburst but hands slide underneath me, picking me up before a word leaves my mouth. Hugging me into his chest, he brushes my hair away from my ear. A feeling of comfort, of ease creeps up my spine.

"I got you," he whispers, the simple words stifling my pain. I throw my arms around his neck and bury my face into him. My chest warms at the affection he displays toward me. I need this, need to feel protected and safe. To feel like my life is worth living, and fighting is not a waste of time.

He takes us into his room and tucks us into his bed, pulling me into his strong frame. I don't fight him; I need this, as much as I may think I don't want it. I need something to cure my broken heart, to help get me over this damaged path I'm on.

His arms are strong and gilded, and my body sags into him for solace. There is something about Lip that has me feeling tranquil. I don't have to defend myself and build a wall, 'cause

Lip just tears that wall down. He stands there in his tattooed glory and controlling way, ready to show me the path of depending on another. He pulls me closer, nearly spooning me.

"I like to snuggle," he growls into the back of my neck. A smile pushes through my sorrow. *Big bad biker with piercings and tattoos likes to snuggle.*

Closing my eyes, I take in the smell of him. Fresh, minty, and spicy. It's odd; ever since I've laid eyes on Lip my heart has seemed to beat off-rhythm, but lying here next to him, our hearts beat in sync, a rhythm of their own that I have yet to understand.

◆◆◆

Thunder strikes and I jump awake. Sweeping my eyes across the way, I notice it's still dark outside, and I'm in Lip's bed. He doesn't look so...hard, when he's asleep. He looks gentle. I cup his cheek, the scruff of it scratching against my palm. Is it so bad that I want to be with him, that I don't want to be alone and surf in a tide of loneliness anymore? His eyes flutter open and pin me in their gaze. I hold my breath as he lifts his hand, his index and middle fingers brushing across both my lips. My body tingles everywhere, and my sex throbs with an intensity so strong I feel my hips trying to rock in rhythm to it.

I hitch my leg over his hips, and his cock instantly begins to harden against my thigh. My hands trail up his hard chest as his dick rubs against me just right. His hands grip my hips, and I literally hear his teeth clench together.

"Cherry," he warns. My eyes dart to his, my heart beating a mile a minute that he's rejecting me.

Thunder booms from above us.

"I'm afraid if I do this, I'll never be able to let you go," he whispers, his brows knitted together. My eyes widen, and a sly smirk fits my face. Playboy Lip wants me to himself.

"Who says you have to?"

Like a match finding its flame, he rolls over on top of me, his knees spreading mine apart. My fingers anchor themselves into his hair. I have to latch onto something because this man, the things he says, and the way I feel when his fingers barely graze my skin... it all feels too good to be true. Like this is a dream and I may float away at any moment and drop face-first into my reality of misery.

"I'm sure there is a rule somewhere that says I shouldn't sleep with a man I barely know, but I just don't care," I mutter, curling his hair around my finger. I know I'm being reckless; the nerves in my chest can prove that. But the urge to feel desired, to feel Lip's hands claim my skin is a stronger, more prominent craving.

"Something you should know about me, babe: I'm a rule-breaker," he states, his voice coming out raw and seductive.

Leaning down, he nips at my underwear, his hands sliding up my legs. I bend at the knee and moan from the amount of pleasure I'm receiving with just the simple contact. I've never felt so worked-up before. With every touch of his skin against mine, I feel like I may explode in a world of euphoria. He brushes my shirt above my belly button with his nose as his hands travel up my hips. Pushing his fingers in my panties, he slides them against my wetness. I buck against him and close my eyes from the intense tingling sensation bursting through me.

"Fuck, you're wet for me," he whispers, the sound nearly making me whimper from the way it does things to me. It's so powerful, so raw.

"Lip, I, uh..." Insecurities start to fill my chest, second thoughts firing in my mind. The first time I'd done this, I was wasted. I'm far from being shit-faced, and I'm feeling very inexperienced at the moment.

"What's wrong?" He stills. My mouth dries as I try to think of how to say it.

"I've, um, w-well," I stammer. "I've only had sex once before, and I was really drunk," I finally state.

"So?" He shrugs, nipping at my knee.

"So, what if I'm- you know- not any good?"

He smiles. He fucking smiles.

"No fucking way you could be bad." He shakes his head and looks down. I arch a brow, unsure what to say to that. "But I'll go slow so I don't hurt you."

He slowly lifts his head, his eyes hooded. "I feel sorry for that last prick you were with, 'cause now that you're opening your legs for me, I'm about to be the last man to be between them," he states, his tone deep and serious. My heart thuds with attraction. His words are so proud, so confident, and I fucking swoon.

"You're pretty sure of yourself, huh?" I joke. Lip pushes himself up from my belly and rests his forehead on mine, his eyes not giving anything away.

"Cherry, I'll be your last 'cause I'll fuck you like no man can compare. I'm not being arrogant, I'm being honest. When I'm done with you, you'll have a hunger for my cock like a starved woman. Now let me fuck you, 'cause that's all I've wanted to do since the day you took my wallet."

My lips part and a weak mewl escapes. God, that's all I've wanted, too, and my body can't take the torture of having such rugged sexiness within reach anymore.

He inserts a finger into my wetness, testing me, and my pussy instantly pulses around it. He turns his hand and flexes his finger in a 'come here' motion, and stars shoot behind my eyelids. My hands cling to his broad shoulders and my toes curl from the pleasure.

"Jesus, I can feel you clench around my finger," he murmurs, his voice low and rough.

My hips ride his finger like a wave. I need that unfamiliar feeling of bliss; I want more of it.

He slowly withdraws his finger and my eyes pop open, finding his focused solely on me.

"Seeing you fuck my finger like that, I can't wait to watch you ride my dick, Cherry." The air is zapped from me, and my lips part to allow a large breath to enter. He has a filthy mouth, but his words make me feel so good. He slowly drags my dainty panties down my legs, the slow pace throwing my senses into hyper-drive. Grabbing me by the knees, he pulls them apart, spreading me wide. He looks at my pussy, his chest rising.

"I want you to ride my tongue like you did my finger," he instructs.

I can't speak as fear fills my chest. *What if I taste bad?*

He lowers his head, his hands on my bent knees, and laves at my wetness.

"Oh, God!" I moan loudly. It's so wet and warm. Every strike of his tongue shoots an unfamiliar sensation from my core through each of my limbs.

"You can call me Lip," he rasps confidently from between my thighs, the sound vibrating against my sensitive skin. I clench my eyes and gasp for air as my body winds up with an incredible sensation. My fingers dig into his shoulders as my hips grind against his face.

He pulls up, my wetness shining against his stubble.

"Not yet," he growls, stopping just before my body erupts into a thousand little pieces of sexual need. He seems anxious, like he can't handle it anymore. Sitting on his knees, he lifts me up and pulls my top off frantically. My nipples pebble against the air. I wrap an arm around his neck, my tits pressing into his hardened chest firmly as he places one hand on my back and lowers us.

He smashes his lips to mine, the taste of me filling my mouth. I arch my body into his and pull my mouth away to grant my burning lungs a breath of air. I wrap my legs around him, his hard length pressing right against my opening. I can't help but rock against it. I want it badly—desperately, even.

"That's it," he growls.

"Lip," I breathe heavily. I can't take this torture anymore. I know I should resist him, shouldn't even be here let alone in his room, but with the look in his eyes when he watches me, the wolfish smile across his handsome face, and the way his fingers shoot a toxic wave through every nerve ending of my body, I can't push him away anymore. I am weak, I am hurting, and I just want to feel good for one damn minute.

He slowly places me back down on the bed and pulls his boxers down to his knees.

Oh. Fuck. His dick is pierced. My eyes flick to his, and he smiles wolfishly, his expression full of ego.

"You on the pill?" he questions. I nod; I've been on birth control since I had Piper. Thankfully for me, they give those with low income—or, in my case, no income—free birth control.

"Good, cause condoms break every time I use 'em," he informs. My eyes widen with that statement.

He grabs my knees and positions the head of himself right against me. My heart beats wildly. *What if it hurts?*

I draw in a tight breath as he pushes the head of his dick inside of me. He stretches me as he pushes all the way in, and I whimper. It burns, my body not used to the size of him. However, the pleasure of him filling me binds with the ache of him stretching me. I can't decide if I want to whimper with pain or moan with satisfaction.

He throws his head back and groans, the sound vibrating through his body. His palms slide along my thighs and up my stomach, the simple action causing the muscles in my stomach to tremble. He hisses between his teeth and applies just enough pressure on my left nipple that a deep, whole-body sigh sounds from my mouth.

He pulls his hips back slowly and thrusts forward, and my lips form an O as that feeling of bliss instantly starts to re-surface.

He gently kneads my tit and lowers his body on top of mine, our bodies trapping his hand on my breast. I clench my eyes shut and don't hold back, moaning as loudly as I can as pleasure erupts in my lower half.

"Damn, I love that sound," he grits through clenched teeth.

His hips keep pulling back and driving forward, the barbell in the head of his cock hitting me just right. I try to breathe but the air just won't enter my lungs as I ride the tide of my orgasm.

My body pulses and clenches around Lip as I come down from my cloud of ecstasy. He shudders on top of me, and his warm cum fills me.

Lightning strikes, lighting the room briefly. Our chests rise and fall rapidly as we just lay here in elation. He rolls over and pulls the sheet with him, covering his wet dick.

Awkward silence fills the room. I brush my hair away from my face and rub at my forehead. Regret surfs through me. *What did I do? Why did I do that?*

"You okay?" Lip whispers. It's like he can read my fucking mind.

"I don't know," I reply honestly.

He rolls over and pulls my bare ass against his still-hard cock.

"You're something else, Cherry," he whispers. I smirk as regret and second thoughts vanish. My brows narrow at the reaction, not sure what it means.

"Cherry? That guy you slept with before, is he the reason you're hurting so bad?" Lip whispers into my ear. My body tenses, and my eyes widen. "I'd kill him, if it makes you feel any better." I shift, turning to look him in the eyes, and find him staring right at me, dead serious.

"I'm not sad about him," I sneer, shaking my head.

"Then what? What makes you cry at night?" he pushes, brushing hair from my face. I inhale a large breath. If I tell him about Piper, this could be over before it even starts, and I don't need him trying to rescue me and making it worse in the end. Eric could hurt Piper just to keep her from me; he's unpredictable.

"You're right. It's about him," I backtrack. I mean, he is somewhat the reason I'm sad. "He just...he didn't treat me right. He lied and betrayed me," I continue, my brows slicing inward with anger the more I think about it.

"Where I come from, betrayal gets you six feet under," he rasps. I roll back over and exhale. Obviously, my world and Lip's world are incredibly different, because instead of Eric being six feet under, it was nearly me.

"He'll pay his dues, Cherry." Lip's words come out as a promise, and I clench my eyes. I don't respond, because I just want this conversation to be over.

4

Lip

SITTING ON THE COUCH, I RUN MY HANDS BACK AND FORTH through my hair. My head is swimming with confusion this morning. I've fucked dozens of women, but I've never felt whatever that was last night before. I've taken Bull's and Shadow's advice and tried not to come off like a fucking Neanderthal toward Cherry. 'Cause really, all I wanted to do last night was bend her over my bed and fuck her stupid. But I didn't; I was gentle. She's so feisty, but deep down that heart of hers is made of a fragile element. She's alone and has nobody to depend on. There's something about her that draws me in. Maybe it's the depths of sadness that pool in her eyes when she thinks I'm not looking. That alone makes me want to have mercy on her.

My compassion for her makes me step over the boundaries I usually set with other women. I blame her misery on my piqued interest in her. Leaning my head on the back of the couch, I sigh loudly. I don't need this bullshit. This is going to confuse things badly. I have an omission, an undisclosed predicament that will drive more than a dagger in Cherry's naïve heart when it's revealed. Clenching my teeth, I stand. I'm an outlaw, a fucking outcast to society. I live by my own rules and thrive on my own demands; it's what's kept me alive so far. I need to set aside my infatuation and get focused.

Walking into my room, she's just waking up, her freckled perky tits flashing briefly before she covers them up. Images of me sucking on those last night string behind my eyes, giving me morning wood.

"Nice rack." I grin as her cheeks flush crimson. I love embarrassing her, saying something brazen just to watch her cheeks turn a sexy shade of pink.

"Here." I toss the phone on the bed.

"What's this?" She peers up at me.

"You need to call your brother. Didn't you say you had a brother? You are obviously alone and need someone. Call him," I suggest, my tone harsh.

She shakes her head and looks to the floor. "I'm not sure if that's a good idea."

"Why?"

"Things are complicated between him and --"

"Call him. Figure it out," I interrupt.

She nods, running her thumb along the phone.

"I got church, but I'll be back later."

"Okay." She smiles up at me, and my chest burns. I gotta get the fuck out of here.

Riding to the club this morning, I think about how things with Cherry have escalated and how quickly. Me caring for her, taking her in. When I'm around Cherry, I feel sane, like I got my shit together. It's opened a side of me I thought was smashed by my father.

I ride into the parking lot and back my bike into its spot. Bobby rides in behind me and parks next to me.

"Morning, brother," Bobby greets. I nod at him and put my bike on her stand. "You all right?"

I shrug. "Never better."

Heading into the club, Bull walks out of his room, a tight-ass little blonde following behind him.

"Let's do this, boys," Bull calls the patched-in members to the chapel, and I sit on my stool, just in case they need me for something. Hawk, our oldest member, grumbles as he follows them in.

"This shit is too early." Locks points at Bull, a cigarette between his fingers. Locks is the VP, and a prick. He's one I'm not sure I can come to like even if it means my patch or not. He has an ol' lady named Babs and he's more than a fucking prick to her. Don't get me wrong; I have a reputation of being an asshole amongst some of the club hoes myself. I've thrown a half-naked chick out of one of the club rooms. Turned one down to fuck another with bigger tits. Shoved a bitch's face into a bed for talking too much while I fucked her. All of it. But I'd never disrespect a woman I owned.

"So, how are things with you and the little redhead?" Bobby asks, drinking milk right from the gallon. I swipe it from him and take a big swig, ignoring him. "You fuck her yet?" he prods.

I normally go into great detail about the girls I fuck, but for some reason I never thought about sharing how I fucked Cherry.

Bobby's eyes widen as he wipes the milk mustache from his lips.

"Oh, damn. That good, huh?"

I level him with a look of anger.

"He got him some of the stuck-up pussy, and now he's whipped." Shadow laughs, sitting down beside me.

My fists clench. I'm not sure if I'm angry with them or her, though. I inhale a breath and try to shake it from my head.

"She's just a chick," I tell them, but really I'm telling myself that. Cherry is getting under my skin deep, and it's got me feeling things I don't know if I want to feel.

"Yeah, I fucked her. Freckles everywhere." I turn the milk carton and muster a smirk.

"Man, I love the ones that have 'em on their tits. She have 'em on her tits?" Bobby asks. The doors to the chapel swing open and the brothers walk out.

"Lip, Bull wants you." Locks jerks his thumb over his shoulder.

"Uh-oh." Bobby chuckles, and I flip him the bird and head into the chapel.

"Shut the door, son," Bull orders. I do as told and sit in a chair. "Cherry, how is she?" he asks.

"Good. Why?" I ask.

"She's from Golds Trailer park. Keep her away from there." I try to think of where the fuck that is; if it's the place I'm thinking, it's miles from here. That place is trash, and dangerous. *Jeez, no wonder Cherry is the way she is.*

"How come?"

Bull raises an eyebrow. I know I'm a prospect and not supposed to ask questions, but I did anyway.

"Got some rival gangs from there, and we don't need the trouble."

I nod.

"You're a good prospect, Lip. I see a patch coming your way soon," Bull states. I smile; the thought of belonging to this club is an accomplishment I can't wait to achieve.

"The Devil is in my blood. I'd wear the colors with pride."

"I'm going to look at an SUV for the club today, so why don't you ride along. We have a local club meeting us before. You do well, you can come with us when we go on our big run in a few weeks."

74

"You mean the one near Nevada?" The boys have been talking about it for weeks. Potential suppliers for AK-47s.

"That's the one."

"Yeah, I'm in." I stand, my palms sweating.

"Good."

Cherry

I LOOK AT THE PHONE, DEBATING ON CALLING MY BROTHER. I bite my lip, unsure. *Maybe I can call and see if there's been any suspicious activity. If there has been, I won't call him again. That's it, that's what I'll do.*

"Hello?"

"Hey, Tyler."

"Lindsay! Where have you been?" His frantic voice makes tears prick my eyes.

"Things have gotten out of control with Eric and the lawyers. You know how I told you that I found the judge being paid off?"

"Yeah?"

"Well, he has people in his pockets, and they tried to kill me. I've been living in my car." I'm crying now.

"Fuck, Lindsay, why didn't you come to me?"

"'Cause I didn't want to lead them to you."

"Nobody has been here. Are you sure you're not over-reacting?"

I growl into the phone. "I'm sure."

"Wait- how do you have a cell phone?"

"This guy, he picked me up on the side of the road. He's really nice—too nice, maybe. He asked me to stay with him, so I'm laying low here."

"Too nice, huh. You know when they say that, that means

something is wrong."

"Yeah, he is really persistent." I laugh. "Don't worry, he has a flaw: he really doesn't like kids." My head falls with the thought.

"Um, that's a problem, right?" His tone comes out low.

"Not really. I mean, as much as I don't want to admit it, I've lost Piper, and I can't do anything about it. If I do, I'll be killed." Saying those words, my heart literally feels like it's being torn in two. I hate myself for not being able to do more with my current situation; being backed into a corner without a safe move forward is a feeling of helplessness I can't overcome.

The phone goes silent.

"You're probably right, Lindsay. I know you love your daughter, and I'm not saying give up on her. I love her, too. But if you really think someone is after you, you should let this shit blow over before you try to get her back."

I nod because I know he's right. It's just hard to accept.

"We should meet up," he suggests.

"You think it's safe?" My eyebrows rise.

"What part of town are you staying in?"

"I'm near the docks, I know that. I can hear and smell the ocean."

"Yeah, I think you're far enough away that nobody would recognize you, and that's if anyone is even after you," Tyler ensures. "I think maybe they were sent to spook you more than anything, make you keep quiet about the judge and all."

"Well, it worked. I'm scared to death," I mutter.

"You want me to come get you? You can stay with me, ya know."

I look down at my hands and sigh. "I know," I whisper.

"You're not going to, are you?"

I don't reply. I don't know what this is between Lip and me, but I want to find out. Not only that but if Tyler's wrong and the judge *is* after me, he'll find me quickly if I'm around that area.

"This guy you're with, be careful, yeah?"

"Yeah."

"Love you, shithead." He laughs, breaking me from my thoughts.

"Love you, turd licker."

Lip

WE RIDE OUT OF TOWN FOR THE POTENTIAL SUPPLIERS. I HAVE no clue where we're going, but I don't care. My palms are sweating and my heart is beating like a fucking beast. This is my test, to show Bull and the club if I'm worthy to be a Devil. Loyalty and respect are something that swims in my DNA, and I need my pack that shares the same dominance. I need that brotherhood, that family that would do anything for one another. Maybe it's because I didn't have it growing up, fuck if I know. All I know is being patched into the Devil's Dust, being called a brother... that's all I want in life right now, and if I fuck this up, I won't have it.

We pull up to a warehouse in the middle of nowhere. No grass, no houses, not shit. Just desert and some aluminum-sided warehouse. I blow out a ragged breath, trying to compose myself. Maybe I should ask Bull for a cigarette, calm my fucking nerves before I have a heart attack.

I pull in behind Locks and park my bike.

A middle-aged guy in a sleeveless flannel shirt walks out of the door to the shitty warehouse, a couple of armed men standing behind him.

I swipe my sunglasses from my face, searching the area for anything suspicious.

"Devil's fucking Dust," the guy chimes.

"Bart," Bull greets, his tone anything but welcoming.

"You looking for good weed, we got it." The guy holds his hands out wide, as if this trashy warehouse is gold or some shit.

"Yeah, let me be the judge of that," Bull sneers.

Bart loses his smile and opens the door to the warehouse. Walking in, there are tables lined with Ziploc bags and scales. Along the back of the warehouse are crates and lights hanging from the ceiling. There aren't any marijuana plants in sight, though, so this isn't the main warehouse where he grows. This is just where he packages.

"This is my top shit." Bart points at some dime bags on a nearby table.

I walk over to the supply and open a bag. The smell isn't strong. I glance inside the bag and notice more seed than bud. My father taught me all I needed to know about marijuana, coke, the quickest way to kill a man—the list goes on.

"It's ditch weed," I state, shuffling the bag around. Bull lifts an eye at Bart and grabs the bag from me.

"Excuse me?" Bart quips, his tone coming off as if I've insulted him.

"It's not top-notch. I can grow better weed out of a pot in my kitchen window." I raise a brow at Bart, waiting for him to fucking lie to my face.

Bull inspects the green and hands it to Locks as I walk over to the table behind this one and find more bags. I open one and the smell of earthy tones nearly knocks me off my feet. It's good. Really fucking good. This is no ditch weed.

"Yeah, it's shit," Locks agrees.

"So, that's your best shit, huh?" I toss the bag of good weed to Bull. He scrunches his face in question as he catches it. "Open that one," I encourage.

Bull opens it and instantly pins Bart with a death glare. "You trying to hustle me bad weed?"

"I mean, you gotta work up, you know?" Bart chuckles and I grit my teeth. I've had enough of his fucking lies and hustling, as I know Bull has, too. If I want to prove myself, now is the time to do it.

I pull my gun from my waistband and put it to the back of Bart's head.

"Do you know who you're fucking with? We don't work up to nothing," I seethe. Our club is the biggest in LA, we have a reputation, and we've worked hard for over the years. "Your disrespect for my club is going to put you in the ground," I promise.

"Whoa! Whoa!" Bart holds his hands up in surrender.

"My boy is right, Bart. Do you know who you're fucking with? Lying to my face is not something I take lightly," Bull explains.

"Okay, okay, how about we give you a couple blocks of Betsy, and for a third of the cost?"

I look at Bull, waiting for his direction.

"This Betsy?" Bull points at the good bag of weed.

"Ye-yeah, yeah," Bart stammers.

"Okay, deal. But you try and give me anything less, I'll have Lip here shoot you in the fucking foot," Bull threatens.

Bart nods, rolling his lips on top of each other out of fear. For a drug dealer, he sure is a pussy.

"Grow some balls, man," I insult, taking the barrel of my gun away from his head.

Bull laughs and pats me on the back. I smirk; it feels good to be in his good graces. As a kid, some local thugs cornered my father once. I grabbed his gun from his motorcycle and took aim, threatening the punks. They ran away in seconds. My dad was not impressed, said I should have pulled the trigger. I never made his fucking ass happy.

"Get my shit together, Bart." Bull points at Bart as we head out of the warehouse.

"You did good, son. You're on that run for sure."

I smile and climb on my bike. This right here, this is the life I long for. Guns, drugs, and violence, but most of all respect. I do what I love and I get respect in the end. This is the only life I know. I'm a sinner. A Devil at heart. I'd make my father smile and my mother pray if they saw me today.

◆◆◆

"So, this is the newest model?" Bull points at the black SUV. He doesn't seem impressed, though. After the deal, the boys went back to the club while Bull and I headed over to the local dealership to find the club an SUV.

I glance inside the vehicle and shrug. I'm not fond of the model, either.

"Too much money for standard shit," I add.

"Think I agree," Bull growls.

I stand up straight, done with looking at the SUV, and spot a cherry red VW beetle across the way. The color of it makes me think of Cherry. I stride over toward it and peer in. It's plain, nothing special, but it's girly. I don't know why the fuck I'm looking at this, why I'm thinking about Cherry, but even with all the events of the day, I can't shake her from the back of my head.

I bet she's never had anything this nice before. A piece of me wants to be the one to give her something nice. It wouldn't be much, though—it looks used.

"Um... Lip." Bull's ugly mug looks at me from the driver's side window. I stand up and he rests his arms on the roof of the car.

"I'm not sure it's your color, brother." He smirks. I roll my eyes and walk away.

"You getting that SUV or not?"

"Not," Bull clips, walking toward his bike.

I went back and bought that fucking car for Cherry. I cursed myself the whole time, walked away at least twice, and tore the contract up in pure panic once. But in the end, Bobby drove it back to my place. Then I gave him shit for the car looking good on him.

Cherry

"CHERRY, COME HERE!" LIP YELLS FROM THE FRONT DOOR, HIS voice anxious and alarming. My brows furrow and I hurry out the front door, finding Lip standing next to a bright red beetle. *Holy shit!*

"What the fuck is that?" I point at the car. I don't know what the hell that is, or better yet, why the hell it's sitting in the driveway, but it better not be for me.

"It's yours." He smiles, and my stomach falls.

"Mine?" I point at myself.

"Yeah. Come check it out." He beams like a little boy. I bite my bottom lip and tiptoe down the hot cement steps. He opens the passenger door and gestures for me to check it out, so I cross my arms and lower my head to look in. It's beautiful, and it even has a hint of that new car smell. The windows are automatic, and I bet the air conditioner even works. It must have cost a lot.

I stand up straight and shake my head.

"No, I can't." I can't accept this. I don't need this.

"Too late. It's bought. It's yours." He dangles the keys in front of me. Emotion rises, causing a painful ache to fill my chest. I've never had anything this nice before; I've never had anyone as nice as Lip in my life before. I don't deserve it.

"I have a car," I defend.

"That is not a car; it's a fucking sled. Actually, I think I've seen sleds in better shape," he insults. I roll my eyes and place my hands on my hips.

"Why?" I shrug and throw up my hands, tears filling my eyes. I don't understand why this guy I barely know would do this for me.

His face softens, and he steps around the door. He cups my chin and grabs my hip, bringing me close.

"Cherry. I thought you'd like it." His voice is low and rough, and my body spikes with arousal.

"I mean I do, but I don't understand why you would get it for me. You don't know me; I could be the worst person in the world." I can't help but chuckle. I'm saying this to a member of the Devil's Dust.

"I bought it 'cause I wanted to. I don't need a damn reason to buy you something." He pauses and blows out a tired breath.

"Yeah, but it had to cost a fortune." *God, she's beautiful, though.*

Lip shrugs. "It was money from my father's will, and it's good to know his fucking life was good for something," he scoffs. I shake my head and look down at my feet. I'm not sure what to even say to that. Lip obviously hates his father, so I guess we have something in common. "When I saw the bright red, it made me think of you." My eyes flick from the car to him. He thinks of me? I'm not crazy. I'm not the only one sitting around thinking about the other.

"You think of me?" I blurt before thinking.

He smirks something adorable and rests his hands on top of the car door.

82

"I mean…" He pauses, looking at me with heavy eyes. "Yes, I think of you, and I can't wrap my damn head around why."

My eyes widen and my mouth parts.

"I love the way your lips part like that." He steps up to me and feathers his index and middle fingers across my mouth. "You do it a lot, like you always have something to say. The way your upper lip perks, and your bottom lip drops in that sexy way, it does something to me," he whispers, his head slowly dipping toward mine. I close my eyes, and my breath hitches in my throat.

His lips peck at mine, simple and sweet, my lips still parted. He kisses me again, this time more demanding and feverous. A fire sparks inside of my chest, my body an inferno of lust. I may dissolve into ash if I don't feel the touch of him against me instantly. He smothers my insecurities, douses the walls I've built to protect myself. He makes me feel like it's okay to open up and feel, to depend on another. I wrap my arms around his neck and hook a leg around him. He bites at my bottom lip and trails his lips across my jaw, his scruff burning my delicate skin. My breathing becomes labored, and my panties dampen. He nudges us toward the car then turns and sits down on the passenger seat, pulling me on top of his lap.

"All I've thought about today is my dick being inside of you," he whispers, pushing my top up over my head. My breathing quickens, and my eyes search his hungry ones. My tits pop out of my bra, the nipples hardening as he runs his calloused palms along them. I loll my head back and sigh from his sinister touch.

"Damn, you're perfect," he whispers. Leaning forward, he sucks one of my beaded nipples into his mouth, the warmth shooting pleasurable sensations down to my toes. My fingers fumble to undo his pants; I need him to fill me, to bring me to the brink of oblivion. He shuffles them down to his knees, and just as eagerly, I pull my shorts and panties down to my ankles. I press each knee on either side of his hips and slowly lower myself onto his pierced length. The seatbelt buckle digs into my leg as his cock buries itself to the hilt. The heat of the summer makes sweat trickle down my back, and Lip's shirt dampens from the sweat beading on his hard chest.

My head falls back and a sigh spills from my mouth as he fills me. A feral grunt leaves him as he drives into me with his hard cock.

"Fuck yes," Lip hisses, his fingers digging into my hips to bring me up and down on top of his hardness. He leans forward and nips at the soft tissue of my breast, and my pussy clamps down on him in response. A low moan vibrates through my chest as he thrusts into me. I rock my hips and impale my nails into his shoulders. Knowing anyone could walk by and catch us makes sensations throughout my body awaken. I push myself up and down faster, wanting that feeling of bliss to overcome me. Lip runs his hands up my back and buries his face between my breasts. I hold onto his head, the hair soft and entwined between my fingers, his hips meeting each of my thrusts.

I feel at peace right now. Being so close to Lip, him inside of me, I feel like nothing in the world matters right now. Pressure builds in my core, and intense tingles rocket through my limbs.

"Lip," I mutter, swirling my hips, his piercing hitting me just right.

"Cher-ry," he draws my name out, filling me as he falls over the edge with me.

I fall against his sweaty chest, my head rising and falling with each of his heavy breaths.

"Does this mean you'll take the car?" Lip pants. I smile and push myself up.

"I'm paying you back for this," I insist.

Lip shakes his head and runs his hands through his sweaty hair.

"Fine, you can pay me back." He grabs my hips and rocks me, a sultry smirk across his face.

Movement catches my eyes from the back window of the car.

"Shit!" I whisper, ducking into Lip's neck.

"What is it?" Lip whispers back. The loud exhaust of a motorcycle sounds, and Lip's eyes go wide.

"That." I tilt my head toward the sound. Lip holds me in place and looks out the car door.

"Shit, it's Bobby," Lip grumbles. I pull myself off Lip's length and frantically start looking for my top.

"Here." Lip hands me my shirt. I snatch it from him and put it on, using the other hand to pull my shorts and panties up.

Lip picks me up at the waist and moves me aside as he climbs out. I glance around the side of the car and find Bobby is sitting against his bike, his arms crossed and a knowing smirk fitting his face.

"Sup, Bobby?" Lip levels him with a death stare.

Bobby juts out his chin, eyeing me. "You ain't busy, are you?" Bobby smiles a Cheshire grin.

Lip looks at me then back at Bobby. "Not anymore."

Bobby steps forward, his hand out stretched.

"I don't think I've met you yet. I'm Bobby," he introduces.

I muster a smile and shake his hand. "I'm-"

"Her name is Cherry," Lip interrupts me. I furrow my brows, not sure why he keeps telling everyone that.

"Cherry, got it." Bobby nods.

Silence fills the air. Awkward, uncomfortable silence.

"I, um, I'm going to just wait inside," I mutter.

"I'll be there in a bit," Lip states, then turns to Bobby. "Dude, what the fuck?" he gripes.

"Forgot your paperwork and shit, brother." Bobby chuckles.

I open the front door, and close it...most of the way.

"She's fucking hot!" Bobby shakes his head, his brows raised.

Lip crosses his arms, and a smug look crosses his face.

"She is. Makes me wonder why she's even fucking the likes of me." My heart saddens with that statement; why would he say that?

"Looked to me like she had no problem with it." Bobby smirks, and my cheeks turn red.

Lip punches Bobby in the arm, and Bobby scowls.

"I won't cock-block ya any longer, brother, just wanted you to get this." Bobby hands him some rolled-up paperwork.

"You didn't." Lip's voice comes cocky and self-assured as he grabs the paperwork.

I gently close the door and sigh. He's so arrogant, and such a smart ass. I can't tell if I love that about him or absolutely hate it. He bought me a fucking car even though I've only known him for a few days. What the hell? Things are moving way too fast. He's so persistent and comes on so strong at times. I roll my eyes, fighting with myself. *But if he didn't come on so strongly, would I have even given him the time of day?*

The door opens and I shuffle forward to keep out of the way.

"Forgot the paperwork," Lip informs, tossing it on the end table.

"Lip, about that. You don't think this," I gesture my hand between us, "is moving too quickly?" Lip bites at his lip ring, his brown eyes find mine, and his brows pull together.

"Maybe, but it makes sense to me. You're sexy, you're fun, and despite that spit-fire attitude you portray, when I look in your eyes, I can see you cracking under that hard shell. You've been strong for so long you just want to be weak for one goddamn moment. You crave human contact, but are too afraid to trust anyone enough to let them in. Well, you can trust me." His eyes go hard and his body puffs out. I draw in a deep breath as my chest constricts with adoration. "You don't have to be strong around me. You don't have to look over your shoulder when I'm around."

I blink rapidly, trying to keep from crying. He steps forward and grabs me by the back of the neck.

"You're with the Devil's Dust now, Cherry; we do things out of the social norm. We make our own rules, we run our own society. We live fast and ride hard. Think you can live like that?"

My eyes trail from his hard chest to his eyes. "I know nothing about your rules or society, Lip," I answer honestly.

"It's easy." He shrugs. "Respect all members, including ol' ladies. Have each other's back no matter what. No lying, no stealing, and no cheating on one another. Live free, ride daily, fuck often."

I smile; it sounds like a fucking dream. My head is buzzing with all this info. I close my eyes and breathe in deeply, trying to process it all.

"I'm starving. I'm going to whip us up something," Lip states, obviously done with this conversation.

"I'm going to shower then."

Later that night, Lip made some kind of amazing pasta. I don't know what the hell was in it, but oh my God, it was good.

◆◆◆

My eyes begin to get heavy with sleep as we watch TV, and I yawn loudly.

"I'm beat, let's get some sleep," Lip suggests.

"Sounds like a great idea," I mutter, untangling myself from the couch. I zombie-walk toward my room, but when I'm a few feet from my door, Lip grabs my hand, tugging me toward his. Butterflies swarm my stomach as a smile creeps along my face. He tucks us into bed and pulls me into him. Man, falling asleep next to him every night sounds fucking amazing. Living his life sounds amazing. I frown, realizing I don't know much about the club.

"Lip?" I whisper.

"Yeah?"

"What happens if someone doesn't follow the rules of the club?"

"For you, not much. For me, it can be brutal. Could be anything from getting my ass kicked, to having Bull fire a round into my leg, or the worst: being out-banned."

"What is-"

"Out-banned is me getting my colors stripped and thrown out of the club." Lip's face goes pale, and his eyes look grave. "If that ever happened, they might as well kill me. Devil's Dust is all I know." His tone is incredibly somber.

"How long have you been here?"

"I dunno; a while, I guess. My brother hates it 'cause he thinks I'm going against the family being here. In a way, I am." He smirks and runs his hands through his hair. I don't respond in fear of him shutting up and not telling me anymore. "My father has an MC he wanted me to be a part of based out of Las Vegas, but I'd never join it. It's sinister and immoral. It knows nothing of the word family, and the fucked-up part is it's mostly my family," he explains. "Growing up, I was no stranger to the criminal way of life. When he got caught moving coke, he tried to get my mother to take the fall. That was the separation of our father-son relationship. My mother was his ol' lady, but she was my mom. She refused to take the fall for my father, said he'd been sleeping around with her best friend and wouldn't go to prison for someone who had no respect for her. My father was killed before he ever had a hearing and my uncle took over, making my brother Zeek president of the Sin City Outlaws."

Wow, I thought my life was Hell, but it seems Lip was from the same part of Hell where I was raised.

"Damn," I whisper. "My mother left when I was a baby. My father wasn't father of the year, either. He hit me. A lot. Eventually, I left, and while I was gone, he did us all a favor and ran off with some woman."

Lip grabs my chin, making me look him square in the eyes, his sudden movements catching me off-guard.

"If anyone ever touches you like that, you come to me. Do you understand?" he questions, the colors of his eyes turning a shade darker.

"Ye-yeah," I stammer nervously. "Sure." He exhales an angry breath, his hand swiping through his hair. I cross my arms, not sure what to say.

"You said something about ol' ladies. Is that what I am now, why you call me Cherry instead of Lindsay?"

Lip's chest stills like he stopped breathing. "Um, no. Being a brother's ol' lady is like marrying a chick in our world."

My eyes widen. "Oh."

"I need my colors before I can have an ol' lady anyway," Lip continues.

"I call you Cherry 'cause I like it. And as much fun as our world may sound, it comes with a price. It can be dangerous, and it's just safer to go by a nickname than your real name."

My heart stammers. I don't need more danger, that's for sure.

"Being an ol' lady isn't like being a wife in the normal world. Your man is gone for unexpected periods, you don't get to know what your man is up to 'cause club work is not to be discussed."

"What's so different from being a girlfriend to a brother then?" I laugh.

"Well," Lip hesitates, "When a woman is claimed by a Devil, she is his property. There is no escaping him. She is his until he releases her."

My lips part in shock. Holy shit. But my chest tingles from the idea, too. To have that kind of security and affection from someone, it's not something you see in the world anymore. I kind of like it.

5

Cherry

TWO WEEKS LATER

THE LAST TWO WEEKS HAVE BEEN FILLED WITH SWEET, MIND-blowing sex. All I can think about is Lip. All I want to think about is Lip. I managed to leave the house yesterday for the first time. Aside from my brother hounding to see me and make sure I was indeed okay, I just needed some air more than anything. I wasn't shot at, and I returned back to Lip's place without a scratch. I still need to tell Lip about Piper. A piece of me, a very sad piece of me doesn't want to in fear that he may not take it well and he'll end whatever it is we have. But the way he looks at me, the way he touches me like I'm the only thing he's seeing, maybe he wouldn't.

A hand slides along my hip and cups my tit, catching my attention.

"I gotta go, babe," Lip rasps from behind me. I groan and roll over in his hold.

"When will you be back?"

Lip shrugs. "A day or two."

I nod. I know this run is something he's been looking forward to. This might be his big moment in getting his patch.

"I'm going to miss you and our late-night sexcapades," I wink. Lip smirks and sits on the bed. He's sweating, nervous.

I lift up on my knees and rub his hard shoulders.

"You okay?" I whisper into his ear. His head lolls back and a staggered breath escapes.

"Everything I know rides on this." His words are raw and emotional; this clearly means so much to him.

"You got this, babe." I run my hands up his neck and into his hair.

"I got this, I do," he repeats, standing from the bed. He gives me the sexiest smile I think I've ever seen as he swipes his hair back with his fingers.

"I'll be back before you know it." He winks.

I stand up and run my hands through his silky hair. "Be safe." I smile, pressing my lips against his.

"No promises," he teases. He kisses me back and rolls me onto my back before getting up. I pull the sheet up over my chest and watch him surf through the dresser for clothes. He shuffles on some jeans and a gray fitted shirt, his toned, tattooed arms stretching the material. He stops, his eyes dragging from the floor to me. I tilt my head to the side, curious at what he's thinking.

"What's wrong?" I ask. He opens his mouth, like he wants to tell me something, but he closes it again and shakes his head.

"Nothing. See you when I get back," he replies on a heavy breath. He grabs his cut off the back of the door and leaves. I frown. He seemed like he really needed to tell me something, like it was bothering him. I nibble on my fingernail, curious if it was good or bad news.

◆ ◆ ◆

I eventually crawl out of bed and make my way to the kitchen. I have been cooking up an egg storm since Lip taught me how to make them. He showed me how to make grilled cheese with apples and bacon, too. My God, it's delicious, but I don't think that would be too great for breakfast. He promised to teach me to cook French toast when he gets back from this run. My mouth waters just thinking about it.

I tried to defy my attraction toward Lip, but now that it's here—now that there's no denying I want him, and he wants me—I need to tell him about Piper. I need to clear the air.

My phone chimes on the counter, catching my attention. I still can't believe Lip got me a phone, I've never had one before. I set the spatula down and open the message.

LIP: I have something I need to tell you when I get back.

I knew he wanted to tell me something. My forehead wrinkles with concern. This is it, though, my sign I need to tell him about Piper. He obviously has something serious he needs to tell me, and this is my chance to tell him, as well.

CHERRY: I have something to tell you, too.

After dinner, which consists of a pizza being delivered, I flip on the TV and relax into the couch. Dozing off, I hear a motorcycle. My eyes pop open, and my heart flutters. Lip. *He must be home early.* I kick the throw blanket off and excitedly pitter-patter toward the door. Opening it, I find Bull standing on the front step, his back facing me. He turns as I flip the porch light on, his face wrinkled with a grievance.

"Bull?" I thought he went with Lip and the boys on the run.

"Cherry, dear." The words leaving his mouth are filled with more grief than my heart can process. My body goes into pure panic, little hairs rising on the back of my neck.

"What happened? Where's Lip?" I look around, like maybe Lip will pop out, surprising me, but he's nowhere. It's just Bull and me.

"Something happened on our run today." Bull looks down, his hands gripping a leather cut.

"Fucking say what happened." My nostrils flare with unease. Bull's eyes flick to mine, clearly surprised by my outburst.

"Lip took the fall for something on our run. He was taken into custody, and I'm not going to sugarcoat it. He ain't getting out for a while."

My eyes fill with tears instantly.

"What?" I croak. My heart sinks, and my nails dig into the doorframe.

Bull steps forward and grabs me by the elbow to hold me upright, making me aware of my unsteadiness from my emotional state.

"What did he take the blame for?" I manage to spit out, both of my hands clutching the doorframe.

Bull shakes his head and looks off.

"I'm afraid I can't tell you that, Cherry. It's club business, which means it's not your business."

"What do you mean you can't tell me?" I sneer, my anger replacing my sadness.

"Our club has rules, regulations. It's not personal; it's to keep not only you safe, but the brothers, as well."

I shake my head, pissed. Lip told me club affairs are just that—club only. I never thought that would affect me... 'til now.

Bull hands the black cut out to me. I scowl, not sure what it is. Maybe Lip got his patch for taking the fall for the club. I take it from Bull and when I open it, a giant sob escapes my mouth.

Lip's Ol' Lady is written along the back of the cut, the Devil's skull patched right under it. Lip must have gotten patched in, and now he's making me his property.

"You're family now, Cherry. We'll take care of you while Lip is away. He did something very brave today, and I will forever be in his debt." I just nod and sob some more. Do I want this?

"I'm sending some of the ol' ladies over tomorrow. They'll help you through this, darling." Bull leans forward, the smell of booze and cigarettes strong, and kisses my cheek.

"Hang in there," he whispers before turning to leave.

I just stand here, unsure of what to say, or what to think. This life, is it for me? I run my finger along the skull. He said I was family now. I never really had a family. My family has been taken from me, over and over. Lip claimed me; I'm his now. A small, pathetic laugh escapes from my mouth, and I pull the cut next to my chest. *I'm his now, and the Devil's Dust will always have my back.*

◆◆◆

The front door swings open and I hear a lot of chitter-chatter fill the house. I swipe at my tears, and my heart races. *I know I locked that door.*

A plump, redheaded lady waltzes into the bedroom, and I shrink into the comforter. Her hair is pinned up and she has on a tight black blouse and blue jeans.

"Who are you, and how'd you get in?" I question, sitting up on the bed. The lady scrunches her face like I'm being ridiculous and holds up a set of keys.

"Bull gave em to me," she explains. This must be an ol' lady he was talking about. I sniff back the snot and nod.

"Baby, you best wipe those tears away and get out of that bed," she sasses. I wince, a little taken back by her forwardness. "You can't lie around here moping," she continues, sitting on the edge of the bed as she pushes my hair from my face.

"I finally found a good guy, and he's taken from me in a blink of an eye," I mumble.

"You look like shit," the lady blurts. My fingers tangle in my hair and I smirk. I can tell she is an outspoken person. I like her already. "I didn't sleep a wink last night; all I could think about is Lip being in jail, or prison. Is he okay? Why is he in there?" I ramble, pulling my legs up and wrapping my arms around them.

"I know it's hard. I do. I'm Babs, by the way, cause I talk a lot. I'm Lock's ol' lady. He's been to jail a time or two, and you get used to it. From what I'm told, Lip admitted to everything, so he'll be on his way to prison and serving his sentence before you know it."

"They won't tell me why he's even locked up," I state, my tone coming off irritated.

"Yeah, that's part of it. This life can be rough, and some can't handle it. We women don't get to know much about the inside of club things. Think of it as Lip's in the CIA, and everything he does is top secret." She smiles and pats my back. I can't help but laugh at her explanation.

"There you go, there's a smile."

I push myself off the bed and run my hands through my hair.

"But you're family now. Our loyalty to one another is thicker than blood. You need something, you get us and we'll take care of it." I sniff the snot back again, taking in everything she's saying.

"Now, how about we get you a shower, and maybe go have a girls' day," she suggests.

"I don't know," I hesitate.

"So, this is the new lady, huh?" A woman with brownish hair walks in, her lips so bright red it's the first thing my eyes land on. She has on black ripped-up shorts, a white shirt, and a leather cut.

"Yup, she's depressed," Babs replies, crossing her arms. *Wow, they make me feel bad for caring.*

"Suck it up, buttercup. You wanna be an ol lady, you better grow a fucking backbone. Our men do what they need to do. They don't need a sobbing bitch back home. They need a strong woman taking care of things while they're away," the brownish-haired lady snaps. I swallow the lump in my throat and stand.

"Damn, Vera, back off a little bit, will ya?" Babs frowns.

"She needs to know now," Vera smarts, rolling her tongue along the bottom of her lip.

"Thanks for the advice, but I got this," I sneer. I don't need some bitch walking in here telling me how to feel.

"Clearly." She stares at me, and I look down at myself. My hair is a tangled mess, I'm wearing the shirt Lip wore the night before he left, and I need to shave my legs badly. I look a hot mess. The only thing missing is the bag of donuts I offed at midnight last night.

"Well, if you got this, then let's go. I really need to get my nails done." Babs pulls her hand up, examining her red nails.

I attempt to run my fingers through my hair, not sure what to do.

Vera sighs loudly and stomps her black-booted feet at me. I fist my hands, ready to punch her if she gets harsh.

"Look." Vera stops right in front of me, her face a tone softer. "Lip is a good kid. I know it sucks, trust me. We all have

97

been here, eating donuts in bed." I look at the bed and notice remnants of the powder donuts. Shit. "Not showering, not doing shit 'cause we miss our man so much. That's why we're here. We're your support system. We may be tough, but we're only like that when we need to be. Bull told us you're Lip's property, and he told us Lip took a big hit for him too. You and Lip are like the fucking prom king and queen of the club right now."

Babs laughs, and I can't help but smirk. That's an image.

Babs grabs the cut off the bed and throws it at me. "Wear that property patch with pride, girlie. Your man did something very honorable, and not only Bull but the whole club will have a high amount of respect for him. You gotta tough cut to fill." I catch it and caress Lip's name. I miss him; he makes me feel things I never have before. But if he picked me to be his property, I'll make him proud.

I look up at the girls who are both now smiling. "I'll wear it with honor," I whisper. "Yeah, sure, I'll go. Let me get some clothes on."

◆◆◆

3 Weeks Later

I sit in my chair, waiting for Lip to be escorted to his side of the glass. I was told he isn't allowed to have contact visits yet because he just arrived, which sucks because I'd do anything for a hug. To smell him, to feel the warmth of his skin against mine. It's getting lonely at the house without him. Piper has been in my mind more than ever because of it. I thought about driving by the trailer park the other day but decided against it. That is a stupid, stupid idea. I want to see Piper—hell, I *want* Piper. I *am* her mother, after all. But I know going over there will put me in the line of fire again. I thought about telling the ol' ladies, but I'm new to the club. And besides, what can they do? I'm not sure the hit that came after me wasn't from a judge. That's not some little trailer park shit that might need the piss kicked out of him; it's someone who could cause some major damage. I don't want to hurt my new family when I just got them. But I *will* get Piper back. Someday.

I shift in my seat and pull my leather cut onto my arms. To wear this, I feel proud, like I'm a part of something whole.

Orange catches my eye, and I look up to see Lip handcuffed and being pushed toward his chair. *Orange. Is that for being new or for murder?*

He looks rough. His lip piercing is gone, and his hair is oily and un-groomed. This guy doesn't look like Lip at all, but rather a maniacal empty shell of Lip. I pick the phone up and watch as his chest lifts on an inhale before he lifts his phone.

"Lip," I state anxiously.

"Sup?" He looks off, not at me. A stabbing pain radiates in my chest, but I furrow my brows and try to shrug it off.

"I miss you. How have you been? Are you okay?" I ramble off all the questions that have been in my mind since the day he was taken from me.

He shrugs. "I'm fine. It's prison." His tone is clipped and dry. He doesn't even seem excited to see me. I pull on my cut, a little sad.

"What is that?" Lip snaps. My head jerks up and I find him actually looking at me.

"This?" I pull on the leather claiming my shoulders. I smile and turn a little bit in my seat to show off the back.

"I gotta say, I wasn't expecting it." I chuckle.

Lip bites his bottom lip and nods. "I gotta go babe."

I jerk in my seat. "What? Why?" None of the guards had said anything about our time being up.

"Time's up," he states, standing from his seat.

"Wait!" I slap my hand against the glass, my teeth gritting with anger. Ever since the day he was taken from me, I have had one thing on my mind every day.

"That day you said you had something to tell me, what was it?" I yell, hoping he can hear me.

Lip trails his bottom lip with his tongue, his eyes searching mine for the first time since I've been here. I feel vulnerable with the intensity of it. Seconds go by which feel like several minutes.

"It doesn't matter," he finally says and walks away. My bottom lip trembles and I cover my mouth with my hand, trying to hold back a sob. I all but run out of there, so confused. He doesn't look like Lip because he isn't Lip. He's built a shell, an ego to survive in prison. I have to be strong for him, just like the girls said. He was there for me when I needed it most, and now I'll be here for him.

Lip was sentenced to six years in prison. When that verdict came in, I fell off the wagon of sobriety. I got so high and drunk that Babs had to put her finger down my throat to make me puke up some of the liquor. I was hungover for three days.

Cherry

4 Years Later

I WOULD LOVE TO SAY THAT ALL THE VISITS WE HAD OVER THE last four years were different, but they weren't. He was distant, his eyes hollow and cold. The Lip I knew was nowhere to be found when I was with him. But he was in prison, and I couldn't imagine what that was like. I was told a couple of times visits were not an option because Lip was in trouble. Not to mention he had extended time added to his sentence because he killed a man in self-defense. The ol' ladies took me in as one of their own, and I loved them for it. Prison wasn't only rough for Lip, but for me, too. Living among the MC, a rougher side of me escaped. When one of them was in trouble, I was there standing behind them, ready to throw down. To say the least, my soul had become corrupted for my new family, but being alone for years can make anyone angry. I was mad, I was sad, I was lonely, and I took it out on anyone I could. Before, I saw a baseball bat as something you did to pass time—little league, even. Now when I see a bat, I wonder whose kneecaps I'm about to crack, and If I should use aluminum or wood.

Who knows, maybe this side of me would have come out eventually. I wasn't exactly raised in the best upbringing, after all. I asked God to feel my pain that day I met Lip, and he must have listened and placed me where I'd be accepted. With the outlaws, where I belong.

◆ ◆ ◆

Staring at the keys in my hand, my heart races when I think about the thought that has been plaguing my mind for several months. Piper. My daughter. Seeing her. I want to see her just once, know that she's alive and doing well. Years have gone by and yet every day I think about her. Think about telling the club, and think about telling Lip, but I don't. I don't tell anyone. Not because I don't want to, but because I'm scared. Lip is not the man I knew. He's distant since he's been in prison; he doesn't say much when I see him, and hardly writes back anymore. He's breaking in there. Prison is making him hard and constantly on-guard. Lip has two more years in that hellhole, and every day seems longer without him.

I tell him every time I talk to him that I'm here, waiting for him, staying strong for him. Just like the ol' ladies told me to. They said those are the main things a man locked up wants to hear. Hell, they're the main things I want to tell him. But even with the club having my back, inviting me to functions and making me one of their own, I feel a piece of my soul missing. Piper is missing. Lip is missing. Therefore, I am missing.

"I could just drive by," I mutter to myself. Just drive by and see that the trailer park is still there, see the house Eric lives in—or used to live in, because who knows if he's even still there.

I bite my bottom lip and step out the front door. *Just a drive-by; nobody will even recognize me.* I get into my car, pull my hair into a white baseball cap I found in Lip's closet, and put on some sunglasses. I flip down my sun visor and look at myself in the mirror. It'll work.

I grip the wheel and my world shifts.

"Shit," I mumble. Adrenaline is pulsing through me so hard it's making me high. This is so dangerous, incredibly reckless. I blow out a steady breath, trying to get ahold of myself.

"If the Devil's Dust taught me anything, it's to live on the wild side," I tell myself. I start the car and drive the long journey toward my daughter, praying for just a glimpse of her.

Almost two hours later, I turn on the road that holds my old trailer. My heart beats violently as I pull up behind a slow van. I attempt to keep my eyes on the road but I keep glancing to my left, waiting for the trailer park to come into view. I try and keep my pace, so as not to draw attention to my car, but when I finally drive in front of the trailer park, everything seems to slow down. My eyes sweep the area frantically, knowing I have only seconds to see her.

I notice a couple of kids playing on an old jungle gym, but none of them stand out. Something grabs my eye, and I turn toward Eric's house. My breath catches and a whimper leaves my mouth. A small little redheaded girl in pigtails bounces down the front steps. She has on the biggest grin, her cheeks rosy red. Everything hits me at once. *That is my daughter. My blood. I've abandoned her. I'm a terrible mother.* Gravel flies at my car, and I look forward to see the van swerving to the right because I just nearly ran into them.

"Shit!" I curse, jerking my wheel to miss them. I veer off onto the side of the road and slam on the brakes, the van honking its horn as it speeds off. I look out the window, ignoring them, needing to see Piper just one more time. All of the kids are looking at me, including Piper now. Alarm ignites and I panic. *Shit!* I grip the wheel and dart back onto the road, cursing for drawing attention to myself as I drive away.

That was her. That was my little girl. She's still here, and still alive. My brows furrow. She had on a really baggy shirt, and jeans that looked like they were boys. What the hell is Eric thinking? I shake my head. He obviously knows nothing about raising a little girl.

Lip

PICKING UP THE PHONE, I LET OUT A LONG BREATH. I NEED TO hear Cherry's voice today.

"Lip?" Cherry's sweet voice sounds, and my body sags against the brick wall.

"Sup?" I reply coolly.

"Hey, how you doing?" she questions. I pick at the cement between the bricks.

I hate it here, but I never tell her about what goes on in here. Gangs and rival gangs are here, and I constantly have to watch my back. I can feel myself slipping into something dark and very familiar. I feel like a fucking DeLuca. I have to stand my ground constantly; if I walk away from one altercation I basically put a bulls-eye on my back, but if I stand up and beat my enemy to a bloody pulp, I draw attention from some of the prison's most notorious outlaws. Not to mention the worst thing that could have happened. I had an FBI agent visit my cell the other day, told me he could get me out of here if I gave him something, anything about the club. I told him to get the fuck out of my cell without hesitation. But I lay awake at night wondering what it would be like if I *did* rat. What if I did give him something, nothing big, and got the fuck out of here.

"I don't know. I'm fucking sick of it here. I needed to hear your voice," I reply honestly. I hear her gasp in the phone, and my chest squeezes. I've been cold to her, I know. I don't want to be, but it's hard in here. I hate her seeing me like this, and I hate that I'm keeping shit from her.

"Lip, are you okay? What's going on? What's wrong?" she rambles, prying me for information. I sigh into the phone and rest my elbow on the wall.

"Just the same ol' bullshit, ya know. Temptation knocked on my cell door yesterday. I needed to hear your voice, remember my way of life, and not pussy out."

"Temptation? Like guys?" Her voice goes soft, like she thinks I might be messing around on her in here.

I chuckle. "No, not like guys. I like the feel of wet pussy, baby."

"Then what? Lip, you can tell me anything," she murmurs. I bite my bottom lip and close my eyes. I want to tell her, but I don't want her to worry.

"Tell me, what have you been up to? Club treating you okay?" I change the subject.

"Umm, yeah. Everything's good." Her voice takes on an unfamiliar tone. Little hairs on my arms rise, worried that something is wrong.

"What's wrong?" I ask, my tone coming off snappier than I intended.

"I'm fine, really." She doesn't sound fine.

"Inmate, time's up!" Guard Geraldo hollers toward me.

"Shit. I gotta go, babe."

"Yeah, I understand. It was good to talk to you." Her voice falls back into that sweet tone again, and my dick perks at it. Fuck, I miss her. I miss her pussy, too.

"Stay out of trouble," I add. I've been told by Bull himself that Cherry is a resilient one. They went on lockdown at the club because they got into some shit a while back, and Cherry ignored his texts and fled. It made me beyond angry, because I was in here and unable to do a damn thing about it. Cherry is a fire that nobody can put out, having a mind of her own. I'm afraid one of these days she's going to burn herself trying to prove to others she doesn't need them to thrive.

"Yeah, we'll see," she retorts, knowing exactly what I'm talking about. She's feisty and stubborn, and I both hate it and fucking need it at the same time.

Cherry

3 Months Later

SITTING IN MY CAR, I WATCH PIPER FROM AFAR. I'VE BEEN coming up here and sitting in the gas station right across from the trailer park, watching her like a creeper. I can't help it, though, and in doing so, I've learned Eric's schedule. He works construction, I think. He came home one afternoon when I was watching Piper play; I nearly had a stroke, but he never even looked my way. He works Monday through Saturday, from sunrise to sundown. Sundays, he comes home at noon. In the mornings, he takes Piper to a trailer next door before he leaves for work, and no longer than five minutes after Piper is dropped off she runs out of the trailer to play in the playground. She's there most of the day with the other kids. She's never dressed in anything nice, though; in fact, she looks like a damn boy.

Looks like today is the first day of school for the kids. A bunch of them are waiting at the end of the trailer park's drive in new clothes and shoes. They all look clean-cut and nice. I wonder if Eric put Piper in preschool this year. I sigh and bite into my donut, needing the sugar. Preschool would be good for her, give her a head start on what to expect.

My heart practically stops beating when I see Piper walking down the stairs of Eric's house. She stops and looks at the door. Following her line of sight, I find Eric close behind her.

"Shit," I mumble, ducking in my seat. Eric waves at her and heads toward his truck. What an asshole—he's not even going to help her on the bus on her first day of school. I grit my teeth and sweep my eyes back to Piper. Her clothes look ridiculous. I glance back at Eric, curious if he just doesn't have the means to provide for her. He's in nice-looking clothes, though, and his boots look brand new and expensive. Does he just not care? Or is he punishing her because of me?

After Eric has driven off, I sit up in my seat. I want to go stand with her, tell her not to be scared for her first day.

The group of kids turns, and Piper's bright smile fades. I frown. *What are they saying to her?* I sit up more in my seat and squint my eyes, trying to see what's going on. One of the other kids points at her dark blue shorts, and the rest of the kids laugh. They are making fun of her. My heart sinks, and I look down at my hands.

God, why does this feel like déjà vu? Glancing back up, one of the kids pushes Piper.

"What the hell?!" I open my car door and jog across the

street. "Hey, you little punk, get away from her!" I holler. All of the other kids scatter, running to the opposite side of the circle drive. I step over and grab Piper's hand to help her up. She looks up and pins me with tear-filled eyes, and my heart slams against my ribcage with such force I can't breathe.

What am I doing? She looks just like me. She even has freckles on her face. I can't be here.

"Thank you," she mutters, her voice cutting me.

"You're—" My voice cracks. "You're welcome," I finish. She looks at the other kids as her tears fall down her cheeks.

"Screw them, they're stupid," I add. Her head whips toward me, her eyes wide. She peers back at them, then back to me and smiles.

"Yeah, screw them," she repeats. I close my eyes and scorn myself silently for my language.

"Why were they picking on you?" I question, opening my eyes to find her looking right back at me. My heart does that panic beat against my chest again, making it feel like I'm drowning in my own guilt and regret.

She looks down, her fingers rubbing on the material of her shirt.

"Because of your clothes?" I assume. She nods.

"How come your daddy doesn't buy you girl clothes? Or clothes that fit?"

She sighs and crosses her arms. "He says I shouldn't worry about what I wear." She rolls her eyes. "He always buys me boy stuff. I think he thinks I'm a boy." I clench my jaw. *That bastard. I can't tell if he's just being a protective father, or a fucking prick.*

The big yellow school bus screeches as it comes to a stop behind me.

"Well, I guess you better go enjoy your first day of school." Her eyes flick from me to the bus and fear consumes them.

107

"Think of it as a big Twinkie. It isn't scary, really." I laugh as she just looks at me, swallowing hard.

"Your first day of school is going to be so much fun. You're going to meet your teacher, and find friends." I pause, smiling big. "And the biggest playground ever is there!" I laugh, my tone enticing. Her lips part into a toothy smile.

"I'm Piper, by the way." She holds her hand out, and I shake it. Her little palm in my hand makes me want to cry it's so small. I don't want to let go, can't help but circle my thumb along the top of her hand, feeling her soft skin.

"I'm—" I choke. I want to say her mother, I want to say Lindsay, but it's too risky. "I'm Cherry."

"Cherry?" Her face scrunches up. She tilts her head to the side, eyeing my leather cut. "Are you a biker?" The bus honks, and Piper jumps.

"You better get going." I finally pull my hand from hers and give her arm a friendly squeeze. She looks up at me and beams with innocence before running off toward the bus.

"Bye, biker lady!" she hollers over her shoulder. I can't help but giggle and cry at the same time. I got to see my daughter off for her first day of school, but the thought of her not even knowing who I am weighs heavily on my heart.

6

Cherry

TWO YEARS LATER

THE CEILING IS SPOTTED FROM WHERE THE ROOF HAS LEAKED over the last few years. My body beads with sweat from the unbearable heat as I lie on the bed and stare up at it. The small air conditioner placed in the window is not keeping up with the fucking heat this summer. Lip put it in trying to cool the house down, but it ain't working. I may just evaporate into a pool of sweat if I lie here long enough.

Lip was finally released from prison about a month ago, the club lawer finally got him off on self-defense and his extended time was taken off. But, things are not like they used to be. Not at all. He's quiet, often looking at me when he doesn't think I'll notice, but as soon as I make eye contact, he looks away. He has this raw energy surrounding him, like something dark dwells within his chest and it might just rip through at any minute.

I thought he would paw me to death, fuck me into oblivion as soon as he got out, but that was hardly the case. He hung out at the club for a few days, getting patched in for his honorable duties. He had to learn the ropes. After that, the club had a big returning home party. I was nervous Lip would cheat on me. The way things were going I wasn't sure where we stood. Instead, he came home drunk and screwed me on the couch. I didn't realize how much I truly missed him until he was inside me. Him coming home after the party tucked all my insecurities away. His hands claiming me, and his hot breath whispering in my ear about how much he missed me almost put all the broken pieces of my heart back together. Almost. Things still aren't right between us. He's not the guy I remember. *We* are not how I remember.

"Heading to the club. Don't wait up," Lip states, striding through the bedroom. I sit up on my elbows and cock an eyebrow. His hair is wet and messy and my hands ache to tug on it. His arms bulge through his sleeveless black leather cut, revealing all of his tattoos and their vibrant color. My eyes sway down to his tight jeans that sculpt that sexy ass of his. His butt is fine, but not fine enough for me to forget him not coming home tonight—again.

"Don't wait up? What's that supposed to mean? What the fuck are you doing?" My face twists with anger. Lip has been a recluse since he's been out of prison. He rides alone, watches TV alone. He's ... alone. I've been alone without him the last six years and want nothing more than to play catch-up, but he has different ideas.

He sits at the end of the bed and shoves his foot into his dirty boot. Turning his head, he eyes me with those drop-dead-sexy brown eyes. "Exactly what I said—I won't be here." His voice is deep and rugged, something I definitely missed hearing every day while he was locked up.

I roll my eyes and swing my legs over the bed to get up.

"Seriously? You've been gone a lot lately," I cross my arms and pop my hip out. "I wish you would talk to me, Lip. Tell me what's going on in that head of yours." I step up to him and run my hands through his wet hair from the shower. He's hiding something; I can feel it in my chest.

Lip shakes his head from my grip and pulls on his last boot. "I ain't got time for this shit this morning." My eyes widen with his tone of voice, and my heart sinks. He's been losing his temper with me a lot lately—with anything, really. The other day, the kitchen drawer wouldn't open so he yanked it open with anger, breaking the entire thing. I've never seen Lip react like that. I'm starting to feel like maybe what we had before isn't what we have now. Maybe we've grown apart. I mean, we only knew each other for a short time before he was locked up, and we didn't exactly have a lot of contact over the years.

He stands up, taller than me by six inches. Stepping up to me, he looks down at me. His dark brown eyes pierce right through me, and I hold my breath.

"Don't be a pain in the ass today." He leans down and smacks my forehead with a kiss, his lip ring cold against my sweaty skin.

I follow him out of the room, my hands on my hips. I have so many things on the tip of my tongue just ready to spew his way, but I can't open my mouth. I feel like I don't even know this man anymore.

"Later," he tosses over his shoulder as he slams the front door.

My breathing quickens, my nostrils flaring to allow the harsh breathing to escape. In a fit of anger, I grab the picture of me and Lip that someone took of us when he first brought me to the club and throw it at the door. The glass on the frame shatters, and it splits in two before falling every which way.

I've waited for his ass for six years. SIX FUCKING YEARS, and this is what I get when he comes back?

He won't even tell me why he went to prison. Club rule. If it's club business, it's none of the ol' ladies' business, meaning none of my business. The time I spent with Lip before he went to prison, he was sweet and would spend every minute of the day he could with me. Most of those tangled in sheets, screwing my brains out, telling me how perfect I was. Sometimes it was as if it were too good to be true. But since he's been out of prison... I haven't seen that man. Prison changes people; that's what I was told over and over by the girls at the club. I refused to believe it ... until Lip got out. He went in a sensual man, but he came out something darker than the caverns of Hell. He's not Lip. When I look in his eyes, I see secrets, I see ... something unfamiliar.

I blow out an irritated breath and look at the clock.

7:00 AM

"Shit." I hurry into the room and pull on a black tank top with a white skull printed on the front, and shimmy on some shorts. I can't say anything about Lip having secrets... 'cause I have one. A big one.

One that is six years old and looks just like me, and I still haven't told him about her. How can I?

◆ ◆ ◆

Sitting in my car, I watch the little girl with strawberry-blonde hair trot down the stairs of her house. She's wearing the clothes I gave her yesterday: a green skirt and a white top with a watermelon on it. Her father is a fucking douchebag. He had her in clothes two sizes too big again, and they were boy clothes at that. I've wanted to tell Lip about her so many times over the years, but I just couldn't. I was going to tell him about her, but I couldn't while he was locked up. I should tell him now, but it doesn't seem like the right time. I groan in frustration.

I drive to the trailer park, thoughts of Lip and Piper filling my head. Over the years, I came often during the week to see Piper; of course, it was in the morning after Eric left for work. I would see her off to school, and to see her grow over the years is a bittersweet moment. I bought a book about lawyering, trying to figure out a way around whatever I'm in, but I can't even read the first fucking chapter with so many legal terms. I pull up to the gas station across from the trailer park and turn the car off. I hate this fucking trailer park. I will not leave my daughter here to grow up. I *will* figure something out. But that's just it, I gotta figure it out, be smarter than Eric and that piss-brain judge. It's risky showing up here, I know, but I can't stay away. I'm her mother, and Eric obviously is not taking care of her like he should.

She looks up and spots me, her cute little freckled face beaming with energy.

I can't help but smile and climb out of my red bug.

"Hey there, Piper! You look beautiful today." She looks down at herself and smiles a toothless grin. "Did you lose a tooth?"

She touches the empty spot in her mouth and nods.

"It came out last night," she slurs. I laugh, but a piece of me breaks. I should have been there to place her tooth under her pillow with her. I rest my hands on my hips and lift my head to the sky, trying to draw strength from the gods.

"Are you okay, Cherry?"

I blow out an emotional breath and muster a smile.

"Mmhmm. What did your dad say about the clothes?" I bite my lip, nervous.

Piper's light of innocence fades into something sad. She

shrugs, kicking the rocks in front of her.

"He didn't even notice. He was drunk last night, and was passed out in his puke this morning." I grind my teeth. I should kill him. I should take Piper and just run, goddamn it.

"Wait, is he home right now?" My body goes stiff.

"Yeah, but he's passed –"

"I gotta go." I give her a kiss on the forehead and turn to leave. The hair on my neck is raised in alarm, heart slamming against my chest in fear. He can't know I'm here, that I'm alive.

"Will I see you tomorrow?" she yells. I turn my head and look over my shoulder. I try to see her every day before school, sometimes after. It's hard because she's not supposed to know about me. She doesn't know me, actually. She knows Cherry... the biker lady who saved her from bullies and became her best friend. I'm all she has.

"Yes, I'll be here."

I climb in my car and peel out of the trailer park before Eric sees me.

Lip

I BRING THE CUP OF ICED TEA TO MY MOUTH AND TAKE A COOL sip, the ice cubes sliding against the glass and cooling my lips as I watch a bunch of club whores washing the guys' bikes. I've been at the club a lot lately. I can't be around Cherry. Those eyes, the way they see right through me, cuts me. I've been meaning to sit her down and tell her something that has turned into the blackest lie, but she pins me with those gray eyes, and that loving smile, and I just... I fucking can't. I wanted to tell her before I was locked up, back when I realized I really cared for her and needed to get shit out in the open, but I kept telling myself one more day, or I'll tell her tomorrow. Now that lie has grown from a small storm into a violent hurricane. I know I'm being a fucking prick to her lately, and it pains me. But I'm in over my fucking head. I can't stand to lie to her anymore, but I just can't be that guy she fell in love with either. It's not me. I'm not gentle, and I'm not sweet. I have a filthy mouth, the urge to fuck hard, and pull the trigger on my gun at any bastard that crosses me. I am not the man any woman should love, especially Cherry.

"Who's that chick?" Bobby points out, grabbing me from my dark thoughts. I glance at him, curious how long he's been standing beside me. He is the prime example of what a surfer should look like, only he's got tattoos and a leather cut on.

"Which chick?" I reply, looking at my glass uninterested. I got enough shit to deal with right now.

"The one who looks like a fucking doll."

I raise my stare and look at the bunch of half-naked girls. One with dark hair that falls just above her tits stands out above the rest. Her cheek bones are a slight pink, standing out amongst her smooth porcelain skin, and her hair curls in the front. Just from standing back here, I can see her thick eyelashes. Her frame is slender and small, sporting a Harley Davidson bikini perfectly.

"Jesus, she does look like a fucking doll," I mutter, taking the last sip of my drink. She's hot, though; if I could, I'd fuck her.

"Dibs," Tom Cat claims, walking up beside Bobby and slapping his shoulder. Tom Cat was patched in not too long ago; he's all right as far as they go.

I laugh, because Tom Cat obviously knows nothing about women. If a woman heard you call dibs, she'd laugh in your face and walk away. Well, the kind I'm interested in anyway. Feisty, stubborn, hard to get.

"Yeah, good luck with that." I chuckle.

"What, you want her? You hopping off the ol' Cherry train

there, Lip?" Tom Cat taunts, running his hand through his brown hair. I glare in reaction.

"You best shut the fuck up if you know what's good for ya, Tom Cat. What I do is none of your fucking business."

His face falls flat, and Bobby looks at me with confusion. I hand Tom Cat my empty glass and stride past the girls.

"Lip!" I stop and look at the group of girls, curious who called my name.

"Hi, I'm washing your bike and was curious if there was anything," she bats her baby doll lashes at me, "special you might need." I inhale a strong breath, not sure how to handle the first piece of ass that has thrown themselves at me since I've been out. She obviously doesn't know Cherry, because every girl who has strutted into this club knows Cherry and I are together.

"Yeah, clean it. You missed a spot, Dolly," I reply coolly, pointing to my Harley tank. Her eyes widen, and she looks back at my bike. The guys laugh behind me, clearly amused by my assholery.

"Where's Bull? I thought we had church this morning," I ask Shadow as I walk into the kitchen of the club. Shadow is the VP now, and is also married to the president's daughter. Yeah, who knew Bull had a fucking daughter? That was one of the not-so-fun events I missed while being locked up. I'm not saying Bull favors Shadow now... but Bull favors him. After I got out of prison, Bull was waiting to pick me up, my patch in hand. Best fucking welcome home gift ever. We had a small party, naked chicks, booze, drugs—all of it. I didn't fuck around, though; my mother taught me better than that. Seeing the pain she went through when she found out my father messed around on her, I couldn't do that to anyone.

"He had an emergency this morning," Shadow mutters,

116

pulling out a tub of ice cream.

I turn and lean against the counter. When I was locked up, a lot of shit went down in the club. FBI was knocking on our door, and I mean that literally. Babs was killed in a hit-and-run, and we even found out that Locks, our previous VP, was a rat. I never did like that guy. During this time, Bull stepped out of reality, too. I got orders inside of prison from Shadow for the last several months I was in the joint. His orders were different then Bull's—more digressed, more violent. Things I never had to do before, Shadow ordered me to do. He was the VP, so I did what I was ordered.

Lots of shit can go down in a six-year period, but it was all worth it because I got patched in as soon as I walked out of there. I look down at my cut and smirk. Feels good to be a member, to belong. But prison changed me in a way, the things I did and saw; my mind slowly became as tarnished and marred as the walls that imprisoned me.

"Bull's gone? What about the drop tonight?" Bobby questions, digging in the fridge.

"It's all set up. It should run smoothly." Shadow shrugs.

"Suppliers paid?" Bobby asks, pulling out a tub of coleslaw.

"Shit!" Shadow exclaims.

"I'll take care of it," I offer.

Shadow looks at his phone and shakes his head.

"If you can, man, that would be great. I need to meet Dani about Zane's school," Shadow states. Dani is his wife, and Zane is his little boy. Shit has changed since I was in prison. I never would have thought Shadow as the prime example of a happy family. I mean, his kids are cute, but I don't want any. Fuck. That.

"Can do," I reply.

"Want me to come with?" Bobby asks, diving a fork right into the container.

.

"Nah, I got it. I gotta go to my mom's afterward."

"See ya tomorrow, brother," Bobby sounds around a mouth full of food.

◆◆◆

The sun is hot on my arms, and the wind is sweeping through my hair. In prison, I thought about a lot of shit. Pussy, good food, a nice bed. But what I missed the most was my bike. There is no therapy like wind therapy. Having the open road at my mercy, my thoughts free to roam where they please. It's a freedom I longed for.

I pull into the shady-looking bar and turn my bike off. Striding inside, the smell of mold and stale beer is strong.

"I was wondering when you'd be here," a guy sitting at the bar states. He looks Mexican, with short, dark hair. He has a tattoo of a marijuana leaf on his dark tan skin. He's wearing a white shirt and black jeans, a gold Rolex shining amongst the shitty bar lights. This place is clearly a front, a way to hide the outrageous amounts of money he's pocketing. I step over to him and slap the envelope on the counter.

"You Bud?" That is obviously not his name, but what the fuck ever.

"Yup. That two thousand?"

"Yeah."

He slides his hand over and grabs the envelope.

"Everything's on schedule then."

"Great," I respond, tapping my knuckles against the counter.

Stepping out of the bar, I inhale a large breath, taking in the clean crisp air. That was easy—no bullets, no hustling. Guess I'll be arriving at my mom's earlier than I thought. I clench my teeth. It's as if I long for violence now. I hate it. Taking pain from another is similar to doing drugs. You're nervous at first, thinking of all the things that can go wrong, but then you push through those unsettling nerves and just do it. You come to find out it's not that bad. You actually get a high out of it; feel fucking great. You do it again, and then again, and the next thing you know, you start craving it.

I glance over and find a black shiny car parked next to the curb with a man leaning against the hood, his legs crossed out in front of him. I squint, trying to figure out if I recognize the man when he turns his head and looks right at me. Fuck.

"Phillip. You haven't been answering my calls." It's Stevin, the FBI agent who hounded me in prison.

"Get the fuck away!" I yell, pointing off into the distance. Stevin grins and stares off. He knows he's putting me at risk.

"So, you've been *ignoring* my calls."

I shake my head before turning and walking toward my bike. "This ain't prison. You have no leverage over me anymore."

"I'd think again. I want you as my informant!" Stevin hollers.

"Not my problem." I step up to my bike, ready to throw my leg over it.

"Yeah, but it will be your problem if your club knows you've been talking to the FBI inside of prison." I stop, my blood running cold as my heart beats to a dangerous level.

"What about the pretty little redhead, huh? I wonder what dirt I can dig up on her." He lifts his shoulders with a Cheshire grin plastered across his arrogant face.

I nibble on my lip ring, not sure what to do. He's threatening not only my woman, but my club. I flick my eyes to his and start my bike.

"Fuck you," I mutter, deciding he's fucking bluffing. If he were going to do that shit, he'd have done it.

◆◆◆

Four hours later, I pull up to my mom's house and see Zeek's bike already parked in the drive. Zeek and I don't get along. He's was my father's pride and joy, running the Sin City Outlaws in Vegas, carrying on the DeLuca title. I said 'fuck you both' and turned my back on them. My uncle is just like my father, and I want nothing to do with any of them. They shoot now and ask later; family is of no importance to them. They care about leverage, rank, and money—nothing else.

"Phillip!" my mother cheers, rushing out of the front door. Her brown hair is pulled into a messy bun, and she has on a Levi shirt with gray sweats chopped off mid-leg.

"Sup, Ma?" I climb off my bike and head toward her, enveloping her small bony frame into mine.

"My boy, it's been too long," she cries into the crook of my neck.

"Mom, it's only been a few weeks," I laugh.

"Yeah, well, I get lonely." She pulls back and slaps at my shoulder. "Your brother is inside setting the table now."

I look at the two-story house, the house that was my mother's starting over chip. She moved here after my father was killed. I came with her and found Devil's Dust shortly after. Ever since Zeek and I moved out, Ma has tried to get us to come over for dinner at least once a month. When I was in jail, she would visit at least once a month. Zeek never came, and I didn't expect him to.

I step inside the house and see pictures of Zeek and me as kids. Mom has them hung all over the living room walls like a fucking shrine. It's humiliating. I can see it now: if I brought Cherry here, my mother would whip out the pictures and laugh at my expense. My mother knows about her, but that's about it. She's asked to meet Cherry, but it's just not the right time.

The smell of pot roast takes my eyes off the wall and toward the kitchen.

"Smells good, Ma." I inhale deeply and walk toward the mouthwatering smell.

"Zeek," I greet, my tone dry.

"Brother," Zeek responds, sitting at the dining table. His dark brown hair is pulled into a small ponytail at the top, the rest of his head shaved. He's wearing a dark blue shirt with rosary beads around his neck, and has his boots kicked up on one of Ma's chairs.

"Sup?" I tug the chair that his feet rest in, making them drop to the floor with a 'thud'.

Sitting in the chair, I feel him staring at me.

"What?" I glance at him from the corner of my eye. He's rubbing his chin, a fucking smirk crossing his face.

"You ever talk to your president about letting us in on some business. I told you we got much better drugs than you're getting, bet money on it," he states, his tone holding a high volume of confidence.

"No, I didn't. I think it's best if you keep your fucking skunk weed in Vegas and out of my affairs, brother," I retort.

Zeek's face falls, the veins in his neck protruding suddenly. "My shit is the best in Vegas, I'll have you know. You can pussy foot around the DeLuca family business all you want, but you *will* be involved one way or another. I can promise you that, brother," he threatens. He swears on our father's dead body that he'll make me a Sin City Outlaw one day.

"Yeah, I'm sure your weed is that fucking fantastic that you can't find a buyer, so you're going to try and hustle me here at Ma's dinner table." Sarcasm drips from my voice. I shake my head and smirk at his flustered face.

"Boys, no business talk at the dinner table. I've told you

that," Mother scolds, striding into the dining room. She has blue mittens on each hand, carrying the crock-pot to the table.

"Hey, Ma, just trying to help Lip out." Zeek leans back in his chair, his face back to its normal cocky appearance. He shrugs and smirks. "But Lip never was any good at knowing what was good for him." I narrow my brows. I'm getting really tired of this back and forth bullshit.

"Zeek!" my mother hisses.

Zeek trails his eyes from me to her.

"Sorry, Ma," he mutters. He's not sorry, but he's about to be. I grab the knife next to my plate; it's intended for cutting meat, but I'm about to cut into my brother's neck if he doesn't shut the fuck up.

Ma sits down and stirs the pot roast.

"So, Lip, when are you going to bring this girl of yours over here for dinner?" My stomach falls. I knew she was going to ask—she does every time I fucking talk to her. I really just need to clear the way between Cherry and me but now I feel like it's gone on too long. When it *is* revealed, when I reveal my omission to Cherry, it'll go badly. I'm not sure Cherry will stick around, and I don't want to go filling Ma's head with fairytale shit of me running off into the sunset with some chick, so I keep Cherry away.

"Cherry? Not anytime soon, Ma," I reply, dipping the ladle into the pot. Ma would love Cherry, and that doesn't make things easier on me. It's for the best. Things are already more blurred than I can comprehend as it is, so I don't need to make it worse by mixing both families together.

"See, doesn't know what's good for him. I haven't seen this bitch, but from what I hear, she's hot enough to fuck twice on Sundays," Zeek insults.

I grab the knife and stand from the table. Rage and anger filling my veins, all I see is red. All I want is to make his fucking skin bleed. Nobody talks about Cherry like that. Zeek doesn't move from his seat, just continues to butter his bread as I stand over him with a serrated knife.

"Lip, sit your fucking ass down now!" My mother stabs the table with a cutting knife, grabbing mine and Zeek's attention. My mother is a badass bitch, regardless of her attempt to play housekeeper. I have seen her stab a woman for disrespecting her before, shoot at a man trying to get into our house, and she knows the perfect combo to get blood out of the carpet. I woke up in the middle of the night as a child finding her scrubbing the living room carpet enough times to know. She is one female you don't want to fuck with. I close my eyes and breathe deeply.

"Zeek, you best shut your fucking mouth. Lip, sit your ass down and ease up." My mother tugs the knife out of the dining table and points it at the food. "Eat, damn it!"

Cherry

I HEAR THE LOUD PIPES THUNDER AS LIP PULLS INTO THE DRIVE, so I turn the shower off and step out to dry off. I pull on my red bra and matching panties before putting on my white shirt and blue jeans.

When I open the door, he's pulling his shirt over his head. His chiseled chest takes my breath away. I'd do anything to run my claws down that in a fit of ecstasy.

"You're back," I state. Lip turns his head slightly before slipping onto the comforter. He said he wouldn't be back yesterday, and he kept his word. "Where were you?" I interrogate.

"Out," he replies. I cross my arms and lean against the doorframe.

"Seriously?" I cock my head to the side, anger building in my chest. It hurts that he doesn't talk to me anymore. I'm furious that I've become that girlfriend who has to question her man every time she sees him because she knows he's hiding something from her. I'm not sure I can do this shit anymore.

He pulls his head off the pillow and pins me with a glare.

"I said I was fucking out. Now let it be," he snaps. I jump with his outburst. *Who does he think he's talking to?* I lean down and grab one of my heels and throw it at his head, hitting it spot-on.

"What the fuck?!" He shoots up off the bed, his body puffed out with rage. I don't back down; he doesn't scare me. If anything, it turns me on. My mind drifts with sexual need, but the glare in his eyes reminds me to stand my ground.

"Where the *fuck* were you?" I question again. He steps up to me and fists my hair roughly. My heart skips a beat; this is not Lip. This is a man I've never seen before. The muscles in his arm flex and dance as he pulls my head back, our eyes locking. My thirst for sex wins, and I mewl in response. I can't help my arousal from the dominant anger radiating off him. This side of Lip has never shown before, it's unfamiliar and a turn on I didn't expect. His eyes widen when he notices my excitement from his roughness.

"I was at my mom's most of yesterday, and then I stayed at the club last night 'cause I didn't get back till really late. Now chill the fuck out," he mutters. He leans down and smashes his lips to mine, his cold lip ring against my warm lips causing a shiver to race up my limbs. I sway into him, wanting him to grab me and throw me over the bed. It's been weeks since he's had sex with me, but it was so distant, I might as well have been fucking my vibrator. I'm so worked up with sexual tension I can barely think straight. He pulls back and my body sags with sorrow.

"Where are you off to this morning?" he questions, crawling back into bed. I bite my bottom lip.

"Um, I'm thinking about trying some yoga. Going to go check that out," I lie. I'm going to see Piper. I hate lying to him, but I have no choice. He can't know about Piper, not yet.

"Fuck that," he grumbles into the comforter.

I grab some flip-flops and high-tail it out of there before he questions me any further.

◆ ◆ ◆

Sitting outside of the trailer park waiting for Piper, I see a couple walking out of a trailer holding hands. The tall blonde releases her partner's hand and he grabs it again, pulling her into a big kiss. I watch them, watch the love and life surrounding them without a care in the world. That was Lip and me years ago.

A knock sounds on my car window making me jump. Piper. I smile and climb out of the car. I look over to where the couple was and notice them gone.

"Can you help me with my hair?" I slowly trail my eyes from the trailer to Piper and notice her hair is a tangled mess. I try and slide my fingers through her red locks, but they get caught instantly. Her hair is dry and rough.

"What happened?" I question, trying to untangle the mess.

"My dad forgot to pick up shampoo, so he told me to use the dish soap," she replies softly.

My eyes widen. *What the actual fuck?*

"Dish soap?" I ask, making sure I heard her right.

"Yeah," she huffs. That explains why it's so dry and tangled.

"Hang on a minute." I get in my car and dig out my keratin spray and brush. I spray her hair and brush it over and over before it finally falls into silky waves.

"You know, Cherry, we have the same color hair," Piper observes. My eyes widen, and my hand stops mid-brush.

"Yeah. Yeah, we do," I reply softly. The yellow school bus pulls up, the brakes squeaking as it comes to a full stop. Thankful for its arrival, I lean down and give Piper a big kiss on the head, taking in the smell of her.

"You have a good day, Piper," I whisper into her hair.

"See you tomorrow?" She tilts her head back and looks up at me. Her eyes are the same color as mine.

"Yeah. I'll be here," I mumble.

Lip

"FIRST ORDER OF BUSINESS. THE DROP WENT SMOOTHLY, BUT the drugs seemed to be of low quality," Bull announces, lighting a cigarette.

"Should we find a different supplier?" Tom Cat asks. He slides his hands back and forth through his hair and looks around the table for a reply.

"This will do for now, but yes, we need someone who isn't growing weed out of their ditch," Bull replies, blowing cigarette smoke into the air.

"Kids today can't be happy with what they get," Hawk grumbles from the back of the table. He rubs at his white mustache that matches his old-ass hair. He's older than dirt and pretty much just says what he's thinking, whether or not it makes sense. I just nod and agree with him half the time, because I never know what the fuck he's talking about.

I could tell the club about my brother and their club in Vegas, but I'm not sure if it's something I want to get wrapped up in. I don't think it's a good idea. People could get hurt, and I would be to blame for introducing them.

"Tonight, we're having a party. Got some girls coming from the Wicked Birds, and The Ghost Riders are going to be here. It should be a fun night," Bull informs, slamming his cigarette into the ashtray. Wicked Birds is a strip club we take profit in, a cover for our illegal expenses. My uncle on my mother's side runs the place. He's a tool, but safe. He wouldn't fuck us; in fact, he hated my father when my mother introduced them.

"Why are we having the Ghost Riders here?" Shadow questions. Bull sighs and lowers his head.

"Because, they are a big club. Their president has connections with some men from the Cartel, and I want those connections," Bull explains. "Maybe they can replace our skunk weed dealer we got."

The Ghost Riders are disloyal. I've seen them turn against their own, and rumor has it they have no rules in their club. They are rapists, murders, all of it. But Bull's right; given their dubious rep, they have respect and connections with every outlaw organization you can think of. Getting them on our good side would benefit the club.

Bull slams the gavel down, dismissing everyone.

Cherry

I STIR MY CUP WITH MY STRAW AND WAIT FOR DANI TO SHOW up. She's an ol' lady I have grown to love over the years. She is the president's daughter and one of my best friends. She met Shadow, fell deeply in love with him and got married. I hate her sometimes. She has the perfect life. Sexy, caring husband. Two adorable children. Big house. Loving father. All that's missing is the pink corvette.

"Hey, sorry I'm late. Did you already order?" She sits down

on the opposite side of the table and tosses her dark hair over her shoulder. You can't even tell she's had two kids, she barely gained over ten lbs the whole time she carried Shadow's children.

"I did, I got us burgers," I inform.

"Sounds good." She pins me with her vibrant green eyes and smiles. "How have you been?"

I shrug. I always tell her I'm doing great and that Lip is amazing, but it's always a lie. I mean, how do you tell someone who has the perfect everything that your life is falling apart?

"Are you okay, Cherry?" She pulls her brows together and gives a concerning look. I want to lie like usual, but I need someone to talk to, someone to tell me what the hell to do. I close my eyes and look down at my glass of Coke. I'm always the one giving love advice. Hell, life advice. Yet here I am at the end of my rope.

"No, I'm not okay. In fact, I haven't been okay for a while." I sit back in my seat, and cross my arms.

"What happened, what's wrong?" The waiter sets our plates down on our table and asks if we'd like anything else. Dani shoos him away.

"Lip." I shrug, the smell of the burgers consuming my thoughts.

"What about him?"

"He's just different. I noticed the changes while visiting him in prison. I didn't think anything of it, because I thought being locked up he was just depressed or something. When he got out of prison, it was worse, and I thought it would go away, but it's not." I shove my plate away, not hungry anymore.

"What do you mean by different?"

"I dunno, like he's hiding something from me. He has this look of darkness I can't explain. There's tension between us that was never there before." I sit up in my seat and blow out an irritated breath. "You know we've only had sex three times since he was released a month ago. is something so nasty and dark sitting between us it's like there isn't any room for anything else."

"Damn, Cherry, I didn't know."

"There are times he doesn't come home for a couple nights in a row," I mutter.

"You think he's cheatin'? 'Cause we will go key his bike right fucking now!" Dani threatens. I can't help but laugh. Sounds like something I would normally offer someone. I've rubbed off on her well.

"I don't know if he's cheating. But if he is, I will chop his fucking nuts off."

"You know the club is having a party this Friday." Dani lifts a brow.

"Really? Maybe I should give an unexpected visit."

"Maybe." Dani smiles wickedly.

7

Lip

THE CLUB IS BLARING WITH MUSIC, AND THE LIGHTS ARE dimmed. The air is filled with smoke and cheap perfume, and a wave of people. I stride to the bar and grab a beer, watching the crowd.

Bull is sitting on the leather couch, a blonde chick wearing nothing but a bright pink bikini bottom dancing on a coffee table right in front of him. She has a nice pair of tits on her, but they'd be better if they were bigger.

Tom Cat has some girl bobbing up and down on his lap, and Bobby and Doc, our club doctor, are in the corner, making out with each other like a bunch of pre-teens. I take a sip of my beer. *I should go home to Cherry.*

"You look awfully lonely." I look over my shoulder and find Dolly leaning against the bar, a beer in her hand.

"I'm not," I reply, dry.

She smiles and steps up next to me.

"I think I may be drunk." She giggles, her dark hair falling in front of her face. I look her up and down. She's wearing some purple skimpy-looking top and black shorts. She stumbles into me, and I catch her.

"Maybe you should go lie down," I encourage, trying to stand her up right. She turns in my hold, her body limp.

"You have really pretty eyes," she slurs.

"Yeah, thanks," I respond, uninterested.

She frowns. "Are you gay or something?"

I smirk, trying to fight through my laughter. I level her with a serious stare and cock my head to the side.

"Why do you think that? Because I'm not interested in some teeny-bopper who can't hold her liquor?" She doesn't respond, her eyes blinking rapidly like she's trying convince herself I didn't just say what I did.

"I don't like girls who spread their legs easily. You're like a fucking penny—you're two-faced and in everyone's pants." Her mouth opens and closes and her eyes flutter. I think she's having an aneurism or some shit.

I hear a familiar giggle and look up. One of the Ghost Riders has his hand wrapped around Cherry's waist, whispering something into her ear. *What is she doing here?* She laughs and tries to pull away, but he doesn't let go. My brows pull together, and my blood goes cold.

I drop Dolly, letting her fall to the floor. Stomping toward the guy, my heart is slamming so hard in my chest my vision blurs. I can feel the poison of the reaper swimming in my veins. I am going to kill this motherfucker. Without warning, I grab the fucker by the throat and slam his head against the brick wall. Cherry screams and jumps back. I pull my knife out of my back pocket and flip it open. Without a second thought, I slam it forward, but my wrist is caught quickly before the blade can make contact.

"Drop it, brother," Bobby whispers into my ear. I shrug him off and try to push through his hold, ready to gut this fucker.

"Drop it, don't do this. Not here," Bobby continues. I grit my teeth and slam the man's head against the wall one last time. Blood drips from the back of his head, splattering the floor.

I release my hold and let the guy fall to the floor in a daze. Cherry gasps next to me, catching my attention, Dani standing right beside her. She looks terrified.

"What the hell?" I slowly look over my shoulder finding Stunt, the president of the Ghost Riders, eyeballing me.

"He put his hands on my ol' lady," I inform him sternly.

"Fuck, Boonie," Stunt scorns, shaking his head. From his tone, it sounds like Boonie does this kind of thing often.

Stunt steps in front of me and squats in front of Boonie. Feeling dismissed, I move forward, grabbing Cherry's wrist, tugging her out of the club.

"What the fuck was that Lip? What has gotten into you?!" Cherry screams, tripping behind me to keep up. She's never seen me react that way, never seen me do anything violent. I've made sure of it, but my mask of 'perfect boyfriend' is starting to fray. I've never seen my jealousy shine its full worth, but I've never cared for a bitch like I do Cherry. To be honest, I'm not sure what the future wrath of my jealousy would look like. I just know it would be dark and bloody. I would have stabbed Boonie over and over and over.

I let go of her wrist feet away from her car and pace. I'm so angry, so worked up I can't think straight.

"Lip! Just—" Cherry tangles her hand in her hair and sighs. "Fucking talk to me, Lip. I feel like I don't even know you anymore." She shakes her head and looks off into the distance. "Ever since you got out of prison, I feel like I'm sleeping next to a stranger," she whimpers, emotion laced in her voice. I stop my pacing and shoot her a glare that speaks volumes of anger.

"That's because you don't know me!"

"What happened in there?" she whispers. I pull my brows

together, my blood pumping with the rapid amount of adrenaline racing through me. Cherry is strong, one of the strongest women I know, but the look on her face is ripping my black heart in two. Maybe if she sees this, sees my dark colors, she'll turn away and I won't have to expose my darkest secret. For the life of me, I can't keep this act up of being her Prince fucking Charming, and as much as it's going to sting having her walk away from me for being an ass, it won't compare to the hurt she'll feel when I expose all my sins.

"Nothing happened in prison. You know nothing about who I really am. I'm not that love-struck boy you were with before. I am a murderer, a fucking monster." When I was in prison, when I was tested on my true worth as a sinner, I did not fail. I exceeded, and now that façade of hiding it for Cherry's sake is gone. This is me. This is who I am.

"This is the real me." I slam my fist against my chest. "Do you still love me now? Do you still want my affection?" I step closer to her. "Huh!?" I shout in her face, the vessels in my forehead protruding. "I am easily angered. I'm hotheaded, and am more fucked-up than anyone you'll ever know," I continue.

Cherry steps up to me, her face not giving anything away. I wince at her reaction, taken aback by it.

"Yes," she whispers. My face goes lax, and my lips part in surprise. "Yes, I still love you, Lip."

"What?" I'm dumbfounded. The girl I knew before was naive and fragile. A man of my kind would surely scare her away. Maybe I don't know the real Cherry.

"It's going to take a lot more than you being a shade darker than gray for me not to love you," she responds, her hand sliding up the side of my cheek. "You're right, I don't know you. You've proven that, but you don't know me, either," she whispers. My chest slams with emotion. "You being rough around the edges doesn't frighten me, not at all."

I grab the sides of her face, bringing her lips inches from mine. How can a woman still love a man after all that? Why have the gods given me such an amazing woman when I clearly don't deserve her? But they did. The gods put Cherry's fragile life right into my bloodstained hands, and I will not let her go.

"I don't know where you go every morning, but I swear to God if you are cheating on me Cherry..." I pause, searching her beautiful eyes. Eyes that make me feel like being a monster is okay. "I will bury you both," I threaten. If I can't have her...nobody can.

"I don't know why you haven't been home at nights, or why you can't look me in the eye. But if you are cheating on me, if you break my fucking heart..." She brushes her lips against mine, and a sharp piercing sensation slashes through my bottom lip. I hiss and pull back; bringing my finger to my lip, I find blood. *She fucking bit me.*

"I'll fucking destroy you," she whispers. My dick strains against my jeans from her hostile words. My cock aches to be inside of her. The way her eyes are hooded with a sense of darkness, I couldn't care less about the fog clouding my mind.

"You're my ol' lady, Cherry. I own your ass, and don't you forget that," I growl, trying to put her in her place, but for the life of me, all I want is to hear her scream my name.

"If I'm your ol' lady, then fucking prove it, Lip," she sneers, her eyes darting over my shoulder. I look at what she's glaring at, finding Dolly leaning against the club house with her arms crossed, waiting for me to return.

"You jealous, baby?" I turn my head and squint my eyes in question, an arrogant smirk fitting my face.

"Prove it," she repeats, stepping up to me, her fingers grasping my leather cut. "You say I don't really know you, so show me the real Lip."

I smirk and tilt my head back. This could either go badly, or be very, very good.

I grab her by the shirt and throw her onto her car, her back denting the hood. She mewls in response and wraps her legs around me. A feral moan vibrates my chest as her hungry eyes meet mine. I push her legs apart and tangle my hand in her hair. Her body arches into mine, her lust-crazed reaction feeding my animalistic need for her. My lips seek hers out like a man-eating beast looking for its next victim. I clench my teeth at the demented thought. That is exactly what Cherry was to me when I came across her six years ago: my victim. She never stood a chance when I showed up in her life. I was sent to save her, but I'm not the saving type. I'm the bad guy, and we don't save people.

Her plush lips fit mine perfectly. I grind my jean-clad dick against her pussy and her head lolls back, her eyes rolling into the back of her head.

Cat-calls and hollering from the club catch my attention. I slowly look toward the noise and find a bunch of the Ghost Riders, and some of the Devil's Dust, standing outside watching us.

I push myself upward and grab Cherry by the thighs, picking her up. With the chaffing I'm getting from the head of my dick rubbing against my jeans, I plan on finishing this elsewhere.

"Where are we going?" Her voice is breathy, full of lust.

"To the garage for some privacy," I respond, nipping her soft jaw. Walking past the club, Hinder blares, singing "American Nightmare". *How fitting.* Cherry had a mouth on her when I took her off the side of the highway, sure, but over the years her innocence was molted into something dark. She took her place as my ol' lady with a shade of something evil. I heard she nearly beat a guy to death with a bat just because one of the other girls in the club needed revenge. Cherry became one of the family without question.

"Show me your horns." I smirk. Her face lights up, and her hands imitate Devil horns. "Sexiest horns I've ever seen." I grin even wider when her cheeks blush. I remember the first time I asked her to show me those sexy little horns, and she literally imitated Devil horns. I'll never forget it.

Walking into the garage, I turn and pull the door down with one hand, while the other holds Cherry around the waist. As soon as the door is down, she slams her lips to mine. My hand slides up her back, pushing her tits against my chest. The smell of her makes my dick twitch and my chest constrict. She smells sweet, like cherry or maybe strawberry. I run my nose along the crook of her neck, taking in her delicious scent. She throws her head back and rocks her pussy against my hard dick.

I grind my teeth, a growl vibrating in my chest. I need inside of her now.

"Cherry," I draw out, slow and husky. "I need you now." I kick tools and trip over a jack, trying to make my way to the back of the garage. Her hands fist my hair, and mine squeeze her tight ass while we make out. Music pauses from the club, before Seal starts playing "Kiss from a Rose." Cherry, still in my arms, her eyes find mine. My heart slams against my chest, my eyes silently telling her I remember this song playing the first night we spent together. She smiles, and presses her lips firmly against mine. I find a bench seat from the club van sitting against a wall and plop Cherry down on it. Before she has time to react, I grab her shorts and pull them off her in one hard tug.

I drop to my knees and pull her panties down her legs slowly. When I take them off, it's like revealing the greatest gift ever. It has to be done slowly and with ease, because what's behind the delectable lace is my undoing. I take in every inch of her freckled legs and silky skin. Her pussy is waxed to perfection, her cunt pink and glistening wet, just for me.

I slide my finger between her lips, and it soaks the pad of my finger. She arches her back and fists her hair, a whimper escaping her mouth. I grab one of her legs and hike it over my shoulder. Gripping her thighs, I pull her ass to the edge of the seat and angle her just right. I flick her swollen clit with my tongue and her hands fly to my head, tangling themselves into my hair for traction. I trail my tongue through her wetness, tasting her. She tastes just as sweet as she smells.

"Oh, fuck!" she cries, riding my face.

I take one of my hands from her thigh and swirl around her clit, causing her body to tense as her legs squeeze me like a vise. Looking up, her eyes are clenched shut and her mouth is gaped open. I hum against her, lapping her sweetness and then her pussy convulses around my tongue. She moans, grinding her clit against my face, her walls clenching as she comes on my tongue.

My dick strains against my jeans, wanting to slam into that tight, wet pussy of hers. I am usually slow-paced and sensual when we screw around, but fuck that. Tonight, I'm going to show her what it means when Lip DeLuca fucks his girl.

As soon as she calms, I stand. I grab a clean grease rag sitting on Bobby's toolbox and wipe my mouth with it. I fold it back like it was and put it back with a smirk.

"Oh. My. God!" Cherry pants. "That was…" she pauses before giggling.

"What are you doing tomorrow?" I ask, unzipping my pants. Her eyes widen. I shove my jeans to my ankles along with my briefs, allowing my cock to spring free. It's hard as a rock and painfully swollen. It's been weeks since I fucked Cherry.

"Why?" Cherry asks, taking her eyes from my cock to me.

I stroke myself, my hand sliding over the barbell in the head of my dick.

"Because when I'm done with you, you won't be able to walk tomorrow."

She laughs and rolls her eyes. I smirk because she thinks I'm playing.

I grasp her hips and turn her around, pulling her ass out. I slide my hand along the left side of her ass cheek and give it a hard slap. She yelps and sticks her butt out further, seeking the vicious contact once again. I wrap her hair around my hand and pull her head back.

"Someone's a bad girl," I whisper into her ear. She moans in response, and my dick beads pre-cum. I knew Cherry was wild, but I never tested the wildcard out in the bed. At least not like this.

I release her hair and slide my hand between her legs, finding her pussy nice and wet. I use the other hand to guide my length between her thighs. As soon as my head feels the heat from her wetness, I slam into her. She whips her head back and moans loudly as she's thrust upon the seat cushion. I close my eyes and grind my teeth, the feeling of her surrounding my cock fucking Heaven. I slowly pull out, taking in every inch, feeling every sensation her pussy has to offer. I hiss with pleasure and look down. The chrome barbell in my head shines with her juices. I watch as I drive it into her once more.

"Yes," she mumbles, meeting my thrusts. I wrap my arm around her and pull her back to my chest. Sliding my hand up her shirt, I lift the cup of her bra to find her perky tit, pinching the nipple as my hips pick up the pace. My balls squeeze tightly, and a feeling of pressure builds deep in my pelvis. I slide my other hand under her shirt and do the same thing, lifting her shirt and bra until they sit just above her tits. She rests her head back on my shoulder, giving me full view of her breasts. They bounce and jiggle with every pound and thrust of my hips. Her pussy clenches, and a whimper sounds in her throat. With that little sound, warmth spreads up my length and ignites in the head of my dick. I drive into her wetness over and over, chasing my release. Just as my dick explodes into nothing but pleasure, her pussy clamps down, milking my cock.

I grab her hair roughly and pull her head to the side as I come down from my release. I shove my face into the crook of her neck and growl, nipping her soft skin.

We still, trying to catch our breath. My legs ache, and my lungs demand air. I slowly pull out of her and a shiver races up my back, my body wanting to return back to the heat her sweet cunt has to offer.

She leans over the bench seat, her chest rising and falling rapidly as she heaves for air. I pull my pants up and shove myself back into my briefs. Sitting next to her, I stare at the bikes and broken-down club van.

She pulls her top down and leans down to grab her panties. After she pulls them on, she lays her head on my lap and pins me with those angelic gray eyes.

"That was…" she pauses.

"Different," I finish for her. It was not our normal fuck session, but after that, I'm not sure I could ever go back.

"Yeah." She smiles, her cheeks sprinkled with freckles. I rub the pad of my finger along the bridge of her nose and down her neck, following the trail of freckles. It was different because it was real.

"You pulled my hair." She laughs.

I laugh with her. "I did." I was always too scared that if I went too hard with Cherry before, or got too rough, it would scare her away. I needed to keep her by my side. I needed to convince her I was everything she ever needed.

"Lip, if this is what it will be like having sex with you, the real you, then I am more than okay with that. In fact, I demand it."

I laugh and rest my head on the back of the seat, threading my fingers through her hair.

"Lip?"

"Yeah?"

"Don't hide who you really are from me ever again." I frown. She only saw a piece of the devil I am—disrespecting and angry. But she hasn't seen me in my element, with a 9mm pointed at an enemy. She hasn't seen my full jealousy flag wave, or my hotheaded temper yet. She doesn't know what she's asking.

"You can't handle who I really am, Cherry." She tenses on my lap, then sears me with angry eyes.

"Don't fucking tell me what I can and can't handle, Lip. I'm not a child. I'm not that scared broken girl you once knew." My jaw ticks with her tone of voice. I'm angry but it's pretty fucking sexy. She's right. We've both grown over the years, 'cause Cherry standing up to me isn't something I'm used to.

"Lip?"

"Yeah," I mutter, my eyes growing heavy.

"Why did you go to prison?" I exhale a long breath. I never told her why I went to prison. Even with her position as my ol' lady, I don't have to tell her, since ol' ladies are not privy to club business.

"I think I at least deserve to know. I have done things for this club. I have accepted them as my family, and I waited for you for six fucking years without knowing the reason you were taken from me," she continues.

I rub my forehead with the heel of my palm. I owe her at least an explanation; it's the least I could do with the way I've been treating her lately.

"We got pulled over on a run. We had just left the drop, and it went bad. Bull ended up stabbing one of their men. I guess they called the police after we left," I scoff. "Fucking pussies. Anyway, when they jumped out of their cars pulling weapons, I knew right away they were after us because of what Bull had done. I was next to Bull, so I reached over and grabbed his knife out of his pocket and stuck it in my back pocket."

"I know why you did it, why you covered for him. I don't blame you. I have come to love this club; they're my family. I would do anything for them," she replies.

I nod, because the bond we share is comparable.

I close my eyes and continue to rub her hair.

Cherry

SOMETHING SLIDES UP MY LEG, WAKING ME. MY EYES SLOWLY open, finding a man standing right in front of me. I jerk upward, and the man jumps back. It's the same guy from the party. Boonie. He swooped in and put his hand around my waist, telling me he wanted his cock sucked. I laughed him off and tried to pull away. Horny men at the club are not an uncommon thing. That was when Lip showed up in a fit of rage I've never seen before. The look on Lip's face, the fury in his eyes. I won't lie, it was unsettling.

I look up and see Lip asleep.

"Psst." I whip my head back to Boonie who is sliding his hand along his neck, imitating slicing his throat. My eyes widen and my mouth parts.

"Don't you wake him," he whispers. "Get off him and come here. Now," he continues. I swallow hard and dig my fingers into Lip's lap, praying it will wake him.

Lip groans, and pulls his head up from the back of the seat. *Thank fuck.* Lip scowls when his eyes find Boonie.

"You have to be the dumbest motherfucker." Lip pushes me

aside and stands. Boonie grins and walks backward, his body becoming one with the shadows of the garage before disappearing.

"That guy is fucking creepy," Lip states. I scurry down to the floor and pull my shorts on. "Did he touch you?"

I bite my lip and look away. "No." I don't want to tell him, because after the way Lip reacted before, I'm not sure he won't kill Boonie.

"Let's go find an empty room to sleep in. The sun will be rising soon." Lip holds his hand out, motioning for me to take it. I grab his palm and follow him. He takes us inside the club where everyone is asleep. The music is still playing, but softly. There is someone passed out on the couch, a woman hanging off the bar with no shirt on, and a man passed out in a pile of vomit on the floor.

"Jesus," I whisper. Lip tugs me down the hall to the last room on the left. His room. He pulls out a key and unlocks it. I haven't been in here in forever. There is a double bed in the middle of the room with a giant shelved headboard. A chair sits in the corner, and the walls are lined with naked chicks standing next to motorcycles.

"I'm going to jump in the shower," Lip tells me, walking into the adjoined bathroom.

I cross my arms and sit on the bed. Sex tonight with Lip was different on so many levels. It was raw. I felt connected to him in a way I never realized I had been missing. It makes all the other times we had sex before seem fake, like he wasn't really there. He never looked at me when we had sex before, now that I think about it. There are too many things running through my head, and things are not adding up. Has Lip always been this devious? Who was that chick in his arms when I showed up? Has he cheated on me?

I leave the room and stalk down the hallway toward the

bar. I need a drink; I can't cope with all of these thoughts. I kick red cups and step over a pair of panties. I slowly look up and find Boonie standing inches from me. If I hadn't looked up, I would have run right into him. I jump, startled, and clutch my chest.

"Fuck," I whisper. He cocks his head to the side, his long gray hair falling over his face as he does. He's large, bulky even. He has on a stained gray shirt and leather cut. The biggest buckle I've ever seen shines around his waist. He frightens me. I've had guys come on strong before, but this guy is on a whole other level.

"Excuse me," I mutter, trying to step around him. He steps in front of me and chuckles.

"Going somewhere, ginger?" I frown; I fucking hate that term. My brows furrow, and anger rushes through me.

"Ginger? Fuck you," I sneer, pushing him. He closes his eyes, throws his head back and laughs, the sound chilling my bones. He lowers his head, his dark eyes targeting mine.

"Oh, I'm about to fuck you. Right in the ass, sweetheart." He grabs my arm and yanks me against him.

"You better let me go, or I swear to God the only thing you'll be fucking is your own asshole when I tear your dick off," I threaten, trying to pull from his grip.

"Ooh, a feisty one. I love 'em feisty." He smiles and inhales loudly, smelling my hair. My body revolts. "You smell awfully sweet. I wonder if you taste just as sweet." Before I can even react to the words leaving his rancid mouth, he bites down on my shoulder hard, tearing the skin. I cry out and knee him in the dick. He releases me, and I fall back against the wall. I grab my shoulder, pain searing through my limb causing me to whimper. The bedroom door slams open and Lip steps out, looking the other way before turning his head and looking toward Boonie and me. His hair is wet, and he has on nothing but jeans.

"What happened?" Lip questions, walking toward me.

He places his hands on each side of my arm and I wince when he touches my bite.

"He fucking bit me," I grit out, looking at my shoulder that shows the perfect bloody indention of teeth marks.

Boonie starts laughing. "Man, I just wanted a taste."

"You're going to fucking die!" Lip points at Boonie.

Lip grabs my chin and lifts it so my eyes find his. "I got this. Go to the room and don't come out."

"Lip, No –"

"Go, Cherry. Now." Lip lowers his head, his eyes serious and gleaming with an unfamiliar flare. I flick my eyes to Boonie, scared for the prick.

"Okay," I whisper.

Stepping inside of the room, the music suddenly gets louder. I clench my eyes shut, nerves bubbling in my stomach. My shoulder blazes with pain, catching my attention from thoughts of what Lip is doing to Boonie.

"Shit," I whisper, eyeing the torn flesh.

I go to the small bathroom, the smell of Lip's shampoo strong. I turn the shower on and undress, taking extra caution around my shoulder. Leaving the water on scalding hot, I rinse off the bite. It fucking hurts to the point I bite down on my inner cheek as the water pelts against it. After it goes numb, I grab Lip's shampoo that smells of fresh mint and wash my hair, the scent of him in my hair and all around me causing me to inhale deeply. I can't get enough. I sit under the showerhead 'til it runs cold. Glancing at my bite, it looks much better, but swollen as hell.

Stepping out of the shower, I grab the towel hanging up and wrap it around me. It's still damp from Lip.

Walking out of the bathroom, hoping Lip has a new shirt I

can wear because mine is covered in blood, he walks in the door. His body is puffed out, and his hands are balled into fists. He looks like a crazed man.

"Lip?" I mutter. His darkened eyes whip to mine, and I wince in reaction. He steps forward and grabs the towel from my body, yanking it off. He envelops me in his strong arms and plows us to the bed.

He slides his knee between my thighs and bites my bottom lip gently. My body comes alive with such a power I lose my breath. He's hungry, and for me.

I arch my body into his and tangle my hands into his hair. Looking between Lip's body and mine, I find small spots of blood.

"Lip, you're bleeding," I state, concerned.

Lip pulls his mouth from my neck and shakes his head.

"It ain't my blood."

My eyes widen, a little shocked. *Did he kill Boonie?* I look at the blood again, panic rising in my chest as Lip's fingers tease my clit. My eyes roll in the back of my head and a small whimper expels from my lips.

I want to stop and demand we shower, but the intense throbbing between my legs says it can wait. The blood on his chest stains my own. The unholy blood of another corrupting what sense of morals I might have buried within me. The sins of the man I am in love with soak deep into my skin, making me the devil's advocate.

Lip grabs my earlobe with his teeth, and my stomach flutters with a thirst I'm afraid will never be quenched.

"You're my woman, and no man gets to touch you, let alone taste you," he snarls, his words sounding possessive. A mewl vibrates in my chest in response. "Only I get to taste you, Cherry," he whispers, his lips moving against the dip in my throat as he speaks.

"Yes," I respond.

My fingers grab at the button on his jeans, undoing it quickly. I lift my feet and pull them down his legs. The craving in his eyes, the adrenaline rushing through us, I need to feel him inside of me. Just as his dick springs free, he pushes it through my wetness and plows into me.

"Damn," he growls, closing his eyes, his jaw clenching. I moan loudly from finally having the contact, arching my neck to where my head is pressing into the mattress. His dick is buried to the hilt, as far it will go. The fit is tight, the feeling of fullness so damn good. He pulls his hips back and pushes forward with haste, and I sigh with pleasure.

The barbell in the head of his cock hits me just right every time he thrusts into me, the bed rocking against the wall loudly with every push of his hips.

"You're not scared?" Lip pants. I open my eyes and find him staring at me intently—he looks high. His pupils are dilated from the excitement of maiming another human being.

"Losing you scares me more," I whisper. "I knew the day I climbed on the back of your bike you were my ride to the dark side."

◆ ◆ ◆

Screams wake me to an upright position. I grab the sheet and pull it over my bare chest. After Lip and I finished our round two, we dropped onto the mattress exhausted. I fell asleep right away.

"Lip!" I yell, shaking him awake.

"What?" he mumbles. He's lying face-first in a pillow, his bare ass sticking up in the air.

"Someone just screamed really loud," I whisper.

"Fuck!" Lip jumps out of bed, nearly falling on his face. He grabs a fresh pair of jeans out of the dresser and looks for a shirt. He looks frazzled, which causes me to tense.

"What's wrong? What's happening, Lip?"

"I got caught up with you and forgot," Lip mutters before opening the door and rushing out.

"Forgot?" I climb out of bed, and my thighs ache. I slowly sit myself back down on the bed and smirk. Lip did warn me that I wouldn't be able to walk today. Glancing down at myself, I notice I need to shower again. Lip transferred blood onto me, and now that I'm not high on lust, I need to clean it off. Now!

I turn the water on and quickly clean up. I want to see what's going on, but a part of me doesn't. I rinse any trace of blood off, and wash my hair in record time. I towel dry and head to Lip's closet for something clean. I find a gray Devil's Dust shirt and put it on, with my shorts from yesterday. Throwing my hair up into a messy bun, I slowly open the door.

The music is turned off, but I don't see anybody. I tiptoe out of the room, scared of what I may see. I step over the panties and cups and find a large puddle of blood sitting under a chair in the middle of the common area. I gasp, my hand flying to my mouth.

"Look, you say he hurt Cherry, then I agree Boonie had it coming. We have your back, Lip," I hear Bull state. I tear my eyes from the gore to Bull's voice, finding him in the kitchen with the doors shut. "Did Cherry see you do this? You can't upset her. You need to keep her happy, Lip." I frown.

"She saw some blood on me last night, but it didn't affect her. How much longer do I have to fucking do this for, man?" Lip questions and I suck in a sudden breath, my fingers digging into the palm of my hands. *What is he talking about?*

"Why?" Bull questions, flat.

"I just... I don't know if I can do this much longer. Things are getting serious, and I can't keep myself from..." Lip pauses, and

I hold my breath.

A cup is kicked behind me, making me jump and turn toward the noise. It's that bitch I saw all over Lip last night. I place my hands on my hips and glare.

"So, I hear you're Lip's ol' lady."

Her mascara is smeared and her lipstick is smudged halfway across her cheek.

"I think you forgot some of your lipstick on some strange dick," I sneer. She purses her lips and raises a brow.

She tilts her head to the side and crosses her arms. "I thought if Lip was taken it would be by someone much prettier," she insults.

"Ha! Run along back home before Daddy finds you missing," I sneer.

"I hope you're as pretty as you think you are. Lip is done with you. He's ridden that tired-ass vagina of yours out and is looking for something new." She smirks and my stomach falls. "He even gave me my nickname around here, Dolly. He must think I'm pretty sweet to call me something as cute as Doll, don't you?"

"You don't expect me to believe that, do you?" I question, my voice coming out more confident than I feel.

She shrugs. "Believe what you want, sweetie. But when I'm wearing that cut and you aren't anymore, the reality won't lick those wounds so well." She sashays by me, and I reach forward and grab her hair.

"If you go near my man, I will rip the hair from your fucking head, do you hear me?" I yank on her hair hard. It snaps and pulls from her scalp, making her scream loudly. Lip and Bull rush out of the kitchen, so I let go.

"Fucking psycho!" Dolly cries, holding her head.

"Jesus, Cherry. Why do you have to be a pain in my ass?" Bull exclaims, catching Dolly. "Come on, darling. Let's get you to your bike, and get you out of here before the Ghost Riders wake." Bull helps Dolly stand and walks her out. *The bitch rides her own motorcycle?*

I want to know if Lip called her Dolly, and I want to know what the hell he was talking about with Bull, but the blood on the floor has me more concerned. *What did Lip do?* I step forward and survey the chair.

"Did you do this?" I ask. I don't need to ask, though, because I know he did. Looking at the blood, I see little chunks that catch my attention.

"What the....?" I bend down to get a better look and find the chunks are teeth. A lot of them. I cover my mouth and turn away quickly, vomit threatening to race up my throat. Lip couldn't have done this. Not the Lip I know. I clench my eyes shut and swallow hard. I'm starting to second-guess how well I know the man I love.

"Cherry, babe." Lip grabs my elbow, his voice soft.

"I'm fine," I choke. I'm not fine.

"Why don't you go home? We need to get this cleaned before The Ghost Riders get up." I nod in agreement, needing out of here.

"Yeah, I need to go see-" I stop, nearly exposing my lies. I swallow hard and shake my arms out, trying to get a hold myself. "I need to go get a few things."

Lip's eyes, which were pulled into a tight scowl, ease slightly. He leans forward and kisses me, but it's not a peck, not a simple 'I'll see you later' kiss. It's deep and hard, his hands grabbing my face.

"Bye, babe," Lip whispers against my lips.

8

Cherry

I HEAD TO GOLDS TRAILER PARK AND FIND PIPER OUTSIDE playing on the poor excuse for a playground. I pull over and park the car. She is so beautiful, and every time I see her I want to tell her I'm her mother and I love her, but I can't. It hurts, words I can't speak eating me from the inside out. I hope one day Eric feels this uncontrollable ache that dwells in my chest. That the judge feels the wrath of karma, and when he steps in the sight of the Devil it shows him no mercy. That's all I have at this point, hope that karma and the scales of justice will punish Eric and Judge Calhoun.

I step out and head toward her. It's Saturday, so her father won't be home till late.

"Hey, Cherry, wanna see me climb to the top?" Piper asks. Her hair is pulled into two messy piggy tails, and she's wearing an outfit I bought her a few weeks ago. It's neon orange and green. It's summery, and perfect with her vibrant hair.

"Yeah, let's see it," I reply. I can't help but smile when I see her. She climbs all the way to the top of the dome and stands up.

"Did you see how fast I went?" She laughs. Just as I'm about to answer, one of the rusted bars breaks and her foot slips. I run to her and catch her before she hits the dirt.

"Are you okay?" I ask, looking her over anxiously.

"Yeah, I'm o-okay," she stammers, still scared.

I set her on her feet and look up at the broken bar. I've tried to coax one of the MC brothers over here to fix it, but they know this side of town is dangerous, and I shouldn't be over here anyway. Lip would freak if he knew I was here. This is a really bad part of town. Half this trailer park is ex-convicts and drug dealers. They won't bother Piper, though, because she's one of their own. It's outsiders who bring the problems to the trailer park.

"Stay off this piece of shit," I demand, grabbing the bar and wiggling it.

"But it's the only outside toy I have," Piper whines before crossing her arms.

I look down at her and sigh.

"Just stay near the bottom of it until I can get it fixed. I'll bring some more tape with me next time I come by."

"Okay, I can do that." She smiles, climbing on the bottom bars. "You know, my daddy doesn't care if I climb on it, and he knows it's broken," she continues.

I furrow my brows. "Your daddy is a dumbass, Piper." I close my eyes and chastise myself, trying to backtrack. "Just, maybe your daddy isn't thinking when he says it's okay."

Piper's eyes are wide, and she's covering her mouth. "What?"

"You said a bad word," Piper whispers.

"I did?" I tilt my head to the side, trying to think.

Piper shakes her head, smiling.

"What was it?" I can't remember cussing at all.

"You said," Piper looks around and cups her mouth with her hands, "dumbass." I throw my head back and laugh.

"Oh, yeah, I did say that," I remember. I forget that ass is a bad word since I use so many other ugly ones.

"Mommies are allowed to say bad words," I point at her, "but not you."

"You have kids?"

"Do what?" I question, still giggling about her cussing.

"You said mommies are allowed to say bad words," she explains. My body tenses and my mouth parts.

"Shit," I whisper.

"You said another bad word." Piper laughs and points at me, nearly jumping with excitement where she stands. My state of alarm dissipates.

"You must be a bad influence." I smile. A raindrop splashes my arm. I glance up and notice a big, dark cloud starting to mask the hot sun. *Fuck, Eric will be pulled off the construction site if he hasn't been already.*

"I gotta go, baby," I mutter. Her face saddens, and she glances back at the jungle gym.

"Remember to stay near the bottom," I remind her. She nods and starts climbing it. I step behind her and pull the back of her head toward me, kissing it.

"I'll see you around."

"Will you come by tomorrow?" she asks.

Tomorrow is Sunday, and Eric usually works till noon on Sundays.

"I'll try, but no promises."

Lip

KANE STRIDES OUT OF ONE OF THE ROOMS WITH A BLONDE CHICK wrapped around his side. He's Native American and is always with a different girl every night. He's a prospect, but not for long. Last week, twins got in a cat fight over him. It was pretty awesome to watch.

"Fuck, man, what happened?" he questions, looking at the blood around the chair.

"You didn't hear?" The blonde looks up and questions Kane. "Dolly said some Ghost Rider member was duct-taped to the chair and had teeth hammered into his skull."

I pull my brows together and pin Kane with a glare. Dolly must have been the bitch who screamed this morning.

"Um, I'm sure Dolly is just making shit up. Why don't you head on home," Kane suggests. The blonde trails her eyes to me before turning and lifting up on her tiptoes.

"Will you call me later?" she tries to whisper. Kane tilts his head, twisting his lips with an unsure gesture.

"Probably not, babe. I told you before I brought you to my room not to expect anything more than a fuck," Kane explains. I smirk and turn around to give them privacy. The blonde stomps past me in a fit of anger.

"Fuck, that ass was tight," Kane whispers, adjusting himself as he watches the girl leave the club.

"Why you telling her to fuck off then?" I ask. Kane smiles a big-ass, toothy grin.

"Her ass is fine but not the rest of her, brother. Little coyote ugly right there." He points at her, his fingers covered in skull rings.

"She didn't look too bad to me." I laugh, crossing my arms. She was actually pretty skanky-looking. Her makeup was caked on, and her clothes were two sizes too small. I have yet to find a woman in zebra print sexy, either.

"Yeah, well she looked a hell of a lot better when I was shit-faced." He gives me a pat on the back and looks back at the chair. "I'll get this cleaned up before anyone starts asking questions."

"Thanks, brother."

Kane and Tom Cat get the chair and blood all cleaned up, teeth included.

"You know you're one fucked-up individual, right?" Tom Cat states, coming back into the club. I lean against the bar and shrug.

"Teeth, brother?" Kane chuckles, standing next to Tom.

"He fucking bit my property till she bled. He had more than enough warning, let alone not abiding by the rules of my club," I explain, my tone stern.

"I agree. I would have snapped, too, if I cared about someone enough to get jealous over," Kane states, sitting on a barstool.

"THE COPS ARE HERE!" Dolly screams, running through the club.

"Fuck," I mutter, standing up straight. Bull throws open the kitchen doors, Shadow right behind him. Bobby runs into the main area from the hallway.

"Everything clean?" Bull asks.

"I'll do a sweep," Kane replies, walking away.

It's not unusual that we get a random search warrant, but it kind of sucks when we get one after a party.

"Fucking get out!" Kane yells from down the hall. I step away from the bar and see Kane escorting two girls out the back door of the club.

"You're an ass!" one sneers.

Kane shakes his head and slams the door in their faces.

"Couple girls who are wanted, apparently," Kane informs. I give a slight nod and turn to Bull.

"Probably prostitution," Bull explains.

"We're clean."

Two men with blue windbreakers and loaded shotguns walk in and step to the side. Then Stevin walks in. My face falls and my heart slams against my chest in a slow, tortuous rhythm. These aren't cops, they're FBI.

"What. The. Fuck?" Bull growls and I swallow. Today might be the last day I breathe air. I thought Stevin was bluffing when he said he'd come after the club himself, but I guess not.

"Well, well, well. The Devil's Dust. Long time, no see, huh?" Stevin smiles that fucking Cheshire grin of his.

"Oh, wait. Except for you, Lip. We've spoken fairly recently, haven't we?" Stevin chuckles, swiping his hands through his hair. My nostrils flare with anger. He knows what he's doing—he's stamping my death certificate.

All the brothers turn their head toward me with concerning looks. *Fuck.*

"What's that supposed to mean?" Shadow growls. I tilt my head back and thumb my fingers in my belt loops.

"Oh, Lip here has been a real sport. Very cooperative with the FBI," Stevin lies. I step forward and one of Stevin's men jumps in front of him.

"You're a fucking liar, and a coward," I snarl, pointing at his face with vengeance. Kane grabs me by the shoulder and pulls backward.

"Easy, brother," he whispers.

Stevin twirls his finger in the air. "Clean it. I want any dirt you can find," Stevin demands, his tone serious. "If there's a fucking Lysol can being used unlawfully, I wanna know!"

I trail my gaze from Stevin to Bull. His eyes are a shade darker and squinted with anger. Shadow's hands are balled in fists, and Bobby has his arms crossed across his chest. They're pissed. I don't blame them. As many rats as we've had in the club over the years, I bet I look guilty as sin.

"What the hell is he talking about, man?" Kane whispers. The agents pull everyone from the rooms, and what women they were with, whether they were dressed or not. The Ghost Riders do not look pleased.

My feet are suddenly kicked apart, and my arms are yanked out. I pull from the agents' grip, turning to push them off me. Without warning, two agents walk up behind me and slam me face-first onto the bar, while another checks me.

"Everyone's clean!" the agent behind me yells.

"Perimeter is clean," one of Stevin's men announces, walking through the kitchen doors.

Stevin shakes his head, an evil smirk fitting his face.

"Ah, you Devil's Dust are tricky-tricky." He pins me with a serious glare before trailing it to Shadow. "I'll be back. You can count on that."

Stevin sneers, stepping toe-to-toe with me.

"If you're done here, get the fuck out," I demand, my jaw clenched. Kane clamps his hand down on my shoulder. It's a good thing it's there; it's grounding me, reminding me to keep calm. Stevin turns his head, his eyes finding mine.

"Let's go, boys!" Stevin hollers.

As soon as they exit, Shadow stomps toward me and slams his fist in my gut. I fall to my knees, coughing and gasping for air. "You fucking traitor!" Shadow roars.

"It's not what you think," I wheeze. Shadow doesn't hear it, though; he rears his foot back ready to drive into my chest, but I dodge it. I grab his boot and twist it, causing him to lose his balance and fall to the floor.

I stumble to my feet and grab Shadow by the neck, pulling him back up. Growling with a fury so deep my throat bleeds, I ram my shoulder into his body, slamming him against the club wall. Frames and shit fall to the floor. I pound my fist into his mouth then drive my other hand into his gut.

Shadow clocks me in the side of the head hard, and I stumble back.

Bull steps between us and raises a hand to both of us, stopping our brawl. Huffing and puffing, I point at Shadow who's bending over at the waist, his lip busted open from where I hit him.

"Fuck," I pant, trying to catch my breath. My head splices with a sudden pain. I touch my forehead next to my eyebrow, finding blood.

"Did you talk to him about anything dealing with the club?" Bull questions.

"No," I seethe.

"Then what the fuck is that prick talking about?" Bull asks. I thumb the blood dripping from my brow and look off.

"He came to me, telling me he could get me a plea deal, get me immunity, protection if I gave the club up. I didn't tell him a damn thing. I was then cornered one night in my cell by the guards. I got the shit beat out of me, all at the hands of Stevin. I got out before he was done trying to pry me for information, so he's been stalking me around town, threatening the club and Cherry."

Bull nods, rubbing his chin with his thumb and index finger.

"You were locked up when it happened, but that fucker there," Bull points at the door Stevin left out of, "He was the FBI agent who came knocking on our door, managed to even infiltrate our club. He's dirty, and he'll be back."

I shake my head, angry that I didn't know more when I was in prison. All I was told was we had law enforcement infiltrate our club. Dani's mother hated Bull and got together with some agent to take the club down under Dani and Bull's nose. The boys said it was taken care of, so I didn't ask any more questions. *Seems I should have.*

I glance up at Shadow who has a softer look on his face. It's one thing to fuck with the club, but when you bring family in, that's a whole other level.

"Get Doc here, get that eye stitched up," Bull orders.

"Nah, I'll be fine," I insist. Bull raises his brow in warning. "Fine, I'll get it looked at," I growl.

Bobby turns and dials Doc.

◆ ◆ ◆

Thirty minutes later, Doc shows up, her blonde hair bouncing off her shoulders and bright green scrubs hugging her figure.

"All right, who shot who?" she teases.

"Lip got his ass kicked," Bobby states, taking a big bite of a sandwich.

"Fuck you, Bobby, I didn't get my ass kicked." I flip him off, and he just smiles around a mouthful.

Doc sits on the coffee table right in front of me, her little black bag sitting on the floor next to her feet. She cups my chin and turns my head.

"There is quite a bit of blood," she whispers.

"I'm fine, really," I insist. Her eyes fall to mine and a sympathetic smile crosses her face.

"I'm sure you are, but I'm going to clean it and at least put a butterfly on it."

"A what?"

She pulls out this little white strip. "It pulls the skin to-gether," she informs.

"Ah." I nod.

She cleans my cut and puts the butterfly bandage thing on within seconds.

"I'm glad we cleared that up, Stunt," Bull's voice sounds. I slowly tilt my head up and find Bull and Stunt leaving the chapel.

"Yeah. I'll see what I can do." Stunt shakes Bull's hand.

"Let's ride, boys," Stunt instructs his men. "Where's Boonie?" Stunt questions.

"We dunno. His bike isn't here," one of the Ghost Riders informs him.

"Fuck, who knows where he is. He probably went out while drunk last night. Let's go," Stunt continues, clearly annoyed with Boonie. "He'll find his way home."

"All done," Doc states, standing.

"Thanks, babe." I sit up and give her a nod.

"No problem." She smiles then struts over to Bobby and kisses him. "See ya for dinner?"

"Damn straight. These fuckers can't cook for shit." Bobby smirks.

"You all right, son?" Bull asks, sitting down next to me.

"Fine," I reply.

"You good?" Bull asks, pointing at Shadow, who looks at me then back to Bull.

"Peachy," Shadow mumbles.

"This Stevin guy needs to eat a damn bullet," I state, irritated that he's trying so hard to get me killed.

"Agreed!" Bull and Shadow say in unison.

"Want me to take him out?" Shadow questions, his words sounding way too eager. Bull's face goes hard as he stares off.

"No, not yet." Bull flicks his gaze to Shadow. "That is one soul I personally want to deliver to the reaper."

Cherry

I ROLL THE WINDOWS DOWN IN MY CAR AND LET THE WARM breeze sweep my strawberry-blonde hair off my neck. Traffic is backed up from a car accident and it's taking forever to get to Piper today. She probably thinks I forgot. Resting my elbow on the car door, I rub my temples. I'm so confused on so many things. There was blood and teeth on the club floor yesterday; I never thought Lip had that in him. I know he takes a spot in the most notorious outlawed club in LA, but the Lip I know is not the kind of guy who shows no mercy. He's goofy, a horny bastard, and sweet.

I blow out a frustrated breath and pull into the drive of Golds Trailer Park. I turn the engine off, throw my sunglasses on the dashboard and slump in my seat. If I didn't know Lip was capable of doing such a thing, to not know Lip might be darker than he portrays... what else do I not know about him?

Looking out my window, I see Piper on the dome jungle gym, of course all the way at the top.

"Damn it," I mutter. She knows it's not safe to be up there.

I throw my hair out of my face, pieces of it sticking to my cherry-glossed lips, and head over to her.

"I thought I told you not to climb up there?" I snap, my hands on my hips.

"It's okay, as long as you stay away from that side," she assures me. She swings down from one of the bars and beams a gorgeous smile.

"This pile of shit is a death trap," I mumble under my breath. The bar that Piper is hanging on to suddenly snaps and she tumbles to the ground.

"Shit!" Rushing to her side, I pull her to her feet. She is so small and weighs nearly nothing.

"Are you okay?" I question, looking her over. She pulls her palm up and hisses, a good-sized cut slicing right through it.

I gently take her hand in mine and look it over.

"Well, you won't need stitches, but you should go clean it up," I recommend. "Does it hurt?"

She shoots her gray eyes from her palm to me, her nose dusted with little freckles.

"Some," she mutters.

"Go get it cleaned up. I'll see if I have anything in the car to fix the bar. But please, stay off the top. You could have broken your leg or something," I state in frustration. She nods slowly and takes off toward her house.

"Piece of shit," I mumble, kicking the jungle gym. I make my way to my car and lift the back hatch for something to cover the jagged edges of the broken bar, but all I find is duct tape.

"Guess it will do." I grab it and pull a big piece with my teeth and fingers. A loud zip sound vibrates my teeth and fingers as I pull it as far as my hand will stretch.

I eye the silver bar, the end of it rusted and sharp as hell. Shit, she might need a tetanus shot. I wonder if Doc would come over and look at Piper's hand without telling anyone. I bite my inner cheek at the thought; I don't want to get anyone else involved with my secrets. Grabbing the bar, I start wrapping the end of it. I need to tell Lip today. It's only getting worse the more I keep Piper a secret.

Something tangles in my hair—a hand. My body stiffens, and my mouth parts in fear. My head is suddenly yanked back and my skull slams into the jungle gym. My head rings, and my vision goes black, my body feeling ten times heavier than before as I free-fall to the ground. The side of my face slams into the dirt. I blink rapidly, trying to break the blurriness claiming my vision. I see someone step beside me, but I can't make out who it is. Blackness envelops me.

"Wake up, bitch!" My body is kicked over, and I cough into the dirt. My head pounds with anguish, making me wince. I push myself up with my hands and remember someone attacked me. I turn quickly and a small cry leaves my lips.

"Eric," I whimper.

"Tell me I'm seeing a fucking ghost. Your ass is supposed to be dead." He points at me, his face beet red from the sun. He's thicker than the last time I saw him, more muscular, his blond hair grown out and pulled into a ponytail. He has on torn blue jeans and a red flannel shirt that's open and showing off his tanned skin. I take a step back and eye him.

"Fuck you!" I push through gritted teeth.

"How long you been around my daughter?" he questions, his upper lip curling.

"You mean *our* daughter? Long enough to know you suck at raising a little girl," I fire back.

His body puffs out and his teeth grit together.

"Run. You better run," he threatens, his tone deep and monstrous.

"You don't scare me." I stand up and straighten my white tank top and glare at him.

"I'm not going away that easy, not this time. I know people now, people who will have you eating your fucking fingers by the time they're done with you," I threaten.

"Yeah. We'll see about that." He juts his chin upward. "I'm going to get my gun. If you're here when I get back, I'll kill your white-trash ass." He turns on the heel of his boot and takes off toward his house. My bravado flees my body, and I begin to breathe heavily. My heart feels like it's slamming against my chest so hard it may combust. I grab my chest and try to calm my rapid breathing but it's no good. I'm panicking. I turn, looking the trailer park over. People are standing on their porches watching, not doing a damn thing about what just transpired. I pick up my pace and jog to my car. As soon as my ass hits the seat, I notice Eric stomping down his porch steps, rifle in hand. I start the car and peel out of the graveled parking, dust and smoke the only thing I see in my rearview mirror.

I glance at the clock on my dash: 1:30pm. I lost track of time, lost in my thoughts about Lip. Eric gets off at noon on Sundays. I walked myself right into my coffin. Eric will hire out, will find someone to kill me. I have to tell Lip. I have to tell the club.

My hands begin to tremble, my chest wracking with emotion. I jerk the wheel to the side and pull over. I can't help it; I let the tears that have been stinging my eyes fall. Throwing my head into my hands, I cry. I cry because the man I love is someone I don't know, because I may never see Piper again. I tilt my head back and take a slow breath. Pulling down the sun visor, I look at myself in the mirror. The corner of my eyebrow is split open, dried blood sticking to the side of my face.

"Shit," I mumble under my breath. I lick my finger and try and rub at it, but more blood just escapes the wound.

I call defeat and slam the sun visor closed. I'm going to need stitches.

CHERRY: Hey. I need a favor.

DOC: What's up?

CHERRY: I have a cut I need you to
look at, but don't tell Lip.

I need to be the one to tell Lip, not her. Seconds feel like minutes as I wait for her text.

> **DOC:** Head over to the hospital. I'll let the front desk know you're coming.

I sigh with relief and pull back onto the highway.

◆ ◆ ◆

"So, what happened?" Doc asks. Her cold hands take my chin and turn my head, getting a better look at my cut.

"I can't," I pause, and inhale a large breath.

"I get it, and you don't have to tell me. But you do need stitches," she informs. Doc is dating Bobby at the club, and is gorgeous. She ran to the club when she was in the worst kind of Hell with her husband, and they took her in right away in exchange for her doctor duties. If anything, she should be an inspiration for me. She is the prime example that someone can escape an ex and everything turning out okay.

She flips her blonde hair over her shoulder and grabs wipes to clean my face.

"This is going to hurt," she warns, her blue eyes promising me it's going to hurt like a bitch. I close my eyes and nod.

Ten minutes later, I can't feel the right side of my face, and I have little beady black stitches snaking in and out of my eyebrow.

"I won't tell Lip you were here, but something tells me he's going to notice," Doc states, a smile on her face.

"Probably," I mutter, pushing myself off the hospital bed. "I'm going to tell him, I just... I need to find the right words, ya know?" I look up at her and find her sympathetic eyes gleaming at me.

"I get it. Sooner is better than later, though." I sigh, knowing six years ago would have been a better time. "They can come out in two weeks," she instructs. "Keep them clean and dry."

"Got it," I reply.

I take the discharge papers from the front desk and head out to my car. Digging in my pocket to text Lip to find out if he's coming home tonight, I notice I forgot my phone in the hospital room.

"Damn it." I turn on my heel and head back to the hospital when a large explosion sounds behind me. Unbearable pressure and heat throw me forward like a stick. The palms of my hands eat the asphalt and the skin on my knees tear. I cough and look up, finding my little red bug in a cloud of black smoke, red and orange flames licking in and out of it.

A bunch of nurses and doctors come rushing out of the hospital doors.

"Cherry!" Doc screams, running to my side.

"I'm okay," I croak.

Doc looks at my car and then to me, her expression taking on one of worry.

"I don't know what you're not wanting to tell Lip exactly, but I'm thinking you better tell him now." I pull my gaze from her back to my car.

"The club will protect you, Cherry; you just have to be strong enough to ask for help."

Lip

My phone vibrates in my pocket. Pulling it out, I notice it's Cherry.

"Yeah?" I answer.

"Lip?" My body goes cold with the sound of her voice. I don't recognize it. It sounds scared—terrified, even.

"Cherry, are you okay?"

"I need you to come get me. I'm at the hospital." The line goes dead.

"Cherry?!" I yell into the phone, but she's hung up. My body turns cold, as if someone just poured fucking ice over me.

"You all right, man?" Shadow asks, lifting a brow.

"Something's not right. Cherry is at the hospital. I gotta go," I say, already standing.

"The hospital? Is Doc okay?" Bobby questions.

"I don't know anything except Cherry is at the hospital and something is wrong," I reply.

"Let's go!" Bull hollers, striding out of the club doors.

Pulling up to the hospital, there is a fire truck sitting in the parking lot next to three cop cars. My hands clench, and my pulse quickens.

As soon as I park my bike, I find Cherry leaning against the building, a cop with a notebook standing in front of her.

"Cherry!" I yell, running to her. She pushes herself off the wall and rushes to me.

She slams her body into me and my arms wrap around her like a shield, protecting her from whatever might have her scared.

"I think we got what we need here," the cop states, walking away.

I tuck Cherry's head under my chin and notice Bobby soothing Doc near the hospital doors.

I glance over toward her car; you can't even recognize it anymore.

I pull back and take her chin in my hand, lifting her face to look at me.

"What happened, Cherry?" Really looking at her, I notice the stitches in her face. *Did she get them from the car?*

"I loved that fucking car," she grits, anger pouring with each word.

"What happened to your face?" I interrogate. She pushes her palms against my chest and looks over her shoulder at Doc. I lift a brow in suspicion and look at Doc, who gives her a curt nod. Cherry nods back, like some secret code shit girls do. Cherry squares her shoulders and lifts her head.

"I need the club's protection."

◆ ◆ ◆

"You all right, darling?" Bull questions from the head of the table. Cherry shrugs. I've never seen her so defeated before; it's like she's a whole other person. The boys notice it, too—I can tell by the look of concern written on their faces.

"You mean besides someone trying to kill me and blowing up my fucking car?" Cherry shakes her head in anger, but her tone is laced with sorrow.

"Why don't you just tell us from the beginning what's going on exactly," I instruct.

Cherry sits up in her chair and rubs her arms.

"I got this ex, and he's after me," she mutters. "Actually, he's not even an ex, since a one-night stand doesn't make someone an ex." She half-laughs. The hairs on my arm stand and I shoot Bull a look, his eyes meeting mine knowingly.

"What do you mean? I need more than that," Bull pushes, his soft tone gone.

"I mean, I've been hanging around the trailer park I shouldn't be around. I know you guys said there were rivals there, that I needed to stay away, but I just," she closes her eyes and clenches her jaw, "I just couldn't."

"What the fuck, Cherry!" Bull roars. She shoots him a look, her expression of sadness replaced once again with anger.

"I couldn't. You don't understand." Cherry pushes the

words out through gritted teeth, tears filling her eyes.

"Why don't you clarify it for us then?" I state, getting tired of these back-and-forth games.

Cherry shoots her beautiful gray eyes to me. They hold a sadness, like a person telling someone they love goodbye. As if they were going away to war and you may never see them again.

"My little girl lives in that trailer park," she mutters, tears falling from her eyes. I wouldn't have even heard her if I wasn't watching her lips. I stand from my chair, my heart pounding dangerously.

"What the fuck do you mean your little girl?" I seethe.

"Just that, my little girl. Eric took her from me, did it just to hurt me. To prove a point. After I lost her in court, I went to talk to the judge. I walked in on Eric and his lawyer paying the judge and my lawyer off so I would lose the case. I told them I was taking them down and getting my girl back. They tried to kill me, I ran and haven't heard anything since," she rambles, her eyes flicking between mine and Bull's.

I throw my chair back, anger filling my chest.

I turn and glare at her. "Who the fuck are you? How can you keep something like that from me?" I curl my lip in disgust.

"Me? Who the fuck am *I*? Who the fuck are *you*, Lip?" Cherry shouts.

"I think this charade has played its course, Lip. I think it's time we tell her." Bull sighs, and my head whips in his direction. The anger that was filling my chest turns into dread.

"What?" I mumble.

"Tell me what?" Cherry shrugs.

"Just know, I ordered this. Me, and I did it to protect you." Bull pulls a cigarette from his pack and lights it. Shadow sits back in his seat and exhales a long breath. A vein pops out of my neck with the sudden amount of blood racing through my body. I feared this day would come. I never knew what I would do when it did come though, because I know I let things go too far with Cherry. But it's here, and now she'll hate me. She'll loathe me.

"Just fucking tell me already," Cherry demands, her brows furrowed.

"The judge to your case, he came and saw me. Asked me to take care of you. To kill you in short. He's dirty, if you haven't learned that already. He's on our payroll, as we're in his. When he told me his predicament, I told him no. I wasn't getting involved in his dirt. Judge Calhoun threw the cash on my table and told me I had twenty-four hours to reconsider my offer or he was tearing my club down and he'd have another club off you. Next day, the local PD ambushed our club. I got my arm broke and my nose busted. Let's just say I took that reconsideration he offered. I told him I would take care of you, and he'd better have my back with any cases turned his way," Bull explains.

The words Bull is about to spew have my pulse throbbing in my ears.

"He handed me your folder after I accepted the order. It contained the usual. Photos, birth certificate, where you lived, what you drove, everything. When I saw your photo, I thought you looked familiar, but I didn't know how familiar 'til I looked closely at your birth certificate. I knew your father. We went way back, but he got on that juice and he was never the same after that. You – I only barely recognized you because you were barely knee-high to a grasshopper when I last saw you." Bull's face pulls together with sorrow. "Your father was an angry drunk, Cherry. I busted his jaw when I saw him get rough with you one time. That was the end of our friendship, and I never saw him again." This is all news to me. I didn't know any of this, didn't know anything, in fact. I was given my orders, and where to find her. That was it. I've tried to get him to give me more over the years, but he just told me what I needed to know was what I knew.

"How did you take care of me? 'Cause you didn't kill me? I'm confused." Cherry frowns, tears streaking her rosy cheeks. I have to curl my fists to curb the urge to wipe them away. To care for her. Old habit. Bull slowly takes his eyes from Cherry to me.

"What?" Cherry follows his gaze. Her eyes widen and her chest rises when she realizes I was sent to hush her. "No," her bottom lip trembles. I stare back, not wavering.

"I'm afraid so. I couldn't order the hit on you, Cherry. When I saw you, all I saw was a little girl who started life with an unfair advantage. So, I sent Lip for you. Told him to keep you away from the trailer park, to keep you safe and make you happy. To do whatever was necessary to make you feel at home," Bull continues. Cherry's eyes fill with tears again, her face angry as she pins me with a look of betrayal. My mouth goes dry, and I swallow the hard lump forming in my throat.

"I was a job," she whispers. "I WAS A FUCKING JOB!" she shouts. She turns her head, tears spilling from her eyes. I feel like a fucking tool; nothing in my life has compared to the hurt that's driving through my chest at this moment. I caused those tears on her face. I'm causing her hurt. Me.

"Try to relax, Cherry. It was for your own good, darlin'," Bull tries to reason with her, but he obviously doesn't know Cherry. She glares at him, her expression telling him to fuck off. I'm surprised she isn't throwing a chair at him—or me, for that matter.

"So, he knew about Piper this whole time?"

"No, we didn't tell him about Piper. In fact, we told him nothing. He was a prospect at the time. I had Shadow track you, and I told Lip where to find you," Bull responds.

She shakes her head; her eyes clenched shut. "Why didn't you just tell me all of this, why make –" She chokes on her words.

"I had my selfish reasons, Cherry," Bull rasps. "This lifestyle isn't all rainbows and unicorns, if you haven't noticed. Everyone has been tested in one way or another in earning a place here."

"Explain. I deserve to know why you couldn't just tell me what was going on over the last six years!" she shouts.

Bull's face hardens. "You were blackmail if that fucker ever broke our agreement," he spits, his tone not sugarcoating a fucking thing. Cherry winces and closes her eyes again. "It was a win-win for everyone. You were alive and safe, and I had my insurance." I glare at Bull's insensitive tone.

"Cherry, I--"

"Don't," Cherry interrupts me. She rolls her lips on top of each other and exhales a long, tired breath. I look at Bull, his eyes giving an apologetic look.

"We aren't even real, Lip. What I feel for you is not even real, is it?" She wipes her eyes and sighs loudly. "We are so done," she cries.

Hearing her say those words, my heart jumpstarts with panic and my eyes sting. I grit my teeth, angry my emotions are getting the best of me.

"I thought fate sent you to protect me, to care for me, but it was all a lie. The only thing that sent you was the fucking Devil himself." She points at Bull, and he sighs heavily.

"Cherry, just stop and listen to me," I demand, my tone harsh.

"We'll give you kids a minute," Bull states, he and Shadow pushing away from the table.

As soon as they leave, I pull a chair up next to her and reach for her hand. She pulls away from me and levels me with a look that has my balls shrinking into themselves.

"Cherry," I coax. She holds a hand up and closes her eyes, turning her head away from me.

I look down at my boots and fumble with my hands. "I'm sorry, babe," I mutter. I feel like shit. I never wanted to hurt her; I was just following orders. This club is my family, my life. I did what I had to, even if I didn't like it.

"Don't call me that," she snaps through gritted teeth. I slowly lift my head to find her tear-filled eyes solely on me. I've seen Cherry cry maybe twice the whole time we've been together. To see her beautiful eyes fill with sorrow, it hurts.

"I was a job. A fucking job to you. I fell in love with you, Lip." She tilts her head to the side, a tear falling from her beautiful eye. "The way you cared for me, showed me affection, did you mean any of it? Or was that part of the job, too? Was any of it real, or did Bull tell you to be that way?"

I draw in a tight breath and run my hand over my head. It's complicated. I tried not to love Cherry, and I'm still not sure if I am in love with her 100%. Over the years, seeing only her visit me in jail, her face lighting up when she saw me come home, falling into pure ecstasy when I fucked her—she grew on me. But when I told Cherry I loved her, it was because Bull had told me to, and not because I loved her. I know I care about Cherry on some level but I can't identify my feelings for her. Are they because Bull told me to portray them, or are they real? I'm fucking confused.

"Yes, he told me to care for you, to be a gentleman."

A whimper escapes her lips. She lifts her hand, resting her fingers against her mouth, as if trying to keep from showing me she's so affected.

"That explains everything. The way you were before, and the way you are now. Your lies were catching up to you. Your mask of lies were SLIPPING!" She swipes a glass off the table, causing it to smash against the wall. "Six years. It was all a lie... for six fucking years. That day Bull showed up with my patch, that was him, wasn't it?" she mumbles. I look down and nod.

"You fucking prick!" She shoves me hard, and anger flares in my chest. "You were the Devil in a mask of a saint." I furrow my brows. *Is she throwing Bible verses at me?*

"You weren't exactly truthful with me either, Cherry," I sneer, sitting back in my seat and resting my hands behind my neck. Her head whips in my direction, her cheeks flushing with anger.

"I wasn't exactly in the position to tell you I had a little girl," she snaps.

I scoff. "Right. Six years wasn't enough time, huh?"

"Fuck you!" She stands from her chair, tears streaming down her face. "I gave more than my heart to you, Lip. I gave my fucking soul." She clutches her chest, and my worthless heart feels as if she just grabbed mine and squeezed. "I may not have been on the right path when we met, but at least I had my soul. I loved you and I loved this club; I thought you all were my family. I'll do anything for family. When an ol' lady wanted vengeance, I was there drawing blood by her side. This club and you blackened my spirit and for what?" She throws her hands out, hostile. "For it all to be for nothing!" she screams, her face turning near purple. "I don't even recognize myself anymore."

I stand and grab her by the shirt, pulling her chest flush with mine. "You're right. You are different. You found who you are and fell into place," I seethe, my patience wearing thin. She acts like she's some fucking angel and I ruined her life. "I was a goddamn prospect; I was following orders, Cherry. You don't think I wanted to tell you?" I jerk her toward me, and she whimpers. "It was just as hard for me as it was for you. Now. Calm. The. Fuck. Down."

"No! You don't get to tell me to calm down. In fact, you don't get to tell me anything anymore. We are done." She shoves me away from her, her eyes holding the look of hatred. "You're a fucking liar," she hisses.

"You're such a fucking hypocrite. Your lie isn't any less than mine. We both lied, both went into this withholding truths from one another."

"You couldn't even look me in the eye since you've been out of prison, Lip. So I guess you can count your blessings that we're done."

I grab her by the face and pull her toward me, my patience with her gone.

"Did it ever occur to you that I couldn't look you in the face because I was living a fucking lie that burned me every time I laid eyes on you? I was falling for you, Cherry, but I didn't know if that was because I was told to or because I really was. You don't even know me; who I am deep down may not be the man you want to love."

She tears her face from my hold, and her eyes furrow. "I guess we'll never know. Huh? 'Cause the man I'm in love with isn't real." She seethes the last part and shoves against my chest hard.

I take a step back and rub at my chin. The idea she has a little girl, a little girl she's been seeing for years and has never told me about, pisses me off more than anything. She's a mother, a role I never thought Cherry would take.

"Yeah, I can say the same about you," I mutter, placing both my hands on the back of my neck. She throws her hair over her shoulder and wipes the tears from her cheeks.

"It doesn't matter. I'm done. *We're* done. I'm getting the fuck out of here and away from-"

"Not so fast, darlin'," Bull states, stepping back into the room, Shadow following closely behind. Shadow gives a sympathetic look; he clearly knows I'm not in the best of situations right now.

"Excuse me?" Cherry huffs.

"It's too dangerous out there, and besides, seeing how I didn't keep my word to the judge, he may come after my club. I don't need him picking you up and trying to use you as leverage or some shit. That wouldn't be good for anyone involved." Bull sits in his chair and kicks his boots up, not seeming nearly as agitated as I am.

"So, what's that supposed to mean?" Cherry questions.

"Lockdown," Shadow replies.

Cherry scoffs and rolls her eyes. From what I heard when I was in prison, when the club went on lockdown, Cherry would go MIA. She's not one to follow orders. It's one of the many reasons why I'm attracted to her.

"You better keep your pretty little ass right here in this club, damn it!" Bull orders. He lowers his head, his dark hair shining against the lights. "If I have to lock you in a room to keep your stubborn ass safe, I will," he threatens.

"FINE!" Cherry shouts, her hands outstretched on either side.

"I'll send Lip to get you some things. The club will be tight with everyone here, so you'll be sharing a room with him." Shadow smirks, knowing the position he's putting me in. Fucker.

"Oh that'll be-" Cherry nods sarcastically and bites her lip. "That's just perfect," she continues.

"Shadow, tomorrow find this ex-boyfriend; I want his every move. Report back as soon as you can and then we'll make our move. We *will* get this figured out, Cherry." She purses her lips and nods. "You can go now," Bull directs.

Cherry shoves past me and leaves the room in a fit of anger. I sigh heavily and fall into the chair. My chest fucking hurts with an ache I've never experienced before.

"You all right, son?" Bull questions, and I nod.

"You love her?" Shadow questions. I shove my hands into my pockets, thinking about that question, not sure how to answer it, when my hands hit my gremlin bell. I pull it out, and look it over. The chrome of it is tarnished, but it still dings all the time. It fucking annoys me.

"You got thirty minutes, inmate," the prison guard yelled before slamming the door. Cherry was wearing a white dress that went to her thighs, with white high heels. My dick instantly went rock-hard. I fucking wanted her, and badly. It'd been too long since my dick felt the wetness her pussy had to offer. I stepped up to her and grabbed her under the thighs, lifting her in the air. The smell of cherries and flowers wafted around me. I inhaled deeply. The smell was a scent of freedom, a scent that reminded me of my lies and sins to a woman who wanted nothing but my cold fucking heart. Why is she sticking around? Why does she care so much about me? I grit my teeth. Because I made her believe I was something I'm not. I close my eyes, and set her back down on her feet. Pulling my fingers away and distancing myself from her is almost as painful as looking her in the eye every day. She laughed, wrapping her arms around my neck.

"I got you something," she whispered. My brows pulled together.

"You got me something?" I questioned. Her face lit up with a flush of pink as she pulled her fist out and opened it. It looked like some sorta bell in the shape of a skull.

"It's a gremlin bell," she informed.

I grabbed it, and it chimed.

"How did you get this in here?" I asked, looking it over.

"I have my ways." She smiled, shrugged then smiled harder. "I

used my puppy eyes and insured them you couldn't kill anyone with it." She laughed. "I saw it at the biker shop. It said it helps keeps evil spirits or gremlins from messing with your bike, and makes your travels safer."

I trailed my eyes from the bell to her. Those gray eyes cutting me, slicing through my walls of shame and guilt. No matter how much of a piece of shit I feel, I just can't seem to spit the words out that she's a job.

"Nobody has ever given me anything before," I muttered. Her face went still, and her lips parted.

"I love you, Lip," she whispers. My balls sunk into the pit of my stomach and my chest constricted with an unfamiliar emotion. I grabbed her by the back of the head and pulled her into me, the smell of her flower shampoo strong. I closed my eyes and inhaled it, and kissed her forehead. I don't think I'll ever be able to tell her, because that will be the day she stops looking at me like I'm her world, her fucking man.

"LIP!" I tear my eyes from the bell to see Bull and Shadow both eyeballing me.

"What?" I mutter.

"Do you love her?" Shadow repeats. The question strikes my chest like lightning.

"I don't know. Before, I would say no, but now I'm not sure." I look back at the bell and rub the pad of my finger over it. "She's grown on me," I mumble.

"Lip, I think it's in everyone's best interest if you just back off. Leave her be. Just let her go, man," Shadow suggests. My chest lifts with every fury-infused breath I take. My brows pull together and my jaw clenches.

"Let her be?" I question. Shadow gives me an off look before glancing at Bull, unsure. "You gave her to me, you put her in my fucking hands, and you fucking patched her in as MY property. That means she's fucking mine." I slam my fist on the table. "Mine! *I* will choose what I do with her. You won't tell me to stay away from her." I stand from the table, and knock my knuckles on the wood. "She's my goddamn property," I reaffirm, my voice deep and rough.

"It wasn't my intention for you to go and fall in love with her, Lip," Bull rasps, swiping his hands through his hair. My brows furrow, then widen. Realization that I may in fact love Cherry sends pain through my chest. Scowling, I point at Bull and Shadow. "Just..." I shake my head, thoughts of love and hate swirling through my fucking head. "Just stay out of it," I mutter before leaving.

9

Cherry

I SLAM THE DOOR TO WHAT WAS ONCE MINE AND LIP'S ROOM. THE impact from the door closing rattles the bottles of beer and perfume on the dresser. I sink down to the floor, my hands tangling in my hair in my moment of distress.

"How can this be? How could this have happened?" I cry. This nightmare of horror is enveloping me. The scythe the Devil himself used to tear my heart from my chest made it so painful the depths of my wellbeing may never be the same again. My bottom lip trembles with the thought of being deceived for so many years. I fell in love with Lip, shared things with him I never have with anyone else. I close my eyes and tears slip down my cheeks.

I knew Lip was hiding something. I fucking knew it. I just didn't suspect it 'til recently, when his mask of Prince Charming started slipping. Funny thing is I preferred the fucked-up, kinky Lip over that bullshit fake Lip he was before. I guess because I always knew deep down he was more than he let on, that he was capable of causing mayhem.

I form fists in my anger. I was so stupid to think some guy off the side of the road would just fall in love with me and invite me into his family as easy as Lip did. I was naive enough to lift my walls, to trust again. I let my wings out and flew with the wind, only that wind turned into a hostile storm and I got swept up in its gust before I knew what was happening.

"Fucking asshole!" I scream. I keep screaming, so loud my throat burns, but I don't stop. I continue to shout, demanding this hurt buried deep inside to leave at once.

I stand on wobbly legs, my voice nearly gone and my throat feeling like I swallowed razor blades. I swipe my arms along the dresser in a fit of rage. One by one, the empty bottles, clothes, and cosmetics go flying across the room.

"Lying son of a bitch!" I shout with my now-raspy voice, gripping the half-naked chick poster hanging on the wall and ripping it down. I grab every picture of slutty twat waffles hanging on the walls and tear them down the middle.

"I hate you! I hate you!" I cry, pulling the blankets and sheets off the bed. The bed that Lip and I fucked in—or what I thought was making love—many times before.

The sheets tangle around my arms, halting me from tearing the mattress onto the floor. How fitting—soft sheets that portray comfort and solace trapping me in a strong hold. I turn and twist, trying to break free, but I fall to the floor in a heap of fabric.

My fury and anger smothered with blankets cocooning me, my emotions spring through me with such a force nothing escapes but a stream of tears and gasping.

Six years of lies. Six years of deceit. Six years of false emotion and underlying secrets. I don't see us ever coming back from this.

◆ ◆ ◆

"Cherry?" I slowly open my eyes, seeing nothing but the gray sheets. I eventually gave in to my feelings and covered my head with the sheets, crying it all out on the shitty floor. I must have fallen asleep.

"Cherry, babe?" It's Dani.

"What?" I croak, my throat feeling like raw hamburger. My eyes burn and feel swollen from crying so hard, and my throat is scratchy from screaming and yelling. I feel worn out... used.

The sheets tug upward and the lights from above beam with such a force I wince and turn my head away.

"Damn, girlie," Dani whispers, her face conveying sympathy. I hold my hand up, stopping her.

"Don't. I don't need that shit. Just go," I demand, pointing at the door, not looking at her. I am not the weak one. I don't cry and I don't have relationship problems. Yet here I am with all of the above. I don't need someone to judge me, or to feel sorry for me. I just want to be left the hell alone.

"Don't give me that shit. Sit up. I got a cold soda and some music." Dani grabs my arm and pulls me upward.

"Anyone ever tell you you're a pain in the ass?" I mutter, sitting upright. I push my back against the dresser and squint at her. She's beautiful—long dark hair, green eyes, and a red slinky top with black shorts. You'd never guess she had two kids with the figure on her.

"Yeah, Shadow tells me all the time." She laughs and I close my eyes. I seriously don't want to think about men right now. "Shadow told me what happened. I'm sorry, Cherry. I'd kick Lip's ass if it'd make you feel any better, but I know it won't." She slides down, sitting directly in front of me. She leans her back against the bed and tosses a soda can between her legs toward me.

"The joke's on me 'cause I really love Lip. Dark, light, all of his shades," I scoff and grab the soda. Anger is slowly replacing my sorrow, but not fast enough.

"I hear you weren't very honest with him, either."

My eyes snap to hers and she raises a brow, waiting for an explanation. Instead, I pop the top to the soda can and let the fizzy cool contents slip down my sore throat.

"Seriously, Cherry, how could you not tell me you had a kid?" she continues. I set the soda down and pin her with a serious glare.

"I wasn't really in the position to tell anyone, Dani. I wasn't a mother. I had my rights taken from me. I saw Piper in the mornings when I could, and I had to be very careful about it. I had very dangerous men after me. I couldn't risk it." Lowering my gaze, I finger the soda top.

"Piper, that's a cute name."

I smile, and then tears prick my burning eyes. "Oh, Cherry," Dani's voice is laced with sympathy. She slides across the floor and embraces me in a warm hug. "It's all right," she whispers into my hair. I slowly push her off me and wipe under my eyes. I have to keep my chin up, got to stop this pity me bullshit.

"I'm fine. Really, I'll be okay," I reassure her. I think a piece of me knew there was more to Lip, a darker, more devious side. An inner beast that was lurking within the depths of his eyes, or the growl in his tone when he was angered. It was always there. I just refused to acknowledge it. I was too set on finding someone that was kind and gentle, making me feel like a fucking princess after Eric killed me emotionally. Now it's time to suck it up, and face the beast that I'm in love with.

"You know I have your back, right?" My teary eyes find hers and my bottom lip shakes with the urge to just bawl.

"How? I'm not an ol' lady. I'm not a part of this club. Lip didn't want me here, Dani!" My voice begins to rise and Dani just shakes her head, a small laugh lifting from within her chest.

"It doesn't really matter what Lip wanted. My dad gave you that property patch, right?" I nod, not sure what she's getting at.

"My dad patched you in. He wanted you as family, and he made you one of us. You can tear off 'Lip's Property', but that Devil's Dust rocker? That's no lie. You're my sister through and through." She gives a tight-lipped smile. My heart pains, not with one of heartache, but one with love and adoration toward Dani. She's strong, she's beautiful, and she's the best damn sister I could ever ask for.

She stands and when I look up, I see a black iPod in my line of sight.

"What's this?" I ask, taking it from her.

"It's mine. I listen to it a lot when I'm in a mood or need my emotions sorted out. Or when I don't know how to feel—the music does it for me."

I nod. "Thank you, Dani." I whisper.

"I gotta get back in there. Zane is probably raising hell with Bobby right now. Keep your chin up, Cherry."

I stand on tired legs and grab the sheets.

"Oh, and Cherry?" I turn, finding Dani halfway out the bedroom door.

"Yeah?"

"If you really love Lip, make him hurt. Show him what he's giving up." She smirks and shuts the door. I furrow my brows, not sure if I want Lip or not. A piece inside of me still does, but my mind is confused on whether it would be smart to forgive him.

I remake the bed and take off my bra and shorts. I'm so tired all I want to do is climb in this bed and sleep. Just listen to music and sleep my way through this lockdown. I flip the lights off and put the ear buds in. The song "Locked Away" by R.City plays. I arch a brow, unsure of the song at first. I've never heard it before. As the lyrics continue, they speak right to my soul, telling my life story. A tear slips from my tired eyes as the song serenades me through reality and emotions I'm trying to deny. The fact that I've wanted nothing but to be there for Lip, and yet here I am, turning my back on him, not listening to a word he's saying. The song guides me through emotions and feelings I can't sort or explain, until my senses are drowned with sleep.

◆ ◆ ◆

The bed dips, the feeling of warmth slips over me, and the smell of fresh mint wafts around me. Lip. I turn onto my belly and look over, finding Lip getting comfy right next to me in the bed. Has he lost his mind?

"I'm sorry, are you lost?" I ask, my voice muffled with sleep. The ride of self-pity is over, and now I'm pissed. I'm fucking angry and really just want to deck Lip in his face.

Lip rests his head on the back of his hands and looks up at the ceiling. "There is nowhere else for me to sleep. The club is packed, Cherry," he explains, sounding irritated, like he's talking down to me. It grates on my nerves.

I push myself up with my arms, grab his pillow from under him and throw it on the floor.

"What the fuck?" He leans over to grab his pillow, and I quickly shove my feet in his back and push his ass off the bed. He lands with a loud thump, and I move over into the middle of the bed.

"You like to lie so much, why don't you sleep with the rug, baby," I suggest in the most condescending voice I can muster.

He pulls himself up off the floor and stands. I can't see him because it's so dark, but I can tell his arms and chest are puffed out and outlined with anger. He's pissed, and no doubt pinning me with the most furious stare. *Good.*

"Maybe you forgot, with your nose so stuck up in the air, but you fucking lied to me, too, princess. So, why don't you lie on the floor with me?" He grabs the mattress and in one swift movement pulls it off the box spring, and I land with a thump.

My mouth pops open with shock. Lip grabs his pillow and fluffs it before lying on the floor next to the mattress.

"There, now we're even. Two liars, side by side." He sniffs. "We're equal."

My eyebrows pull together, and my fingers dig into the mattress. "Yes. I lied to you, Lip, but I had no choice!" I shout.

Lip sits up and leans in, his face nearly touching mine. "Neither did I!" he shouts right back.

We sit like that, nose to nose, our breaths angry and hostile but in sync with each other. I've never seen Lip so angry, so furious. Before he was locked up, if someone disagreed with him, he'd look at me and brush the other person off. I used to think he was just down to earth and didn't sweat the small stuff. I didn't know he was just being a fake.

I pull away first and lie down, my back facing him.

◆ ◆ ◆

The sound of yelling and stomping in the hallway wakes me from my sleep. I slowly peel my eyes open and find myself hanging halfway off the mattress. I raise my hand to wipe the sleep from my eyes, finding Lip's hand entwined with mine. My palm is warm and sweaty, and he's as close to the mattress as he can get. His eyes pop open and quickly find me raising our joined palms.

"Shit," he whispers, snatching his hand from mine. I shove

my sweaty palm to my chest and look away.

"Jesus, what the hell is going on out there?" Lip questions, looking at our closed door.

"I'm not sure. It woke me up, too," I mutter. Lip sits up and hikes his knees, resting his elbows on them before swiping his fingers into his messy hair. My thighs clench; God, I love it when he does that. I close my eyes and shake my head. *No, don't react to him.*

"I'll go get us some breakfast," he insists, standing.

"I can't eat," I state. My stomach is still in knots from everything, and the sound of food isn't appealing. Lip arches a brow as he shoves his legs into some jeans.

"You should eat something," he insists. I scoff and tilt my head to the side.

"Screw you," I snide.

"Whatever, starve. That'll really show me," he mutters, grabbing his shirt off the floor and slamming the door behind him.

I flex my fingers and grit my teeth.

"Gah!" I scream. This man fucking infuriates me!

Who grabbed whose hand last night when we were sleeping, me or him? I shake my head and stand to find some clothes. It doesn't matter. I need to focus on getting out of here and figuring out a way to get my daughter back. Those are my top priorities right now.

Lip

I STRIDE DOWN THE HALLWAY, THE SMELL OF EGGS WAFTING throughout the club. Hopefully, the ladies got together and made the whole club breakfast and not just their kids.

"Give that back!" Addie shouts, chasing Zane down the

hallway. I jump out of the way as the two sprint through. Addie is Doc's kid, and Zane is Shadow and Dani's. I don't know how old they are. Zane is small, and Addie is bigger. I don't do well with kids. I think it goes back to my childhood or some shit. Or that's what the shrinks in prison said, anyway. My dad was a tough ol' man and made my life a living hell. He *called me a pussy, told me I should have come out of my mom sprouting a vagina instead of balls.*

"Phillip, you better hit that damn baseball like a DeLuca!" my father shouted from the stands. I swallowed hard and pulled the rim of my baseball cap down. My father looked huge sitting in the bleachers with the rest of the parents. He had on blue jeans and a white fitted shirt that covered his strong torso firmly, and of course he had on his leather cut, displaying that he was an Outlaw to everyone sitting in the bleachers. The president of the Sin City Outlaws motorcycle club, to be exact. My father shoved his boot onto the seat in front of him and gave a firm nod, his tanned Italian skin shining with the sweat the sun caused. I took a big breath and turned on the base to face the pitcher, determined to hit this fucking ball into the next field. I was going to prove to my father I was worth a damn, that I wasn't the son he was ashamed of. My brother Zeek was my father's pride and joy, always getting into trouble and getting caught in the traps of the law. My dad wanted me to be just like my brother, but I'm going to show my dad that I can shine in a way that doesn't involve criminal activity.

The pitcher looked behind him at his other teammates before looking back toward me, a sly smirk across his face. Tommy Ricci. My father told me plenty of times how I needed to hang out with Tommy, let him rub off on me, that I could learn a thing two from him. But Tommy's just a punk. He's mean to the girls, and a fucking ass-wipe to those who call him a friend. He steals, too; I caught him stealing from our teacher's purse the other day. I, of course, didn't say anything. I'm starting to think my father wants me to be bad, that it would make him love me more.

Tommy threw the ball, and I swung.

"Strike one!" Shit. I hit the baseball bat on the base and gripped the wooden bat. Tommy chuckled and threw the ball again. Another strike.

"Come on, boy," my father sounded from behind me, his tone laced with humiliation.

Tommy lowered his head, his eyes digging into my insecurities. He threw the ball, and I closed my eyes and swung again.

"Strike three! You're outta there!"

Fuck. I just let the other team win.

"Great job, Phillip," one of my teammates slammed into my shoulder leaving the field. I dropped the bat and slowly turned, finding a fuming father. I strode off the field, and my father rose from the bleachers. He unfolded his large frame from them and stood above me. I shrank in his shadow. He gripped the back of my shirt and dragged me to the car.

"You are a disgrace to the DeLuca name. You don't get your sense of failure from me, that's for sure." He tugged on my shirt and pushed me into the car. "You don't even look Italian, for Christ's sake." He lowered his head and shook it, his boot kicking the rocks at his feet. I crossed my arms and tried my hardest not to cry in front of all the other kids and parents. Being ten years old was a tough age as it was, but having my father breathing down my neck was even harder.

"Let's go, Phillip. See about getting you into some fucking ballet classes or something."

Screaming snaps me out of my childhood memory, and I

continue toward the kitchen. I rub my eyes, burning from lack of sleep. I couldn't stop watching Cherry last night. She's fucking beautiful. There is something about being free from the lies that I had to live with so long, being let go from the pressure the club bestowed on me. I see Cherry in a whole other light. She fucking lied about having a kid; her defiance turns me on, yet pisses me off. I love how wild she is, how broken and against the wind she can be. It keeps me on my toes. I need a girl who stays interesting, who can bust my balls. It makes me want to tame her and stand proud that she's mine. I tug my bottom lip between my teeth. It doesn't make me less angry about her lying, though.

Addie runs into the kitchen, slamming the door into the wall.

"Jesus!" I yell as Zane shoves me out of the way.

"Welcome to breakfast," Tom Cat states, thrusting a paper plate of scrambled eggs into my chest. I take hold of the plate and shake my head.

Dani shifts in her seat, bouncing her newest baby Delilah on her hip.

"Damn it, Zane, I said to stop chasing her!" Dani parents.

"He's fine, Dani. He's just being a kid," Bull interjects, shoving a pile of eggs into his mouth.

"Ya know, I thought we were bad-ass bikers. When did this place turn into a playpen?" Tom Cat mutters.

The door slams open and Cherry walks in. The sight of her makes me choke on an egg. She's wearing a black ripped-up tank top, her breasts nearly popping out, and some blue jean shorts that used to be jeans, frays and strings hanging out along her freckled skin.

"You all right there?" Tom Cat questions, slapping my back. I pound on my chest and take a deep breath to clear my air pipe.

"Yeah," I croak. Watching Cherry's ass as she walks to the stove, I have to turn and face the wall. My dick is growing at a fast rate inside my pants, and has no signs of dissipating. Her throwing a wall between us makes her that much more tempting. She's like the forbidden fruit of the MC garden, and I want it. I want to break every rule, give into temptation and damn the consequences just so I can have her one last time. I want her without knowing in my head she's a job. Just her and me, no lies between us. I want to explore the feelings I have slicing into my chest like a searing knife.

"Boys, let's get to the chapel and work out this mess, shall we?" Bull stands from the table and wipes his mouth with a napkin.

"Shouldn't I come?" Cherry asks.

"Nah, not right now, darling. Let us figure shit out first."

"I want my daughter, Bull," Cherry blurts. My dick just took a nosedive, the reminder of her lying to me a complete turn-off. I bite my lip with anger. I never thought she would lie to me, that she could be so manipulative, and that pisses me the fuck off. I became a pussy, and I let my guard down. Bull told me to be that fucking Prince Charming, and I did, for a while. But when I got out of prison, seeing Cherry standing tall to be my woman, I just couldn't hold up the act anymore. I wanted her to know the real me.

"First order of business: Cherry and this fucking mess," Bull states on an exhale. "If any of you are lost, here are the facts. Cherry got herself in a mess with Judge Calhoun, and he came to us to take care of it. I made Lip the distraction, and kept her in line. But apparently, our beloved Cherry has not been so honest with everyone. She was supposed to be gone, dealt with. But now they know she's here and a problem, and now it's our problem." Bull clears up the confusion.

"I'm sorry, maybe I'm just the morbid one here, but why

didn't we just kill her ass or pay her off to go somewhere when this shit happened?" Old Guy questions. I grit my teeth at his boldness.

"Well, we were going to, but I know Cherry from when she was a baby." Bull shakes his head. "I couldn't kill her, or put her out there knowing she'd be killed, so I made the call and kept her under radar. So, now that we're all up to speed, they know we didn't kill her, and they're going to come here with retribution."

"What a fucking mess, man," Bobby mutters, running his hands through his hair.

"I agree," I throw in.

"Shadow, find this boyfriend, or baby daddy, whatever the fuck he is today. Find out what he knows, and who is after her exactly," Bull orders.

"You got it." Shadow nods.

"I'm coming with," I state.

"No!" Bull points at me.

"What the fuck you mean 'no'?" My nostrils flare with anger.

"You're too distracted, and I don't need fuck-ups," Bull explains.

"I'm not distracted," I scoff.

"I disagree, son. If you would've left the table last night and pounded your frustration out on some young piece of tail, maybe. But when I offered my room to you last night, or even a fucking cot in the main room, you turned both down to be with her in your room." He points at me with a steady finger. "*That* is fucking distracted."

"Agreed." Shadow laughs, and I narrow my brows and level him with a 'shut the fuck up' look.

"You stay, Lip." Bull slams the gavel down. I flex my hands in irritation.

I'm so fucking confused and angry. I hate Cherry. I want

Cherry. I want to hurt her and fuck her. I'm a complete fucking mess.

I used to blame the job on my confused feelings. I tried to build a barrier of what was real and what was fake, but that dam I built of guarded emotions soon begin to crack, my affection and desire to care for her splintering through the wall that held me together. Now that the mission has been lifted, I can feel those small cracks spidering into something unstoppable. I care for Cherry, whether I want to admit it or not. She's mine, and I'll kill any motherfucker who tries to step in front of that.

Cherry

I PLACE MY EMPTY PLATE INTO THE SINK AND HEAD BACK TO THE bedroom. I ate some, but I just don't have an appetite. I feel like everyone is staring at me. A shiver runs up my spine with the sudden unease. Everyone knows I was just a job to Lip. They're probably thinking, "That poor girl. She went and fell in love with him, and none of it's even real."

I slam the door behind me and grab the mattress, shoving with all my might to put it back on the box springs. After finally getting it in place, I crawl onto the bed. My eyes prick with the urge to cry. I inhale a steady breath through my nose and close my eyes. *I will not cry. I will not cry.*

The way Lip acted as if everything was just a job conflicts with my heart. I swore he loved me, the way he looked at me when we were together said so. The way he cared so much about my wellbeing, that couldn't have all been because of him being ordered to take care of me... was it?

A small knock sounds at the door. I roll my eyes and sit up, folding my legs under me Indian-style.

"What?" I snap.

Dani steps in with Delilah, her youngest, on her hip, Doc following closely behind her.

"You all right?" Dani asks, sitting on the bed. She flips her hair over her shoulder and pins me with sad green eyes. I tear my gaze from hers and look at Delilah, who's picking up a ripped-up poster piece.

"Shit, Delilah, no," Dani scolds, grabbing hold of the poster.

Doc takes Dani's place on the bed and reaches for my face. She takes hold of my chin and turns my head slightly, looking over the stitches in my eyebrow.

"How do they feel?" she questions, trailing her manicured finger over them.

I shrug. "Okay, I guess. They itch some," I reply.

"Yeah, try some Vaseline. I'm sure with all these horny men around here, you can find some." She smiles, and I can't help but laugh.

"Are you going to hide in here the whole lockdown?" Dani spits, holding Delilah on her hip.

"Wow, to the point, huh?" I chuckle.

"Well, I mean, it's no secret you're avoiding everyone." Dani laughs and my cheeks warm with humiliation.

"Ease up, Dani; I don't blame her. This club..." Doc shakes her head. "Let's just say, it can be unconventional sometimes. That order your dad gave Lip was fucked-up and you know it." Doc looks over her shoulder and furrows her brows at Dani.

"No, I agree it was. But it's what had to be done." Dani shrugs. The depth of her loyalty to this club is something I envy. No matter how wrong The Devil's Dust can be, she always has their back.

"Regardless, Cherry is a human. She has feelings. Lip could have been a little less, I don't know, personal about the whole thing." Doc tilts her head and chews on her bottom lip. "Did he say he loved you? Did he make love to you?"

I turn and look out the window next to the bed. The sky is dark; I wonder if it will storm.

"Well, did he?" Dani questions.

The tears I was trying to hold back fill to the rim of my eyelids and spill over.

"Once, but the way he made love to me before was so intimate, as if he was telling me he loved me through sex. I figured he was just a guy who didn't do the mushy shit that he conveyed how he felt through his actions." I fiddle with my fingers. "Lip was very persistent when we met, and came on so strong. He and I were in a wave of lust, in a sea of tangled sheets every other day. Maybe that's all it was, though—lust. Or maybe I fell in love so quickly I became blind."

"Ouch. I can't even imagine," Doc mutters.

Dani leans in close, placing her hand on my knee. "I love this club. I'll do anything for this club. But the reason why we came in here was to tell you that you are one of us, through and through. Lip went too far in that- that job. We'll make his ass pay," Dani promises.

"Damn straight," Doc agrees.

I laugh and wipe at my cheeks.

"Thanks, guys, but you'll probably just make it worse," I advise.

"Probably," Dani agrees. "But we'd do it for you."

"I'm good, but thanks." I smile.

"You need to find out if you were just business to Lip, or if it was more," Doc adds. "I see the way he looks at you. He cares about you, Cherry." I lower my head and bite my bottom lip. I am not sure if I want to know though. I'm scared that I was nothing but a job and Lip was just a really good actor.

"Don't act like you don't want to know. You love him, Cherry, and if you walk away without finding out, you'll always wonder if he really loved you," Doc tells me. I roll my eyes and pick at the blanket on the bed.

Delilah giggles, and my eyes shoot to the little girl. My heart aches. I want Piper so badly. I just want to hug her, to have her little arms wrap around me and pull this bitterness from me.

"This will all blow over, and before you know it, you'll have your little girl back and she'll be here with ours." Dani smiles, her tone optimistic.

"Yeah, then you can go crazy with us." Doc laughs.

My heart sinks, my stomach turns, and I feel like I may puke. The thought that I may get my daughter back is too much for me to even handle. I want it. I want it badly. I never thought it was a possibility, though.

The door opens and Tom Cat pokes his head in.

"Dani, Doc, you might want to get in here. Zane got a Hot Wheel stuck in Addie's hair." A loud scream sounds from the hallway. "Yeah, she's pissed. Zane thinks it's funny, though." Tom Cat chuckles.

Dani and Doc give each other a knowing look before both hurrying out the bedroom door.

As soon as it shuts, I sigh with relief. I don't know how many more therapy sessions I can have with those two. They make me... feel. I don't want to feel. I just want to lose myself into a tomb of darkness, not feeling anything. A tranquility of never-never land. A land where nothing bad ever happens, and the only feeling you experience is numbness.

◆◆◆

I wake with the sound of thunder and groan. Slowly sitting up on the bed, I see a plate of food next to the door. I missed dinner, or was it lunch? Bringing my knees up, I rest my elbows on them. I survey the room—it's trashed. I sigh with a sound of dread. *Maybe if I clean this place up, it will help the way I feel.* I crawl off the bed and kick at some posters. I grab the iPod Dani gave me from the dresser and swipe through the songs, landing on "Look Good For You" by Selena Gomez. My eyes perk with the lyrics, ideas swiping through my mind. As much as I don't want to care if Lip had any real feelings for me, I know I truly do care for him underneath all my resentment. I bite my fingernail and eye the dresser. I wonder if I walk into the club wearing something so revealing what Lip would do. Would he care, or would he shrug it off now that the orders have been lifted? If he reacts, then I know I was more to him than a job. If he doesn't do anything then I know my place, and I'll need to move on as much as it may hurt to do so. But at least I won't beat myself up thinking *what if.*

I grab the dresser drawer and start rifling through it, finding a small red dress wadded into a ball in the back. Perfect.

I pull it over my head, the silk material clinging to my thighs. It's skintight, showing off my curves perfectly. I spot some black heels under the dresser and put them on, too. With all the guys in the club, I can surely get at least one to look with these. If I can make Lip jealous then I know I have some effect on him.

I throw my head over, shuffling my hair, giving it that sexy volume. The door opens and I throw my head back, finding Lip staring right at me. I smirk and run my hands through my hair. *Here we go, the truth is about to be revealed.*

His nostrils flare, and his hands clench. My heart stammers against my chest, not sure what his reaction means.

"What are you doing?" he asks, his tone of voice low and rough, the sound of it doing things to me.

I shrug, not really sure myself.

He rubs at his chin, his eyes undressing me from head to toe.

"Can I help you with something, Lip?" I cock my head to the side and furrow my brows.

His eyes are hooded, his chest rising and falling rapidly, but he doesn't respond. Feeling nervous, I pull the dress down some and step toward him.

"Excuse me." I try to move around him, but he catches my elbow.

"You are not going out there in that." His eyes narrow as I snatch my elbow from his grip and grimace.

"You don't get to tell me what to do anymore," I seethe before walking past him, heading down the hall.

I catch Bobby at the end of the hall, and his mouth pops open. He punches Kane in the arm, not taking his eyes off me, and Kane smirks at me. Before I can take another step, my world goes upside-down and I'm thrown over a broad shoulder. Using my hands, I push myself up to find Lip's fine ass.

"Lip, put me down!" I shout, but he doesn't respond.

He struts into our room and slams the door, plopping me down on the bed.

"Take it off, now!" he orders. *Looks like I made him jealous.*

"Why? Why do you care?" I ask, my fingers digging into the sheets. His face is red, veins popping out on his neck. He looks me over once more then thrusts forward, his hands grabbing the top of the red dress, tearing it right down the center, leaving my bare tits and black thong. He growls in his chest and backs off.

"You're mine, goddamn it! Mine, whether you wanna be or not!" He shoves his face inches from mine, shouting in my face. I turn my head, looking at the wall. He's angry—good. *Welcome to the club, buddy.* He straddles me and pushes his weight onto my torso, pressing me into the mattress firmly. I gasp as his mouth crashes down onto my neck.

"Lip!" I holler, trying to push him off. He sucks hard, causing a sharp pain to rise from my neck. He finally releases his hold on my shoulder, his dark eyes pinning me.

"You pull that shit again, I will throw you over that bar and fuck you in front of every brother in this fucking club," he threatens. He slowly stands and leaves, slamming the door behind him.

I grit my teeth and scream. Standing from the bed, my tight red dress hangs over me like a robe. I hurry to the bathroom, turn my head to the side and notice the dark hickey on my neck. He claimed me.

I guess that answers that. I wasn't just a job to him. He does have feelings for me. But can I forgive him for lying? I frown; I lied, too, though. Can we get through our lies?

I change into some ripped jeans and an orange shirt, then set out to tell the girls what just happened. Maybe they can tell me what to do next.

Getting closer to the main area where everyone seems to congregate, I hear yelling and shouting. I follow the noise to outside of the club. The Ghost Riders are here, and are head-to-head with the Devil's Dust. I cup my mouth, my heart slamming against my chest in fear.

"All I'm saying is he never showed up back at the club, and he was last seen here," the president, Stunt, points at Bull. Stunt turns his head and lowers it in a menacing way, pinning Lip with a look of death. "And your man here had beef with him for laying hands on his cunt." I scowl at his insult.

Lip pushes Bobby out of the way and puffs his chest out in that way he does when he's angry. Stunt's shoulders rise; they're nose-to-nose, and my palms are sweating with fear.

"You better watch who the fuck you're talking to," Lip threatens. Stunt swiftly darts his hand behind his back and pulls out a black gun. Gasping, I step forward, but Dani quickly grabs me by the shoulder to stop me from going any further.

"I know exactly who the fuck I'm talking to," Stunt growls, holding the barrel of the gun to Lip's head.

"Do it. Fucking do it, you pussy," Lip taunts. A whimper travels up my throat in pure fear. Lip is insane; I've never seen him look death in the eye with guns blazing and not give a fuck. He's always been so careful, and not one to take on a confrontation. But that was before he went away, before the truth that he was just acting like Prince Charming. This is the real Lip. This is who he is. Reckless, no regard to reason. Yet here I am on my tiptoes, ready to run to his defense. I still love him, whether I want to or not.

"Lip!" I cry, trying to get his attention. He slowly turns his head and his hard face softens when he sees me. He looks down, like he's pained that I'm seeing him like this.

"Look, your man was warned about messing with my property. He hurt her, and I retaliated. I did what I had to, to protect her," Lip confesses, his attitude of 'I don't give a fuck' gone. My eyes dart toward Stunt, curious if he'll shoot Lip.

"Come on, Stunt. If anything, this ass-wipe did us a favor," one of the Ghost Rider members adds.

"Doesn't matter. He was a brother, have some loyalty," Stunt snaps.

The guy steps up; he's shorter and has a big beer gut. "He nearly got me killed after he fucked an ol' lady from another club, who just happened to be property of a fucking president. He was reckless, he had no loyalty and you know it." The guy looks at Lip. "Let the boy go and let's go home."

Stunt gives Lip a sideways glance as if he's thinking about it. I survey the Devil's Dust, noticing Bobby's hand on his weapon sitting in the back of his jeans, and Bull's handling his pistol in his holster. They'd go to war with another club to protect Lip. They're a brotherhood; I envy that about this club. Loyalty is the common DNA that runs in their blood—they all have it.

My hand is grasped by a smaller palm. Looking to my side, Dani gives me a tight-lipped smile and squeezes my hand. She'd have my back no matter what—I know it, and I feel it. I'm family.

"Yeah. Fine, but we ain't open for business anymore," Stunt responds, replacing his weapon back in his waistband.

"I think that's best," Bull agrees. Everyone seems to relax as the Ghost Riders retreat back to their bikes. Now that the show is over, everyone starts going their separate ways, but I can't seem to move. My eyes are glued to Lip. He told that guy to kill him, and in doing so, I realized I still care for Lip, that I want to try and work through our lies. But does he? Lip eventually strides toward me, his teeth biting on his lip ring.

He stops in front of me and crosses his arms, his stance cocky. I rear my hand back and slap him in the face hard. His head whips to the side, his arms uncrossing to grab at his face.

"Don't ever do that again," I sneer, tears filling my eyes. He removes his hand, revealing a bright red handprint. I huff and return to the room, angry that he makes me care, pissed that I love him, and furious that I ever climbed on the back of his bike.

◆◆◆

Dinnertime rolls around, which consists of burgers and chips. I grab a tomato from the fridge and start slicing it up for the tray of sides.

"Cherry, I don't like 'matoes. They taste weird," Zane says, lifting on his tiptoes to watch me slice it.

"You think so?" I laugh. He scrunches his nose and nods.

"Yeah, I'm not a big fan of them, either," I agree.

"My mom says I should eat them 'cause they're good for me." Zane sticks his tongue out, and I giggle.

"Well, mommies know best." I smile. Zane acts like he's going to gag and runs off. I shake my head at him and grab an onion to slice next. As soon as the knife cuts through it, I feel the room shift and my back tense. I glance up and find Lip grabbing a plate. Seconds go by, but they feel like minutes. I peer up from under my lashes and find Lip staring at me once more. My breath hitches, and a sharp piercing fills my finger.

"Ouch!" I gasp, shifting my eyes to my finger. Blood gushes out of my finger. *Fuck, I've cut it.*

Warmth presses along my back, and a hand grabs mine.

"Is it bad?" Lip asks, his smell and touch making me shift on my feet. I pull my hand from his and hiss.

"It fucking hurts, I know that," I state. I look at my finger and notice a small cut.

"First-aid is in the bathroom in the main hall," Tom Cat tells me, grabbing a tomato.

Lip grabs my wrist and pulls me around the island in the kitchen and out of the double doors. He drags me down the hall and opens the main bathroom door.

"Sit," he instructs, pointing at the sink.

"I can put a Band-Aid on myself." I roll my eyes but still sit on the sink's counter.

He leans down, pulls the kit from under the sink and takes a Band-Aid out. He grabs my wrist and surveys the pad of my finger.

"You nicked it pretty good," he mutters.

"It's your fault," I whisper. His brown eyes flick to mine and I scowl.

"I'm pretty sure you were too busy checking me out and forgot what you were doing." He smiles wolfishly.

"Yeah, that was it," sarcasm drips from my voice. "Pretty sure I just suck at cooking."

Lip's mouth lifts at the corner into a small smile. "Not

arguing that." He winks. My mouth falls open, and I give him a slap to the arm.

"Hey, I'm getting better," I defend, laughing.

He turns on the faucet and slowly places my finger under it. The cool water splashes into the cut, making it sting. I hiss and yank it from the stream.

"Ouch, that hurts!" I yell. An evil grin fits his face and he pushes my hand back under the water.

"You gotta clean it." He chuckles. "Stop being a baby." I furrow my brows and roll my eyes.

He dries my finger off with a clean cloth and gently wraps it with a Band-Aid.

"There, all fixed up." He smiles, holding my finger up to display a Spongebob Band-Aid.

I laugh. "Thanks." Spongebob makes me think of Piper, a small sting in my chest resurfacing.

"Shadow will be back tomorrow with details on Eric and everyone involved," Lip states. It's crazy how he can still read my mind, even after this many years.

His hands rest on my knees, and the simple touch of his palms sends shivers up my thighs. I slowly shift my gaze from his hands to his face. His eyes are hooded, and his mouth is parted. Silence fills the air, and the tension becomes thick. I bite my bottom lip and hop off the counter. Just as I'm about to walk out, he grabs my arm, stopping me. His forehead wrinkles, and his eyes display a sense of sorrow, like he wants to apologize but doesn't know how. Almost as soon as they arrived, the wrinkles disappear, and he lets go of me. I bite my cheek, feeling a little defeated, and walk back to the kitchen.

◆◆◆

I wake from my sleep and feel heaviness on my waist,

something rubbing against my clit. I moan and slowly open an eye. The weight across me is Lip's arm. He's lying in bed with me. I shift my ass, rubbing my clit along whatever is causing me so much pleasure in my sleepy haze.

A moan escapes Lip's mouth in my ear. I lower my hand and grab onto whatever is gliding along my panty-clad pussy. The unmistakable barbell in Lip's dick greets my palm.

"Fuck, I love you, Cherry," Lip groans into my neck. My eyes widen, my fog of sleep lifting at once. I turn on my side and see Lip waking up at the same time. His hooded eyes find mine and we just stare at each other. He must have slept in the bed beside me, and our bodies found each other in the midst of sleeping. He pulls the sheet up and looks under the blanket, I assume at his dick. He shrugs in an apologetic way and grabs a spare pillow, shoving it between us. I shake my head and laugh, and he laughs with me.

"You're in my bed," I mutter, my mind playing back and forth if I really heard him say he loved me or if I dreamed it. Lip tilts his head to the side and a sly smirk crosses his face.

"Technically, you're in *my* bed," he counters.

"Technically, you're on *my* side of the bed," I smart.

He chuckles and pats the pillow. "I'll stay on my side. Promise."

Silence falls between us, and he brushes the hair from my face before cupping my cheek.

"Before my mom left, she told Tyler and I that 'dishonesty condemns you, sinning betrays you'," I whisper.

Lip shrugs. "What the fuck does that mean?"

"It means dishonesty often looks like the simplest route, getting you out of the path of trouble. However, that simplicity is a façade, 'cause it eventually comes back to bite you in the ass, making you tell lies to cover yourself. Before you know it, your sins have not only betrayed you but condemned you." I look at Lip. "I never knew how true those words were 'til recently." I think my mother spoke those words from personal experience.

"For what it's worth, I'm sorry, Cherry. I'm sorry for everything." His apology strikes me right in the chest. "I coaxed you into caring for me, into loving me. As much as I regret hurting you, I don't regret having your love. Not one bit." Emotions spill from the wound, and an uncontrolled sob escapes my lips.

"Come here," he whispers, pulling me into his arms. I clench my eyes shut, my heart and mind playing a battle of what is right and wrong. I don't want to be next to him. I don't want to give into him this easily, but a piece of me is exhausted from being pissed off at him.

Tears stream down my cheeks, but the hurt isn't nearly as bad as it was yesterday. There's something about being in his arms that takes the pain away. Even though he caused the pain. The day I stole Lip's wallet, he stole my heart.

10

Lip

MY HANDS CHOKE MY COFFEE CUP. ZANE AND ADDIE ARE already up and screaming their fucking heads off. My head feels clouded. Seeing her in that damn dress and the way the guys were eyeballing her, I went mad. The look on Cherry's face yesterday when I went head-to-head with Stunt fucked with me above all else, seeing her care for me even after everything that's happened. I know I have some feelings for her; the orders have been lifted and the cloud of what was business and what I honestly feel for her are displayed out before me. Do I tell her how I feel exactly and risk her rejecting us? I close my eyes, fucking confused. I don't know what I want.

"Give it to me, brat!" Addie screams, running past me. I wince and take a small sip of my coffee. Seconds later, a Barbie flies past me, a small pink shoe falling into my cup.

"Dude, you fucking cheated!" Tom Cat yells at Kane over a game of cards.

I sigh and push up from the stool.

"Fuck. This," I grit. I've been stuck in this fucking club too long. Shadow is taking his fucking time, I tell you. *I need out of here.* I stomp down the hall and into my room. Cherry is on the bed, her foot tapping as she listens to music. God, she's beautiful. Her reddish-orange hair is down and fans out along her freckled shoulders. I love it when she wears red; it makes every freckle on her body stand out. Her head slowly trails from the window to me, and my stomach feels like it's been fucking punched.

"Wanna get out of here?" I ask. She pulls an ear bud from her ear.

"Huh?"

"You wanna get out of here?" I repeat.

Her eyes give this weird look, and her brows furrow.

"Um, I thought we couldn't leave. We're on lockdown," she responds.

"I gotta get out of here, I'm going to go nuts," I state. She laughs and looks down at the iPod.

"I don't know," she mutters.

"Come on, come with me," I insist.

Her eyes peer up from under her lashes, a small smile curling the corner of her lips.

"Okay, just one ride."

◆◆◆

Cherry's arms are tight around my waist, the smell of her wafting around me is making my dick press against my jeans. I miss the smell of her. I miss everything about her.

I don't know where the fuck I'm going; I just drive. Sometimes, just driving without a destination is what the soul really needs. No boundaries, no limitations—just freedom.

Clouds pour in overhead, and thunder booms. Cherry's

arms choke my abdomen, so I pull off onto some gravel side road. I haven't seen a house or store for miles. Driving up the graveled passage, I spot a willow tree at the bottom of a hill.

I pull the bike over and park it.

"What are we doing? It's about to storm, Lip; we should head back," she encourages. Rain splashes off her cheeks, making her hair curl at the ends.

"We'd get hammered in the storm if we turned back now." I point to the tree. "That's our best option for now." I press on the small of her back and walk toward a small barb-wire fence.

I push the wire down and she leans on my shoulder as she climbs over.

Lightning strikes with a loud crack, and she squeals. I laugh, grab her hand and sprint toward the tree.

"Oh, my God." She laughs as we make it out of the rain. She bends over, throwing her hair down in front of her and shaking it loose of rainwater as I lean against the tree and smirk. She's fucking beautiful. That red top is soaked and her nipples poke through her tiny bra perfectly. Little beads of rain slip down her long legs and my cock rises in my pants. I have to look away and adjust myself. Fuck, I miss her.

"Cherry," I start.

She turns, pinning me with bright gray eyes.

"When I took that job to be your protector, I didn't know what I was walking into."

She throws her hand at me, dismissing me. "Lip, I don't want to talk about it. It's done." She purses her lips and crosses her arms. Her stubbornness pisses me off. I grab her by the elbow, turn her and slam her against the tree trunk.

"You are going to fucking hear me out, damn it. You don't want to be with me, or have anything to do with me afterward, that's fine. But goddamnit, you *will* hear my side." I rest both of my hands on either side of her head. "I thought it would be easy to walk away when I signed up for the job, but that was hardly the case when the only girl I've ever cared about walked away from me." Her mouth snaps shut and her face goes still. I look her in the eye and know I'd better spit out what I gotta say.

"I was still a kid when I agreed to be your babysitter, I was only nineteen. But when I found you, you were hot and feisty and not at all what I expected. I was immediately attracted to you. Looking at you, and comparing you to me, I knew you wouldn't want to be with me if you knew who I really was. A monster, insane, a fucking devil. Bull knew it, too. So I became that guy, the one my mother raised and my father hated. The one women dream about and guys despise. It wasn't a front, it wasn't a lie—it was me. It was a small piece of me, however. A part I never thought I'd see again."

She turns her head and clenches her eyes shut, like she doesn't want to hear anymore. But I'm determined to break through that barrier she's trying to protect herself with, that barrier she made in promise of never forgiving me.

"When I was thrown in prison, I thought you'd leave, that it would be over. I hoped it would, 'cause my feelings were blurring with what I was told to feel and what I was really feeling. But you didn't leave, didn't walk away even though I wished you had. I had to face you, and lie to you, to someone I was truly falling for. You deserved better than that. You deserve better than me. When I was in prison, you're right, I did change, because you weren't there to ground that better side of me. That good guy was buried, and that monster I used to be came out tenfold. I'm more devil than saint, and I led you to believe the opposite, Cherry. When I got out, I couldn't lock that side of me out anymore, and I sure as hell didn't want to make you believe I was better than I was. I knew you cared about me, loved me even." I brush my lips against her cheek.

"But I wanted you to love who I really was and not who I was told to be." I cup the back of her head and bring my lips to her ear. "I want to love you, and have your undying love without the club in my ear, without the fear of you running from your crazy ex. Just us, Cherry. 'Cause goddamn it, you got in under my skin and I can't get you out. You're like a fucking poison. I've had a taste, and now I'll never be right again."

She slowly turns her head, tears running down her face.

"You really hurt me," she mutters, her lips trembling with emotion. My chest constricts and I grab her face, bringing it close to mine.

"I know, and I'll never do it again, Cherry," I promise.

Her fingers dive into my hair, and her legs clamp around my waist.

"I'm sorry, too, Lip. I wanted to tell you. But I was too afraid of not only losing you, but putting myself and Piper in danger," she murmurs.

"I know. We both fucked up," I add, circling the apple of her cheek.

The wind gusts, blowing her hair around her face. I kiss her sugary lips and slip my tongue inside her warm mouth, tasting her. Hands slip under my shirt, and her nails dig into my skin. The pain makes me hiss, but the wolfish look on her face has me lowering my head and smirking at her.

"I know in my head I should give you up, walk away. But my heart wants you, and I can't for the life of me turn my back on you," she whispers, a raindrop sliding down her face and finding purchase right on the edge of her upper lip.

"I told you when you met me, I'd damage you for any man left in my wake."

I grab her by the thighs and push her back against the tree. My hands slip under her wet top, grasping her firm tits. She leans her face in and sucks my earlobe into her warm mouth, and my cock throbs painfully as it strains against my jeans. I turn us and lower her feet to the ground gently.

Grabbing her wet top, I pull it over her head, leaving her in nothing but her white lacybra. She looks so innocent in it, so I leave it. She grabs the hem of my shirt and tears it off my head, her arms shaky, movements rushed. I grab her by the wrist and pull her close to me.

"Don't rush," I demand.

She blinks, the raindrops weaving through the vines of the tree, planting themselves on her freckled skin. Her hands fumble with my jeans, and she shoves them down. My dick springs free, and I moan with relief. I undo my boots and kick my jeans off the rest of the way.

Cherry lies on her back on the ground, and her chest rises as she takes a large breath. I crawl on all fours over to her and hover over her, right in her line of sight.

My hand slips up her soft thigh, the pads of my fingers soaking up the raindrops. The feel of her silky skin against my palm nearly makes me blow my load. I undo her shorts and find her white lacy thong under it. I swipe my index and middle finger along the thin fabric and pull the dainty material down her legs.

Pushing her knees open, her wet, pink pussy is ready and waiting for me. I thumb her clit, and she bucks against my touch. A sly smirk crosses my face at how well her body responds to me. Leaning down, I kiss her clit, suck it into my mouth, and then nip it hard. She moans and squirms her hips along my face. The taste of her is sweet with a tone of musk. I love it. I could eat her pussy all day. The swirl of her hips as she rides my face is something I'd never get used to.

I push myself up and plant a kiss right above the apex of her thighs. Grabbing her hips, I flip her onto her knees, and she catches herself before she face-plants right into the green grass. Having her on all fours is fucking exotic. I rub my palm along her right ass cheek, my fingers nearly touching her wetness, teasing her. She flips her head back, her hair splaying across her back.

"Jesus, Cherry," I mutter, caressing the skin of her back with one hand and her ass with the other. "That day I picked you up from the side of the road, I never intended on letting you go."

She turns her head, her mouth pouty and eyes heavy. I can't help it; I grit my teeth and smack her ass. She lolls her head back and moans, "Yes!"

"Don't you ever leave," I mutter, rubbing the red handprint staining her skin. "Do you hear me? You're mine; you can't escape me." She doesn't reply, so I slap it again.

"I won't," she moans. I grab the base of my dick and position it right along her wetness. Swiping the head of my cock back and forth through her lips, jolts of pleasure pulse through it with the simple contact. I can't take the torture any longer, so I push the head in and her back lifts as I fill her tight cunt.

I close my eyes and relish in the feel of her warm, tight pussy. It's like I've never felt her before, like it's our first time together. Maybe it is; now that we don't have burdens breathing in our ear, we're free to feel and do as we please.

Thrusting into her hard, she moans loudly. The storm thunders all around us, and I drive my hips into her once more. I notice her fingers dig into the grass and her body trembles with pleasure. I lean over her, my chest on her back, and grab both of the damp cups of her bra as I pound into her over and over. Pressure builds in my balls, and my cock is as hard as it gets. She moans, pants, and growls, sounding like a fucking animal as I give her everything I got. I give her Phillip fucking DeLuca.

"Oh, my God, Lip!" she shouts, but nobody can hear her screams of pleasure, so I don't let up.

My knees slip on the wet grass, and my toes anchor themselves into the dirt beneath. I nip on her back before kissing it softly. I slip my hand up her chest and onto the base of her neck.

Her legs open up and her pussy becomes wetter—she's getting close. As I reach around her hips, swirling her clit, her sex clamps down on my dick and I can't hold back anymore. My knees give out and I fall on top of her, causing her hands and knees to collapse. I thrust into her a few more times as I reach the end of my release.

Realizing I might be crushing her, I roll over and look up at the tree's vines.

"Oh. My. God." She pants between each word. I just nod, out of breath.

She rolls over and I watch her out of the corner of my eye. Her hands and knees are grass-stained, her skin flushed from coming. She rolls over onto her stomach, her red ass glowing amongst her soft skin.

"The storm passed," she says, pointing to the sky. I look out into the distance and see the sun splitting behind the dark clouds. Sitting up, I grab my briefs.

"We'd better get back. They'll be looking for us."

Her head hangs. I can tell she's over-thinking something.

"What?" I ask, pulling on my clothes.

She shakes her head and sits up. "What does this mean?"

I bite at my lip ring, unsure. I know she means us having sex. What does it mean for us? Where do we stand?

"I'm not sure." It's the truth.

She gives me a pained look; I hurt her feelings again. What did she want me to say, that we're a happily-ever-after couple? It would be a lie.

"Look, I could lie to you, tell you what you want to hear. I don't know where we stand, but I know I want to move forward with you, Cherry. Lies breed resentment, and we'll be right back where we were."

Her face relaxes with that, and a smirk crosses her face. "You're right."

"Come on, let's get back," I hold my hand out and she grabs it. My hand tingles as if it's the first time she's held it. Maybe I can actually feel now that I'm not told what to feel.

◆◆◆

Pulling into the club parking lot, I notice Shadow backing his bike into his spot. I pull in right next to him, and Cherry's arms tighten around my waist. She's been waiting for Shadow to return. Turning my bike off, I take my helmet off and eye him.

"You get anything?" I question.

Shadow takes his helmet off and swipes his hand through his hair. "Yeah. Eric and the judge are working together, it seems. Let's find Bull and figure out how we should proceed."

"And Piper, is she okay?" Cherry blurts.

Shadow nods. "Yeah, she's fine from what I can see."

Cherry's body sags in relief. I help her off the bike and brush hair from her face.

"Let me take care of this," I state.

Her hands cup mine and her gray eyes look right through me, telling me I'd better not fuck this up.

◆◆◆

"Boys!" Bull hollers, waving us all to the chapel. All the patched-in brothers head toward the table, sitting in our regular spots.

"What did you get, son?" Bull questions Shadow.

"Well, Eric met up with Judge Calhoun twice. They're working together to find Cherry. I tailed one of Eric's goons and cornered him; he was easy enough to get information out of. He said the judge wants Cherry dead and is paying Eric to find the highest bidder. Between Eric's shady friends and the judge's high-profile resources, it won't take them long to find her," Shadow informs us.

Bull runs his hands along the scruff on his cheeks.

"I say we go visit this judge, put an end to this order. Then we go retaliate on this Eric fuck, show him what happens when you fuck with ours. We owe that much to Cherry," Bull suggests. "All in favor?"

Everyone around the table agrees.

"Let's get this done tonight, before they figure us out and we're ambushed." Bull knocks his knuckles on the top of the table and stands.

When the doors open, Cherry is outside pacing back and forth.

"What happened? What's going on? What are you guys going to do?" Cherry rambles. I grab her upper arms to calm her.

"We're going to end the hit, and I'm going to teach that Eric fuck a lesson. You need to stay here with Kane and Tom Cat," I explain.

"Piper, what about Piper?" Her voice cracks. I bite my bottom lip and tighten my grip on her arms.

"I'm going to bring her back, Cherry. I will. I'm going to do right by you, show you that you're safe with me, no matter what kind of monster you may think I am."

She cups my cheeks and purses her lips. "You're not a monster, Lip."

"Stay here, Cherry. I mean it." I demand.

"Lip! Let's go!" Bobby hollers.

I pull from Cherry's grip and point at Kane. "You protect her, or I'll break your face," I threaten. Kane smirks, not fazed at all by my promises.

"You got it, brother."

Lip

We follow Shadow for what seems like forever, passing the ramps I met Cherry on until eventually we pull up on a nice, three-story house. There are lights shining upon it, and the landscaping looks expensive as hell. This must be the judge's house. Shadow stops a block away, turning off his bike.

"There's no other way in. He has the place armed, and I can't seem to hack through it." Shadow shrugs.

"So what, we just go knock on the fucking door and say 'excuse me, but we're here to fucking break your knee caps'?" Sarcasm drips from my voice.

Bull laughs.

"Pretty much." Shadow chuckles.

We pull into his driveway and park. I shake my head; I can't believe we are just going to walk up to his front door. As we go, we pass a koi pond and a camera on the side of the house.

"Should I just knock?" Bobby shrugs.

"Nah, ring the doorbell." I smirk, jutting my head toward the lit-up doorbell button.

"This is humiliating." Bobby shakes his head and rings the bell.

Minutes later, the door slowly opens, and the judge is scowling at us. He's bald and has on little glasses. He's sporting a beer gut, with a white shirt and suspenders attached to some black slacks.

"The Devil's Dust, I've been expecting you," he greets.

"Come in." He turns and Bull steps into the house.

"Have you now?" Bull states.

"Seems someone went back on their deal," Judge Calhoun scoffs, sitting down in a high-backed brown leather chair.

"Yeah, well, I know the girl and just couldn't do it. I tried to keep her out of your hair, but what can I say—she's a mother wanting her daughter." Bull shrugs. Judge Calhoun nods and looks at the floor.

"Right, I understand. That's why I hired out this time. She will be dealt with," Calhoun threatens. I step forward angrily.

"Sorry, but that's not going to work." Bull sits in a chair across from the judge and crosses his legs.

"Well, I'm afraid that's not up to you. She is a threat, not only to me, but also to my brother." Calhoun looks up from Bull to us. "My brother is Senator Calhoun, and if word gets out that I'm dirty, he's ruined."

I sigh heavily. *This cannot be happening.*

"I advise you to reconsider your options. Cherry doesn't want to burn you, she just wants her kid," Bull tries to negotiate. The judge laughs and reaches for a tumbler filled with amber liquid.

"No deal. Now get out."

I grab my knife from its holster and step toward Judge Calhoun.

"I'm about to make you reconsider," I snarl.

"Whoa!" Bull jumps up and grabs my arm.

"You kill him, you'll go down. He has cameras everywhere, and we drove up to his fucking house. Witnesses, Lip." I flick my gaze from Bull to the judge.

"I'm not about to walk away," I inform.

Bull scoffs. "Me either, son. I'm not saying we aren't going to do what we have to. I'm just saying we need to go into this slowly." Bull smiles wickedly. He doesn't want to kill the judge;

he wants to torture him into reconsidering.

I nod, getting his point. The judge laughs a full belly laugh, thinking he's won. I step forward, grip the butt of my knife and slam it into the top of his hand, anchoring it into the arm of his chair.

His mouth pops open, his eyes wide as saucers. His hand releases the glass of amber, and it shatters into a million little shards as it collides with the floor.

He jumps upright in his seat and starts to heave in excruciating pain.

"All right, let's try it this way," I taunt.

"Kill the hit on Cherry," I suggest. He heaves again and tries to grab the knife, but whimpers when his fingers apply more pressure. Looking down, he shakes his head.

"No, I won't do it," he croaks.

Bobby walks up and pulls a knife that looks damn near identical to mine out of his pocket.

"You wanna try again?" Bobby smirks. The judge looks up and his face goes pale with fear, but he doesn't give in.

"Your loss." Bobby shrugs and thrusts his knife down toward the judge's other hand.

"Wait!" Judge Calhoun screams and Bobby stops, the blade of the knife a hair's width away from the judge's palm.

"Oh, did we have a change of heart?" Bull grins.

"Fine, I'll lift it," the judge pants. "But you'd better keep her mouth shut or the deal is off. She'll die before she ever sees a trial against me." His brows furrow.

"The kid. We want the kid, too," I add. Bull turns his head, looking at me like I've lost it.

"I can't, that's all I got." Judge Calhoun shakes his head.

I step forward and push down on the knife, enjoying the sound of the blade crunching through tendons and veins. He hollers out and tries to grab my hand to stop my assault.

"We want the kid," I repeat.

"Okay, o-okay. I'll draw up the pa-paperwork, I'll--" he stammers. "I'll get you the damn kid, just get this fucking knife out of my hand!" he screams.

I hunch down, my eyes meeting his dull ones. Grabbing the knife and fisting it hard, I twist the blade sideways, making sure it leaves a scar.

"I want this to be a reminder the next time you slam that gavel down. Make sure you're being honest and doing what you think is right by law and not by greed. This scar will remind you of why you're on that stand, and what your duties really are, and that greed will only grant you pain and scar your soul in the end."

Just when I think he's about to pass out, I pull the blade out and wipe it on my jeans.

"So, we're good?" Bull cocks his head to the side, eyeing the judge.

"We're good. Now get the fuck out!" Judge Calhoun points at his front door.

"Great." Bull smiles wolfishly.

Walking out, Bull cups my shoulder and smiles at me. "You did good, kid. It takes a man not to kill another who wronged his family."

I smirk, but inside I'm on fire. I want to kill that bastard, and as much as Bull doesn't want me to, I will one day. That's a promise.

Cherry

PACING THE FLOOR, I BITE ON MY NAILS. THEY'VE BEEN GONE A long time. Worry sears through my chest like a hot blade.

"Girl, you're making me dizzy watching you go back and

forth. Sit down and have a shot or something." Dani sighs, sitting on a stool.

I shake my head. "I can't. I can't stay here any longer." I head toward the door, and Dani jumps from her seat.

"Cherry, you can't leave. Orders are you have to stay here!" Dani yells, following close behind me.

I push the doors open and walk toward the club's SUV. Seeing that my car was blown up, it will have to do.

"Cherry!" Dani screams, walking out of the club. "You can't go by yourself, it's not safe!"

I turn to look over my shoulder at Dani and slam into something hard. I trip backward, nearly falling on my ass. Looking at what I ran into, I find a man. He's hard to make out with the shadows of the night smothering his features. An evil laugh sounds from behind the figure, and I look toward it, noticing a bunch of motorcycles and other dark shadows.

"Cherry, is it?" The voice is eerie and raw. I don't respond, trying to crawl backward. The figure steps forward, grasping my forearm harshly. I twist and pull from his grip, but he's too strong. "She's right, you know; there are bad guys lurking around at night." He chuckles, the sound menacing.

He snaps his fingers and two guys step forward, grabbing me by the arms and lifting me from the ground.

"Dani!" I scream frantically, fear constricting through my chest.

"Kane! Get out here!" Dani screams.

"Put her down now, fucker!" Kane hollers. A nervous sweat builds along my spine as I look over my shoulder, finding Kane pointing a gun at the guy I ran into.

"You shoot me and my men will kill you, take your women, and burn your club to the ground," the guy threatens, his tone cool. His silhouette outlines his muscled body, and the fear I felt before turns into terror. *Who is this guy?*

"What do you want?" Kane questions, lowering his gun when he sees he's outnumbered. My heart sinks that he's giving in and my hands tremble, terrified.

"You tell your president that the Sin City Outlaws want to do business and, when he agrees, Lip will get his bitch back." My eyes go wide. *How does he know Lip?* "Lip knows my number when he's ready to talk."

The guy holding me turns, and two guys standing by an unfamiliar van open the back doors.

"No! No!" I scream, trying to get free.

"Stop fighting, bitch," the guy growls, practically throwing me into the back of the van. I land with a hard thud; the wind knocked out of me, I gasp and wheeze. Before I can sit up, my hands are pulled behind my back and zip-tied. I try to protest but seeking oxygen is more important. A man with a thick beard and defined cheek bones grins wildly, placing a bag that feels like wool over my head, sealing my vision into nothing but complete darkness.

Lip

MY HANDS STRANGLE THE HANDLEBARS OF MY BIKE, ANGER fueling my reason. Someone will pay for the hurt Cherry's lived with the last six years. I can feel the demise of someone's soul heavy on my shoulders as I ride into the night. I will become the reaper tonight, taking what I want, what I crave: blood.

We pull into a closed gas station and back our bikes into the shadows of the building.

"There, that's the trailer park." Shadow points across the way. Jesus, it looks like a dump. A piece of me saddens knowing this is where Cherry grew up, that this is where her little girl is growing up. Guilt shifts through me. I wonder if she would have told me she had a little girl if I had never said I didn't want kids.

"Where does Eric live?" I question, pushing my shame to the side.

"The nice house at the end of the circle drive," Shadow informs. I nod, surveying the house. It's nicer than the trailers, but not by much. The roof has shingles missing and black tires anchoring tarps to the roof. The door is hanging off its hinges, and there's trash littered all over the porch. It's a dump.

"Right, so let's go around the side and enter the house from the back. Surprise this fucker," Bull instructs.

"You got it," I mutter, adrenaline rushing through my veins.

We head across the street, sticking to the tree line skirting around the trailer park. Dogs bark and cats hiss as we pass, but nobody even glances our way. Finally making our way to the back of Eric's house, I spot a little girl sitting on the back steps, sniffling into her hands. I stop in my tracks and put my hand up, stopping the boys.

"What the fuck?" Bobby whispers, eyeing the little girl.

"That's Piper. Cherry's daughter," Shadow tells us over my shoulder. My eyes widen, and my heartbeat stutters. As if the little girl could hear my heart stopping, she looks up, and I'm pinned by this little girl who looks identical to Cherry. I never thought I wanted kids, but to see someone so small, so innocent, and holding a piece of Cherry in her, I rethink that. I feel the need to protect the little girl, to harm whoever caused her tears to spill.

I step forward, my hands up in the air to show I mean no harm.

"You okay?" I ask. She wipes her tears and nods.

"Who are you?" she whimpers.

"I'm Lip," I introduce. I look over my shoulder at the guys, and they're all watching the interaction with wide eyes.

Glancing back at the girl, she cocks her head to the side, looking me up and down. I look down at myself, curious at what she's looking at.

"You're wearing one of those jackets like Cherry wears." Her eyes perk up. "Is Cherry with you?"

I smile at her excitement that I may have Cherry with me. "She's at our club. I'm her friend," I inform.

Her excitement fades. "Oh, well, I'm Piper." She smiles shyly.

"Why are you so sad, darling?" Bull whispers, stepping up beside me. Her smile fades, and she looks over her shoulder.

"My daddy burned all my clothes Cherry got me." She points behind us and we all turn, finding a barrel smoldering. "Daddy doesn't like me looking like a girl, and I'm not allowed to talk to Cherry again." Her dad sounds like a guy with anger problems, taking his frustration and fury out on Piper.

"Does your daddy hurt you?" I ask, my chest puffing out on its own accord. She looks down and her head falls, but she doesn't answer.

"Why don't you come with me, and let us have a talk with your daddy?" Shadow offers. I plan on doing way more than talking to this fucker.

Piper shakes her head. "Oh, no. I can't go with strangers. Daddy would be mad." Her eyes widen with fear.

"It's fine; Cherry knows us. We're here to take you to her, sweetie."

"Piper!" a voice yells from inside the house, and Piper tenses.

I hold my hand out. "Come on, you're safe with us. Promise."

She looks over her shoulder once more, and the screen door is slammed open. She jumps from the bottom step.

"Get your fucking ass--" he stops. The tall blond-haired guy looks us over, his face turning into a deep scowl.

"Who the fuck are you?" he snarls. His button-down shirt flaps in the wind, and his jeans are unbuttoned.

Bobby holds his hand out to Piper, and she walks toward him.

"Don't you think about it, Piper," Eric sneers.

"Come on, Piper. You're okay, sweetie," I encourage. Her eyes peer at me nervously. She's scared to go with us 'cause she doesn't know us, but she's terrified to go back into that house.

"I got you," I whisper. She nods strongly and grabs my hand with force.

I lean down and brush her hair from her ear.

"Go with Bobby; he'll keep you safe," I whisper.

"Piper, get in the damn house!" Eric hollers.

Bobby grabs her other hand and they walk away together, Piper looking over her shoulder at us every couple of steps.

Eric stomps down the steps, but Shadow and I step in front him, stopping him.

"Going somewhere, brother?" I scowl.

"You better get out of my fucking way!" he growls. Having enough of this, I grab my knife and shove it in his gut without warning. His eyes widen, and his puffed-out chest deflates. Slowly, he lowers his gaze to my knife, buried deep.

"How about we go inside, huh?" I ask, pulling my knife from his flesh. He shakes his head, fear surfing in the depths of his eyes.

"You ain't got a choice, I'm afraid." Bull chuckles.

Shadow and I drag Eric into the house, and he starts to holler for help.

I punch him in the mouth to shut him up, his teeth colliding with my skull ring. He quiets instantly and starts to whimper. Bull pulls out a kitchen chair and I kick Eric in the chest hard, throwing him into it.

"You tried to hurt my property," I begin. His brows furrow in confusion. "Cherry is my property," I clarify. His eyes recognize the name, and his brows scowl.

"You mean Lindsay? Yeah, I know the little gutter slut," he growls. I grit my teeth at his insult and stomp forward. Pulling my fist back, I slam it into his nose, a loud crack sounding from impact.

"You won't talk about her like that," I warn. He groans with pain, his nose busted all to hell and bleeding down his chin and chest.

"You know what happens when you fuck with ours?" Bull questions, pulling his gun from his holster.

"Look, man, I didn't know she was with some gang," Eric stammers, and I smirk.

"Doesn't matter if you knew or not. What you did was shady, and maybe the law around here won't deal with you because they know your daddy, or your last name is respectable, or they think you're better than Cherry. But where I come from, our justice system has a way of dealing with those who may escape."

"Wha- what's that mean?" He looks between Shadow and me.

"That means, you're going to die tonight." I lower my head and glare.

"Please, no," he whimpers, but it sounds fake.

"The little girl, why do you dress her like a boy?" Shadow asks. I furrow my brows.

"Do what?" I question.

"The little girl. Every day I've seen her, she's in boy shit." Shadow shrugs.

"Because she reminds me of her fucking momma," Eric spits, doesn't even hide the hatred in his voice.

"I don't get it, why do you hate her so much?" I cock my

head to the side.

"Cherry reminds me of my no-good mother. Getting knocked up on purpose, just so she can live off my paycheck for free. Well, not this guy. Fuck Cherry; she ain't getting shit from me, including the kid she got knocked up with." My chest rises and falls rapidly, anger burning my veins to the point I can barely breathe.

"Cherry ain't like that," I manage to say. My vision doubles with the amount of fury poisoning my blood.

He scoffs, and my jaw clenches.

I hold my hand open to Bull, requesting the gun. He obliges without haste.

"Please kill this piece of shit before I do," Bull growls, sharing my amount of hatred for this motherfucker.

Taking the gun from Bull, I turn to aim it at Eric. Suddenly, he hollers out and jumps from the chair, slamming right into me before I can pull the trigger. We fall to the floor, the gun knocked from my hand. A fist smashes into my eye, ripping skin and causing blood to pour, distorting my vision. Pulling my fist back, I punch him as hard as I can in his broken nose. He screams with pain and flies off me, hitting his head on the kitchen cabinet. I scramble to my feet and grasp the closest thing near me, the kitchen chair. I slam it over the table, breaking off a leg as Eric drags himself from the floor, huffing and puffing.

"Give me your best shot," he pants, taunting me.

Gripping the busted leg hard, I swing it, slamming it against the side of his head. The impact vibrates through the piece of wood into my hand and his head whips to the side as he falls into the kitchen sink. Stepping forward, I grab him by his neck and slam his head into the tiled counter. The bright letters of a Drano bottle catch my attention, and I grab it.

"Hold him!" I order Bull and Shadow. They both step

forward and grab his arms. "Turn him," I instruct, opening the bottle. They spin his body so he's facing me and pin him against the counter.

Eric's eyes widen when he realizes what I'm about to do, and he clamps his mouth shut.

"That won't help." I chuckle. Gripping the side of his jaw, I apply pressure to his pressure points, his mouth slowly opening as he begins to yell. I shove the bottle in his mouth, his teeth catching the sides, and I squeeze it as hard as I can. Instantly, he starts choking and gagging on the chemical. I squeeze it one last time and notice blood sputter from his mouth. I pull back and Bull and Shadow let go of his arms. He falls to the floor, choking and vomiting, his hands clawing at his mouth as he sways back and forth on his knees. Black chunks of blood spill from his mouth as his nose begins to bleed and his eyes cry crimson. The chemical is eating him from the inside out. It's fitting, really—his toxic threats and shameful greed burned Cherry from the inside out for years.

"Finish it." Shadow hands me the gun. I grasp the cold metal and aim it at Eric's cold heart. "This is for Cherry," I croak and pull the trigger. Eric's body jumps as the bullet collides with his heart.

My phone rings, and I growl in frustration.

"Jesus," I curse, grabbing my phone. "Yeah?" I snap.

"We got a problem, brother," Kane nearly yells in my ear.

"What?"

"Cherry was taken. Some club called the Sin City Outlaws took her, and said we ain't getting her back 'til we agree to do business with them." My eyes widen, and my heart stills. "The way the man talked, sounded like he knew ya," Kane continues.

"He wouldn't." I look up at Bull, who eyes me curiously. "You just let them take her?" I snap at Kane.

"Dude, Cherry stormed out of the MC and walked right into

the barrel of his gun. I tried to step toward her, but he was going to kill her," Kane breathes heavily into the phone. I clench my jaw in anger.

"We're on our way." I hang up the phone. "My brother took Cherry," I inform Bull.

"I'll get this cleaned up of any traces and meet you at the club," Shadow states, and I nod. Shadow is the best at cleaning up DNA and traces of evidence..

"Thanks, man." I pat him on the back as Bull and I practically run out of the back door and race toward our bikes.

"Your brother, as in the one from the other motorcycle club?" Bull questions as we hurry.

"Yeah," I reply.

"Thought you said he wouldn't be a problem?" When I first joined the club, I told Bull about my family, and he said as long as they weren't a rival club he didn't care. As far as I knew, they weren't. 'til now.

"Well, he wasn't but lately, he's been asking me to go into business with him, or to trade clubs. I thought he was just being a pain in the ass," I tell him honestly.

"Well, now he's a problem." Bull shakes his head and I stop in my tracks, eyeing Bull.

"A problem I will deal with. He's crossed a line," I grit.

Bull places his hands on his hips and inhales a large breath. "So you're saying you'd go head-to-head with your brother?"

I take a deep breath, the thought of brother vs brother, club vs club, surfacing through me.

"You know that's blood against blood," Bull interrupts my thoughts.

I nod. "I know where my loyalty lies, and it's not with my flesh and blood," I scowl.

Getting closer, I notice Bobby hopping in the shadows.

"No, that's not how you play hopscotch." Piper giggles.

"We gotta get to the club, brother," I tell him, getting on my bike.

"What's up?" I look at Piper and then to Bobby, second-guessing telling him Cherry is in danger in front of her.

"We got a problem, is all," I inform, starting my bike.

Bobby hands Piper a helmet that is way too big for her and helps her on. I think about telling Piper to get on my bike, but rethink that idea. I'd be too nervous with her on my bike and likely kill us both. It's best if she rides with Bobby. He's ridden Doc's daughter around before, so he knows how to handle a kid on a bike.

"You go slow with her, goddamn it." I point at him, my tone threatening. Bobby smirks and starts his bike. Who knew I'd like a kid, that I would be protective of her as if she were my own.

"No problem."

Cherry

THE VAN ROCKS BACK AND FORTH, AND ROCK MUSIC IS BLASTING loudly so I can't hear anything. I have no idea where I am. My heart beats rapidly in my chest, the adrenaline pulsing through me, making me high. I clench my eyes shut, tears threatening to spill. *Lip will come for me. The club will save me. I will see Piper again.*

The van comes to a stop, and the music is shut off. Silence fills the air and is more deafening than the rock music. My body trembles in fear as I hear the doors to the back of the van being opened. Hands grab me and pull me from the van but I fight back, kicking and screaming to get free.

"Jesus Christ, this one's squirrelly," a man says, his voice thick with an accent.

The bag is ripped from my head and I blink a couple of times, my vision blurry from sitting in the darkness. A rusted, metal building sits behind a bunch of guys, one streetlight shining barely enough to see in front of me.

"Do you know who I am?" a rough voice asks. I squint, trying to make out the man standing in front of me. He has scruff lining his tanned cheeks and the top of his hair is pulled into a ponytail, with the rest of his head shaved. He's big and tattooed. "Well?" he continues.

"No," I mutter, eyeing him from head to toe. If I didn't hate him so much right now, I'd be attracted to him. He's sexy in a menacing kind of way.

He pats at his patch. "Zeek, the name's Zeek," he informs. I shrug, still not knowing who the fuck he is.

"Really, lil bro never told you about me? I'm hurt." He laughs, sarcasm dripping from his voice. I shake my head confused. *Lil bro?* My eyes suddenly perk. *Lip. Zeek is Lip's brother.* My eyes shoot to his.

"Aw, so you *do* know who I am." He grins. Lip told me how much he disliked his brother, how his brother was like his father. Evil. My heart sinks further into the pit of my stomach. *I'm screwed.*

"I'm the president of the Sin City Outlaws, and right now, I own your ass," he sneers, pointing at me.

I scoff. "Fuck you," I grit bravely.

His brows furrow in and his jaw clenches. "You will respect me, bitch," he seethes.

I scowl, but I don't say anything.

"I think she needs to learn her place around here, brother." Another man chuckles, walking up beside Zeek. He has thick, black hair and really tanned skin.

"Bow to my president." He points to the ground.

"I don't bow for any man," I whisper, swallowing hard.

"Wrong answer," the thick-haired man growls. He stomps forward and kicks me hard in the back of the knees. My legs give out and I fall knees-first into the ground. I want to holler out with pain, but I won't give them the satisfaction of knowing they hurt me.

"Looks like you're bowing to me now, but I'm not just any man." Zeek squats in my line of sight and smiles hard. "I'm the fucking king of Las Vegas, baby," he states proudly. I turn my head, not wanting to give him eye contact.

"You're going to be a dead king," I mutter, staring off into the darkness. Hands grip my chin, pulling me to look into Zeek's dark eyes.

"You sure do have a mouth on you, *putana.*" His teeth grit together. I jerk my head from his fingers, nearly falling over in the process.

"What now, boss?" one guy asks.

"We wait. Lip will call soon."

The guys stand around smoking, some talking in English, others in another language. I hear a familiar giggle, and my eyes shoot toward the crowd. Two guys shift on their feet and my eyes land on Dolly. *That fucking traitor.* She smiles and looks my way. Her grin quickly fades, and she purses her lips as she walks toward me.

"Well, well," she taunts, sashaying.

"You're a dead bitch," I snarl.

She flips her hair over her shoulder and laughs.

"Yeah, keep telling yourself that, honey. I don't think you realize who you're messing with."

"You're a fucking traitor, club-hopping like the whore you are." I smirk, but she just smiles wider.

"You don't get it, do you. I've been with the Sin City Outlaws this whole time, relaying info about Lip back to Zeek." She tilts her head to the side and gives me a sympathetic smile. "I'd do anything for Zeek," she mutters.

"I hope you like dying for him, 'cause when I get a hold of you, I'm going to stuff your mouth with those fake-ass hair extensions," I threaten. Her eyes furrow in with anger.

"Get!" Zeek snaps at Dolly as he walks up beside her. She turns, glaring at Zeek, and he grabs her face hard.

"Don't mouth me; do what you're told," he scolds. She pulls her face from his grip and stomps off.

"You thirsty?" Zeek asks me.

"No," I reply seriously.

He squats in front of me.

"Aw, don't be like that. This," he waves his finger between us, "it's just business, nothing personal."

My lip curls. "Gee, that makes everything better," I respond, sarcasm lacing in my tone. He nods, a half-laugh escaping.

"I don't get why we have to go through all this trouble, Pres," a man with a big gut states, his hair curly and long.

"I told you, Uncle wants Lip in the family business, one way or another. This is the only way," Zeek announces, looking at his shoes.

"Fucking family, they're nothing but problems." The guy shakes his head, walking away.

A phone suddenly rings, and Zeek jolts upward.

"You better hope that's your Prince Charming. I'm getting tired of waiting," he tells me.

Someone hands him a phone, and his eyes lift.

"Phillip, so nice of you to call," he greets casually. I can literally hear Lip hollering into the phone.

"Brother, brother. She's good, no harm. But that will change real quick-like if you and your club don't want to be friends." Zeek chuckles, the sound menacing. His face suddenly falls, and he rubs at his chin.

"Yeah, we'll see you soon." He hangs the phone up, and I

swallow hard. Hope surfaces in my chest that I won't die today, that Lip loves me enough to save me, and I'll see Piper again.

11

Lip

"WE'RE MEETING AT THE DOCKS. LET'S GO," I INFORM THE boys.

"Let's take care of business," Bobby states.

Dani steps forward, taking Piper into her arms. Piper's eyes shoot to mine in fear. Climbing off my bike, I hunch down so I'm the same height as her and she walks into my arms.

"Don't worry; I'll be back and with Cherry. Dani is a real good friend of mine, she's really nice," I comfort. Dani squats next to me, holding a picture of Cherry. Piper holds her hand out, taking the picture.

"You like toys?" Dani asks, smiling. Piper nods.

"I have a bunch with me if you wanna come check them out 'til Cherry gets back." Piper looks at me, silently asking me if it's safe, if she should go. My heart grows for Piper, the fact she is seeking me out for security is something I can't help but love.

"I'll be back before you know it," I whisper. Piper takes Dani's hand, her eyes not as wide as before but still unsure. I hesitate, not wanting to leave her.

"It's fine; I got Piper. Go do what you have to do, Lip," Dani states.

I nod and climb on my bike. Starting it, the rest of the guys jump on theirs and we head out.

◆ ◆ ◆

Nearing the docks, I don't stop, or slow down for that matter. All I see is red, an ocean of red with a tide of betrayal. My brother is a traitor, and he'll pay for it. My father would roll over in his grave if he knew his two sons were head-to-head.

We drive into the docks, the smell of salt strong and the winds heftier as we pull up to an old building, rusted and decay-ing, a street lamp lighting a small circle. Within the circle are a bunch of motorcycles and men standing around. I wave my hand, encouraging the guys to follow me in.

I search the group for Cherry but don't see her. My jaw clenches. *I swear to God, if he hurt her bullets will fly.*

Parking a few feet away, the Sin City Outlaws turn, facing us.

"Brother, so nice of you to join us," Zeek announces, his hands tucked into his torn jeans.

"Cut the shit, where is she?" I snarl.

"Cherry, you mean? She sure is a piece of fineness. I can see why you're so protective of her."

I reach around my back and pull my pistol out. "You got about two minutes to show me my girl, before your brains are sprayed everywhere," I threaten.

"First business, then the girl," he quips, his tone missing its humor.

"I told you before, no deal." I sniff and look up at him.

"Then no girl." He shrugs, grinning.

I point my gun, and he quickly pulls his own from his waistband.

Zeek and I, gun to gun. I used to play hide-and-seek with him, play video games with him as a child, and now I'm going to kill him.

"The way I see it, neither of us is going anywhere then," I sneer.

"What are your terms?" Bull asks, stepping up beside me.

I turn my head, giving Bull a sideways glance, my arm still outstretched.

"No, we ain't doing business with him," I add. Bull widens his stance and thumbs his belt loops.

"State your conditions, son," Bull states, ignoring me.

"I supply, and you make sixty-percent profit," Zeek replies, his eyes never leaving mine.

"What are we talking about here? Drugs, Guns, Women?" Bull questions.

"Drugs. Pick your poison; I move it all." Zeek smiles proudly.

"Don't do it, man," I warn Bull.

"Why? Why should we go into business with you?" Bull asks Zeek.

"You mean besides getting your bitch back?" Zeek laughs, and the rest of his men chuckle. "'Cause I got the best shit on the West Coast, and," he looks at me, "my uncle will not give up until he gets Phillip in our pockets one way or another. He's blood. He'll either accept that, or be buried for his betrayal of the DeLuca name," Zeek threatens.

"Don't be stupid, man," Bobby whispers into my ear.

"No! Deal!" I holler. "Your idea of family is not ours. You keep your shitty drugs and the DeLuca's toxic DNA on your side of the West Coast." I curl my lip in anger.

Zeek snaps his fingers and the crowd breaks. I see red hair

flinging back and forth as two men push and shove Cherry through the group of men.

"I killed our father, my own flesh and blood. The man who brought me into this world. Don't think I won't kill your bitch—or you, for that matter." My eyes widen, and my hand grips my gun harder. I never knew he had anything to do with Dad's death. I'm shocked; I thought Zeek was dad's favorite. Goes to show how loyal the DeLuca name really is, and that strengthens my belief to stay the fuck away from it.

Zeek snaps his fingers again and points to the ground in front of him. A guy kicks Cherry hard, making her fall to her knees and land right in front of Zeek. I step forward, wanting to save her, but the click of Zeek's gun stops me.

"Not so fast, brother," Zeek warns. Looking at Cherry, she has streaks of tears marking her dirty face. Her knees are bleeding, and the stitches on her face look to be torn and bleeding, as well. I lift my gaze from Cherry to Zeek. My chest constricts seeing her in such distress, and my hands fist at my side. An urge to hold her and tuck her hair behind her ear surges through me. I love Cherry, no doubt about it. I've never cared so much about another person in my whole life. Zeek is a dumb motherfucker for touching her.

"You'll pay for this," I growl.

"One last time: you in, or out?" Zeek questions.

"I will never go into business with you, Zeek. Get that through your head now. I won't put my family in danger because of our uncle's power trip," I reaffirm. He takes his aim from me to Cherry, and I react. I jump forward, throwing Cherry out of the way just as a bullet leaves Zeek's gun. Cherry screams as we fall to the ground hard, and my right shoulder burns with such intensity my eyes water.

"Bobby, get Cherry!" I scream, rolling over to aim my pistol at Zeek's arm. His eyes widen, and I pull the trigger. His body jolts backward and he falls to the ground. His men scatter, and Cherry is yanked from under me.

"Just me," Bobby mutters, dragging Cherry to safety.

Rising to my feet, I run behind a green trashcan. My shoulder screams with pain; looking at it, I find blood oozing from it, trickling down my back. I've been shot. Better me than Cherry, though.

I peek around the trash can and a bullet goes zipping past me.

"Shit," I curse, jumping back behind the dumpster.

Aiming my weapon first, I look around the trash can again and spot Zeek beside the building, aiming his weapon at me. Seems that bullet in his shoulder didn't slow him down. I fire, and a bullet zings as it ricochets off the building.

"You done yet?" I holler.

"Not even close!" Zeek shouts, firing his weapon. Looking over, I find Bull firing his gun at men above me and Bobby holding Cherry behind the bikes.

Enough of this back-and-forth bullshit. I take a deep breath, glance at Cherry one last time and step out from behind the can. I spot Zeek instantly and fire my gun. I fire and fire until I run out of bullets, spraying and praying one hits Zeek's worthless ass.

He shouts with distress and falls back. I smirk, knowing at least one hit him. His men catch him, and silence fills the air. A loud girlie scream sounds near Zeek, and fear hits my chest that they have Cherry. Checking my guys, I see Cherry is still with them, so I look back at Zeek and that's when I see Dolly crying over him. That fucking betraying bitch.

Knowing his men will retaliate, and I'm out of bullets, I turn and run back toward the bikes with the rest of the Devil's Dust.

I slide in behind Tom Cat's bike, and he helps pull me behind it.

"I got ya, brother," Tom Cat states, standing up to walk in the line of fire. I grab his pants leg, stopping him.

"Don't; he's got more men than we do," I add.

Tom shakes my hand off his leg.

"He disrespected ours. He needs to pay, or the rest of the West Coast will think they can walk on us," he explains, and walks off.

"Fuck!" I yell.

"Here." Bull hands me a gun and I cock it, loading a bullet into the chamber.

"Cover him!" I yell to the boys. I aim over the bike and start shooting Zeek's men as they pop up over the rooftop of the metal building.

"Die!" shouts from the side of the building, catching my attention. Looking over, Zeek wobbles out with one arm wrapped around his mid-section, where blood pours down his shirt, and his other hand holding a gun aimed at Tom Cat.

"Tom Cat! To your right!" I warn. Tom Can turns and I aim, but Zeek is faster and pulls the trigger first. Tom Cat falls flat to the ground.

"Aaaah!" I scream, running out from behind the bike. Pulling the trigger, a bullet slams into Zeek's chest. He falls to his knees, staring at me as the light of our childhood fades before he face-plants.

I fall to Tom Cat's side as he begins to choke and suffocate on blood. I grab the back of his neck and pull him close.

"Bull!" I scream. Bull runs from behind the bikes and drops to his knees beside me.

"We gotta get him to the hospital now," Bull states. Glancing at the Sin City Outlaws, they seem to be doing the same, looking over their president, not concerned with us.

"Let's get him there then," I tell him.

"Lip, we need to get Cherry there, too." Bull looks at me

with wide eyes.

"What do you mean?" I stand, worry snaking through my chest.

"Your bullet. It went through you, and hit her."

Bobby comes running up to us.

"I called Doc; they have a helicopter on their way. Should be here any minute," Bobby states, his hands rubbing through his hair anxiously.

"I got Tom, go to Cherry," Bull orders. I look Tom Cat over one last time, his eyes pinning me.

"Thank you," I mouth.

"Broth--" He chokes. "We're br-brothers," Tom stammers, and tears threaten to prick my eyes. Tom Cat is a brother of loyalty, a brother who would risk his own to protect my life. Whereas my own flesh and blood betrayed me and wanted to end my life.

Sprinting toward Cherry, she's leaned up against a bike and panting heavily. Blood soaks her skintight top right below her breasts.

"Baby," I whisper, pulling her head to me.

"You. Get. Piper?" She takes a breath between each word.

"Yes, I did. She's ours now," I state, brushing the hair from her face.

A small smile creeps across her face. "Ours?" she whispers, and I nod. The helicopter zooms above us, and I look up. *About fucking time.*

"You're going to be fine, baby; the medics are here."

"I'm really cold," she mutters, her eyes looking distant. Glancing down at Cherry's gunshot, I see blood pouring through her fingers, and I panic.

"OVER HERE!" I scream at the medics.

Two people dressed in blue jumpsuits sprint toward us and place Cherry on a stretcher. As they strap her in, medics begin to scream and holler and I turn into a fucking wreck.

"We've lost a lot of blood on this one!" someone shouts. Tears prick my eyes, and I tug on my hair.

"Do something! Fucking do your job!" I scream.

"I got a heartbeat!" a medic with long hair hollers, and I can't help but smirk with relief.

"Sir, we can't do our job if you're yelling at us!" one of them yells at me. Ignoring them, I jog alongside them and grab Cherry's cold hand.

Lowering my mouth to her ear, I whisper "I love you, Cherry."

They push Cherry in the chopper beside Tom, and a man with chubby cheeks pulls a sheet over Tom's face.

"Time of death, 11:23AM."

My eyes widen and my mouth drops open, the need for vengeance taking root in my chest. Before I could yell at them to do their job better, the helicopter took off. My world spins, and my heart races. My woman is hurt, and I've lost a brother. 11:23AM—a time I'll never forget, because at that time I realized I'm not invincible, that I can't fix everything, and I can lose everything with the snap of a finger.

Cherry

"BABY?"

Blinking, the word echoes in my head, and I wince.

I lift my hand and wipe at my eyes, and a warm palm cocoons mine.

"Cherry, baby, you had me so fucking worried." Looking over, I find Lip staring at me with tear-filled eyes.

"Lip?" I croak, my heart beating faster knowing he's close.

Using my hands, I push on the bed to sit up, but my side buckles under the pain.

"Don't, you were shot." Lip frowns. *That's right. Zeek tried to shoot me but Lip jumped in front of him and took the bullet—well, most of it.* It went through his shoulder and hit me. I look down and pull my shirt up, finding a huge patch.

"You lost a lot of blood, but they got to you just in time," Lip states. "They had to remove the bullet in surgery, but everything went smoothly."

He pauses, like he's searching for words. Finally, he looks up at me again, sadness taking over his features.

"Cherry, I have something to tell you." Lip sits on the bed, grabbing my hand. Hairs on my neck rise, and my eyes widen.

"What?" I whisper.

"Tom Cat, he--" Lip looks up, tugging his lip between his teeth.

"What about him?" Tears begin to leak from my eyes.

"He didn't make it, baby," Lip mutters, tears falling down his cheeks.

I close my eyes and cry, a terrible sob escaping my lips. To lose one of our own, it's a pain that roots deep within the chest. It never goes away.

"Come here." Lip pulls me into his arms, and I hug him right back. I cry hard and loudly. Tom was one of us, and we lost him. I loved Tom; he was so friendly—horny, but friendly.

"The funeral is tomorrow," Lip states.

"I'm going," I add. I will see him one last time and pay my respects, regardless of what kind of shape I'm in.

"You can't, baby. You need to stay in here and –"

"Fuck that, Lip, I'm going!" I shout, wincing from the pain in my side. Tom gave his life for us, and it's the least I can do.

Lip smirks and runs his fingers over my lips.

"I'll see what I can do," Lip mutters. "Cops came in a little earlier for your statement, but Doc pretty much told them to fuck off. I told them what the rest of the guys did, that we were ambushed by some guys but couldn't make 'em out. We're The Devil's Dust. We have enemies everywhere." He winks. "So if they come back, you need to stick with that story," Lip states. I furrow my brows and nod. "The cops ain't going to be handling this; you know as well as I the justice system is fucked. The Devil's Dust will be taking care of this, babe." Lip brushes my hair from my face and kisses my forehead. I don't argue, because he's right. I don't trust cops to take care of this, not after my last run-in with the justice system.

"But they believed you?" I ask.

"They pretty much know we're lying, but they have no proof." Lip shrugs.

"Can I come in yet?" someone hollers from the doorway. My eyes widen with excitement; I know that voice from anywhere.

Lip laughs. "Yeah, come in."

Piper rushes in wearing a pink little dress, and hair shiny and combed. She looks so youthful and happy.

"Piper!" I cheer with excitement. To see her, it makes me want to move mountains, regardless of the pain I'm in.

"Cherry!" Piper chimes. She crawls onto the bed, and I cry harder as I pull her into a big hug.

"Easy now." Lip laughs.

I hug her tighter, her little heartbeat pounding against my chest. I take in the smell of her, the feel of her skin against mine, and I swear to God I'll never let her go again.

"I missed you," she whispers.

"I've missed you," I whisper back.

I sit her back and look her over.

"You look so pretty." I pull on the fabric of her dress.

"Thank you. Lip took me shopping," My eyes pull from Piper to Lip, shocked.

"Yeah?"

Lip shrugs, and I think my ovaries just exploded. Badass

biker taking my daughter shopping is something for the books, for sure. I look at Piper, my daughter, and smile.

"Piper, I need to tell you something," I mutter, my brows furrowing inward. I don't know if now is the right time to tell her I'm her mother, but I can't hold it in any longer. I've had to keep it secret for six fucking years, so now is as good as time as any. Pushing little strands of hair behind her ear, I tilt my head to the side.

"I'm your mom, Piper."

Her eyes furrow and she nibbles on her bottom lip as she takes in the words I just spoke. Finally, she looks up from under her lashes, her face unsure.

"I always wanted a mommy like you. You know, sometimes when we were together, I would think of you as my mommy." She smiles, and what was left of my heart explodes into warmth. Tears leak out of my eyes uncontrollably.

I pull her close and cry into her hair. I finally have my daughter. Finally have my flesh and blood. I didn't die, but I certainly went through Hell to get her. I'd do it all over again, too.

"I'll make up the last six years for the rest of your life, Piper," I promise.

◆◆◆

Tom Cat's funeral was beautiful, but sad. I think Lip took it the hardest. He lost a loyal brother to one he can't stand. Tom's casket was draped with his leather cut before the service, and it was hard to see. Bull walking up to the casket and whispering he was a true brother, and he'd see him on the other side, before thumping his knuckles on the casket... was even harder. The song "Last Ride" by Wiz Khalifa played and made everyone bawl into a fit of sobs. Dani picked the song, and I think I may slap her for playing something so perfect yet so sad at the same time.

I set an empty glass into the sink and slowly head out of the kitchen. My side is killing me from where I was shot, but I won't dare leave because of the pain. Clubs from all around are here to pay their respects, and it's beautiful, really. People passing us on the sidewalks and in cars look at us like we're monsters living on rage and fury, but when you get past that stereotypical bullshit, we're family. We have each other's backs and love one another just like any other family. To a lot of men, this is all they have. Some returning back from serving their country and needing that family they lost while they were away, or some who grew up on the wrong side and need guidance—we accept them all. I love being a part of something so great, because I know as well as anyone that sometimes people just need a second go at trying one of the hardest things there is to master: life.

"Piper, wait for me!" Zane hollers after Piper as they run across the room. I smirk; Zane is going to be such a player.

Dani walks past me and I stop her. "Have you seen Lip?" I haven't seen him since we got back.

"I saw him heading down the hallway earlier," Dani tells me. I nod and head down the hallway in search of him. Him getting Piper for me is something I will forever owe him for. But since I've been out of the hospital, he's been somewhat distant, like he doesn't know what he wants. Or maybe it's just Tom Cat's death weighing heavily on him, I'm not sure.

Slowly opening our door, I find Lip sitting on the bed, his elbows on his knees and his head in his hands. Crying. To see such a strong man crying, it cuts me. *Should I go in, or leave him be?* I step in, deciding to comfort him. After the many times he was there when I was crying, this is my chance to repay that favor. He looks up and wipes at his face.

"I'll be out in a minute," he croaks, his voice heavy with sorrow.

I sit on the bed and grab his hand. His bloodshot eyes shoot to mine, and I frown. I hate seeing him so broken.

"You okay?"

Lip's body eases, his tense shoulders sagging.

"No, I'm not. My flesh and blood killed one of my own." Lip shakes his head, a tear slipping down his tanned cheek. As much as it hurts to see him like this, it kind of turns me on to see him so vulnerable, too.

"It's not your fault, Lip," I state.

Lip scoffs. "I shouldn't have let him go out there."

"Could you have really stopped him? He knew what he was doing, Lip," I try to assure.

"Probably not; his ass was stubborn." Lip chuckles, wiping his cheeks. He smirks and squeezes my hand.

"How are you and Piper settling in?" he questions, changing the subject.

I shrug. "Good, I guess. I think I'm going to stay with my brother for a while. He really wants some time with Piper and I can't leave her side. Not right now," I explain, a piece of me wanting Lip to object. It would put my fear of him not wanting Piper in his life aside.

Sitting in silence, I shift uncomfortably.

"Where are we, Lip?" I finally ask, sick of the games. I can't read his mind, or his body language for that matter.

"I don't even know." He shakes his head, and my chest aches.

I nod and stand. "Lip, I care about you, I do. But we don't know each other, not really. Besides, I have a little girl, and you don't even like kids." I take a deep breath. "I won't give her up, I'm sorry."

Lip nods, he doesn't disagree, and doesn't try to stop me.

"Yeah, I think we just need a moment to decide where the fuck we're going in all this." Lip looks down at his hands, and my eyes threaten to spill hot tears. "Tom's death, you getting your kid back, and I killed my brother. Everything is just happening so fast," he mutters.

I nearly sob in reaction. I have to get out of here or I'll lose it.

Lip's bloodshot eyes glance up at me. "I care about you, Cherry. I do. I just need some time to process shit. I don't want to hurt you again, and I don't want you to come back to me because you're familiar with me. You know?"

I bite my lips together to keep from sobbing and nod. I get what he's saying, but it doesn't make it any easier. "I know what you mean," I mutter, my head lowered to keep from looking at him. I lean down and kiss his cheek, and he grabs at my hand as I walk away.

◆◆◆

Tyler shows Piper how to pluck the strings of his guitar, and I can't help but take picture after picture. To see them together, in one room, it's something I'm not sure I'll ever get used to. Piper's hair is braided over one shoulder, and the torn blue jeans and pink top she's wearing looks adorable on her. She didn't know what to think when I bought her clothes that actually had pink on them and fit. I wanted to cry and curse Eric at the same time at her reaction.

"There ya go, you got it." Tyler laughs, placing the guitar fully on Piper's lap. Looking the guitar over, it's close to the one that was in Lip's spare bedroom. I frown; I miss him so much. Everything reminds me of him. I heard a motorcycle yesterday, and I ran out the front door in nothing but a tank top and panties, thinking Lip was there to take Piper and me home. But it was just some old guy, although he seemed more thankful for the peepshow. I'm starting to question my sanity.

Grabbing my phone, I check my messages for the fifth time in the last hour, but there's nothing. He hasn't texted, hasn't called, and it's been days. Maybe he's decided he can't love me and Piper, that he just doesn't have enough love in him for that. Glancing from the phone to Tyler and Piper, I notice Tyler smile as wide as I've ever seen it, but it fades quickly as he looks me over.

"You okay, Cherry?"

I sigh loudly and toss the phone on the couch cushion.

"Still hasn't called?" Tyler purses his lips, and I shake my head.

"Screw him. If he can't accept you and," he looks at Piper, who is still playing the guitar, "then he doesn't deserve you or her." I bite at my bottom lip, because the thought of Lip not wanting to be in our lives after bringing us together is almost too much.

"He's just going through a lot with Tom's death and all," I defend, and Tyler huffs in irritation. I roll my eyes. Tyler wouldn't understand; he's never been with a chick after a week let alone falling in love with another person.

"I mean, at what point do you say, 'hey, enough is enough', Lindsay? A couple can only handle so much bullshit." Tyler shrugs, and I wince at my civilian name. I've grown to hate it compared to Cherry.

Cocking my head to the side, I narrow my eyes at Tyler's flippant tone. I don't agree with him, because I don't think a couple that cares about one another should ever just walk away when things get tough.

"Never," I respond. Tyler narrows his eyes in confusion.

"I think when two people love each other, you never get to that point. You never give up, and you never reach the point of enough," I clarify. Tyler's face looks like he was just slapped with reality, and it makes me smirk. One day, a girl is going to turn his world upside-down, and I hope to God I'm there for it.

"Hey, kiddo, let's go raid the cookie jar," Tyler suggests. Piper's eyes go wide, and she hands Tyler the guitar. Watching them enter the kitchen, I pick my phone back up, my fingers aching to type his number into a message. My phone dings and my heart jumps with it. Opening my messages, I find a text from Dani.

> **DANI:** Family get-together next week at the beach. You better be there with Piper.

I'm not sure if I should go; it feels weird not knowing where Lip and I are. My phone dings again.

> **DANI:** You're family. Be there or I'll just come and get you.

I laugh. I love that woman. Piper told me how nice Dani was to her when they met, that doesn't surprise me though. Dani is an amazing person, and family means everything to her. To know that I am her family no matter what, it's refreshing. I sigh and tell her we'll be there.

12

Lip

ONE WEEK LATER

"Lip, you coming to the get-together?" Dani asks, stacking trays of food. The club decided to have a big BBQ, trying to lift everyone's spirits after Tom's death, but I just can't wrap my head around it. Growing up, my mother was Catholic, and my father wasn't so much. When someone passed who was close to us, my mother made us mourn religiously, while my father went to the club and got his dick sucked to grieve.

"You need to go, been moping around here for a fucking week," Bull scorns. "I get it, brother. We all loved Tom Cat, but he gave his life so you fucking had one. Now get out there and fucking live it," Bull demands, his tone angry.

"Live it, as in go and find Cherry?"

Bull nods. "Please, I can't take this shit anymore. You always looking at your phone, hiding in your room—I'm about to buy you a box of tampons, son." Bull smirks, and I scoff.

Cherry staying at her brother's has nearly killed me. Seeing where she used to lay in our bed and where she used to throw her hair shit all over our bathroom counter, I feel like a piece of me is gone. I stay here at the club mostly so I don't have to notice her absence, or smell her scent around the house. All a reminder of how I fucked up, how I fuck everything up.

I want her in my life, and I want Piper in my life—that much has become clear to me. But how do I reassure her I want her daughter in my life? How do I say, 'hey, you fucked up, and I fucked up. Let's move forward'?

"Where is it?" I ask, knowing Bull is right. I need to get out of this fucking place for a while.

"The beach." Dani shrugs. "Should be fun, the kids love it there," she continues.

"I don't know," I mutter, grabbing another beer. I glance at my phone again then shake my head at myself and sigh. Here I am acting like a fucking chick checking my phone, hoping she calls me first. Knowing Cherry, she's waiting on me to come to her.

"Cherry will be there," Dani sing-songs. "You can stop checking that phone and just go to her, ya know."

My ears perk at Cherry's name. Just hearing another person say it drives the nail of loneliness in my heart. I saw a redheaded girl sitting at the club bar the other day, and my heart stopped, thinking it was Cherry. It wasn't her of course, and I looked like a damn fool for swinging the strange chick around by her arm like a crazy asshole.

"I don't know how to make things right," I answer honestly. Dani sighs heavily, flopping her purse on the counter.

"You guys just need to start over, forget everything that went wrong. She misses you, ya know. She wants to be with you. But she doesn't think you want to be with her because of her daughter." Dani's eyes furrow inward with an accusing glare.

"But I do," I flick my eyes to Dani's and she smiles sympathetically. "I wasn't sure at first, but I—" I lower my head and exhale a frustrated breath. "I'm miserable without them," I confess. "When I met Piper and saw how fragile she was, all I wanted to do was protect her. She reminds me of Cherry so much, and there's this piece of me that just wants to be their protector, their main source of security."

"Then fucking tell her that," Dani huffs. "You both fucked up, you both told some shitty lies. Nobody is worse than the other in this, but Cherry being my partner in crime, I'm just going to say that you are the fucking asshole in this. You need to go to her and stop with the pride bullshit." Dani lays it out there, no beating around the bush. As much as her flippant mouth angers me, she's fucking right.

"Thanks for the advice," I grumble sarcastically and stand from the counter. As much as Dani's words make sense, but why would Cherry believe anything I said after all the lies I've spoken? Why should she?

I saunter into my room in the back of the club and slam the door. I never thought I wanted kids, never thought I'd love someone, but now I don't know how I could live without Cherry and Piper. The way she's on my mind day and night, the thought that another guy is looking at what's mine, I know without a doubt I've fallen for her. Me running to her and spewing a bunch of apologies, though? That ain't Cherry's style. Hell, that ain't my style.

I spot Cherry's property patch lying on the floor. Stepping forward, I grab it, the smell of her making my dick swell. Bull gave me Cherry, and I fell in love with her. She taught me how to balance my dark and light. Without her, I'll dissolve into my own shadow. I can't help the man I am, but for fuck's sake, I'm not going to be the man who lets the one girl he's ever loved slip away.

Fisting the cut, I turn to the door, taking long strides out of the room.

Cherry is mine, whether she wants to be or not. I won't let her walk away that easily.

"Dani, wait up!" I holler.

I follow Dani and some of the guys to the beach, the whole time my heart slamming against my chest. What if she tells me she can't right now, that she needs to focus on Piper? I shake my head. Fuck that; I won't let her push me away with that bullshit.

I pull up to the beach and prop my bike on its kickstand.

"Good luck, brother." Bobby smirks, patting me on the back as he walks past. Asshole.

Red hair catches my attention, and my heart sinks. *There she is. Fuck, she's beautiful.* She's wearing a two-piece mint green bikini, her red hair vibrant as ever with the sun shining through it. She still has that patch on her stomach, though, where she was shot. She and I will have matching scars now, ones that prove our devotion to one another. How many couples can say I took a bullet for my significant other?

I stomp forward, sand filling my boots, Cherry's cut in my hand. A guy with long, blond hair and flowery trunks walks up to Cherry, and my jaw clenches. He's fucking flirting with my girl, and that isn't happening.

Striding up beside Cherry, I sneer at the punk.

"Sup?" He juts his chin out, but I don't respond. I convey all I need to say in my death stare. The guy stammers, looking around awkwardly like he just realized there are a bunch of Devil's Dust bikers around, and walks away like a fucking coward.

Cherry turns, and I swear to God the words I was going to

speak lodge in my throat. Fuck, she's breathtaking.

"Really, Lip?" she huffs. "We were just talking." She shakes her head.

I wanted to come off half-decent when I approached Cherry, but after seeing that punk flirt with her, I can't think of anything but claiming her ass in front of everyone. Using one of my hands, I fist her hair and pull her head toward mine.

"You're mine, Cherry. I won't let you walk away, and I sure as hell won't let some punk try and take my place," I scorn. Her lips part, and her eyes grow heavy with lust. "I want you in my life, and I want Piper in my life," I mutter, easing my grip, my fingers flowing through her red hair. "I fucked up. I fucked up bad, babe." My eyes narrow as regret stings my chest.

"I'm not going anywhere, Lip, and we want to be a part of your life, too," she breathes heavily. "But we are a package. It's me and my daughter or nothing."

My eyes go wide, and my jaw tenses. "Cherry, I wouldn't want it any other way. What kind of a man do you think I am?" I grimace.

Cherry tries to fight a smile, turning her head. "I don't know. The kind I can't seem to escape, I guess." Pulling her gaze back to mine, those gray eyes drive right into me.

"Damn right. You and I are something our worlds didn't expect, baby, but I'd be damn if my world didn't have you in it." I grab the sides of her face, pulling her lips close to mine.

That gorgeous smile breaks through, and I can't help but smirk in response.

"I've missed you, Lip," she whispers.

"God, I've missed you," I groan. Closing my eyes, I breathe her in, the scent of her comforting.

I smash my lips to hers, pushing my tongue through her sweet lips, the taste of fruit filling my mouth as I devour her in front of fucking everyone. My mouth begs yet demands, her mouth accepting yet teasing. Pulling away from her, I kiss her bottom lip tenderly.

"I'm sorry I didn't come back, Lip. I wanted to, but I needed to know you really wanted to be with me and Piper." She frowns and brushes her hair from her face, scowling.

"Don't you ever fucking leave me again, Cherry," I snarl angrily. "You're mine." I hold up the cut, and her eyes look it over.

"Be my ol' lady," I demand rather than ask. She glances at it again then eyes me. "I'm about to place it on you in about three fucking seconds," I threaten. Her eyes flick to mine, and I smirk.

She giggles, but it soon fades. "If you hurt me, Lip..." She pauses, her lips parting that sexy way they do. "I'll kill you this time."

"Won't happen," I whisper against her lips. "I love you, Cherry. If I've learned anything in this, it's you have the power to destroy me." Her cheeks flush with my confession, and her fingers mess with my cut.

"I'll tell my brother that Piper and I are moving back then," she says, smiling.

"I already told some guys to go pick your shit up already." I smirk, and her mouth pops open with shock. A speaker set up on a table plays "Never Going To Be Alone" by Nickelback. Glancing back at Cherry as she pulls the cut on her, I can't help myself.

"Show me your Devil horns?" I ask in the sexiest draw I can muster. A smile curls her lips and she sticks her tongue out, her hands pulling up two Devil horns.

"Leather, Devil horns, and some tongue action... Fucking sexy." I wink and tug her close. She laughs, slapping me in the shoulder.

"LIP!" Piper hollers, running toward me, Zane right on her

tail. I scowl at the little fucker and pick Piper up.

"I love your swimsuit," I admire, poking at the penguin-sequined suit. I took her shopping for some clothes, and I swear to God I'll never shop with a girl again. It took Piper two hours to pick out four outfits, and she then had to try every one of them on. I thought I was going to die sitting in that fucking store.

"Thanks. My mom got it for me." She smiles, glancing at Cherry.

My phone rings, and I set Piper down.

"I'm going to take her to get some food before it's all gone," Cherry states, grabbing Piper's hand.

"Yeah, I'll be there in a sec, babe."

Not recognizing the call, I accept it out of curiosity.

"Hello?"

"Brother," Zeek rasps into the phone, and my eyes widen, my fingers curling around the phone in a death grip.

"You're supposed to be dead," I snarl. After the helicopter took off, the Sin City Outlaws were gone. The only thing left was a pool of blood where Zeek was laying. I thought for sure I had killed him.

"An outlaw doesn't die so easily, I'm afraid." He chuckles. "This isn't over... brother," he snarls before the line goes dead.

My nostrils flare with rage, and my hand nearly crushes the phone.

I'll kill that son of a bitch if it's the last thing I do.

Epilogue

Cherry

ONE MONTH LATER

EVERYTHING'S BEEN GOING SMOOTHLY SINCE PIPER AND I MOVED back into Lip's house. Lip and I are stronger than ever, and the sex is mind-blowing! I ground Lip's beast that dwells within, and help bring out the good he never thought he was capable of. I can actually say I have all of Lip now, and I wouldn't have it any other way. Convict, angry, furious, but also gentle and caring. He's Lip, and he's mine.

Lip completely redid his spare bedroom into My Little Pony for Piper, and spoils her beyond any little girl's imagination. It's crazy to see him care for her so much after swearing he never wanted kids for so long. But he's wrapped around Piper's little finger, and he wouldn't have it any other way. Piper has taught Lip and me a lot about life that we never knew we were missing.

I finally feel at peace—well, as much peace as I will allow

myself. I'm constantly looking over my shoulder expecting someone to take my happiness away, to steal my hope and devotion right from under my feet, but it hasn't happened yet.

Lip seems on edge since his brother threatened him. He suggested a lockdown, but I refused. I couldn't put Piper in a lockdown after just getting her settled in. I don't want to scare her. I know Lip is planning on revenge, but I'm pleading with him not to ride into Vegas to revenge Tom's death, that it's too risky. He said nothing has been decided yet, but I know he and the club are discussing tactics. The Devil's Dust and The Sin City Outlaws will be enemies for life now. Blood has been spilled, tainting any lines of respect that might have been there.

So far, nothing has happened—no eerie phone calls, nobody trying to kill us. I think the bad blood between Lip and his brother isn't going anywhere, but I believe as long as each club stays within their territory, no blood will be shed. *If* they stay on their own territory that is. Lip's mom sold her house and bought an RV, said to fuck with both of the boys and is traveling the country one campground at a time. She said the boys have too much of their father in them, and she couldn't stand to see them shed their own bloodline. I don't blame her, though. What do you do when both of your sons are trying to kill each other?

"Hey, Mom, is it okay if we go visit Zane?"

I scowl. Dani's son has really been sniffing around my daughter's trail since she's been here.

"I think tonight we're staying in to watch movies," I counter. She shrugs and starts playing on her iPad that Lip got her. She's actually very easy to raise; I haven't had much trouble out of her, thankfully.

Piper has asked about her dad once. I didn't really know

what to say to her, 'cause I don't know what happened. Lip won't tell me, either, saying if I never know then I don't ever have to worry about lying to Piper.

So I told Piper her daddy went away for the bad things he did and I don't know when he'll be back. She seemed sad at first, but hasn't said a word about him since. I hate that it had to come to this between Eric and me, but one thing a man should know is you don't come between a woman and her child. Ever!

"Time for the movie!" Lip hollers.

Climbing off my bed, Piper and I head into the living room where Minions is playing on the TV. Lip didn't want kids when we met, but I swear to God, he's the perfect dad. He knows all of Piper's quirks. Like she doesn't like ketchup on her hot dog but on the side, and how she loves veggies so he always doubles her portion at dinner. It's the little things. We sit on the couch, getting comfy, and I rest my head on Lip's shoulder while Piper snuggles into his ribs on the other side of him.

"Hey, Lip," I whisper as I think back to the other day. Lip had mentioned he wanted to knock me up. I don't know if he was joking, speaking in the moment, or serious, but I'm about to find out.

"Yeah?" he replies around a mouthful of popcorn.

"I stopped taking my birth control," I mutter. He pauses for a second, and my heart stammers.

He pulls me close. "Good," he mutters into my forehead.

I smile; our family is about to get a little bigger. I've grown since I've met Lip, and I think he has, too. We've both learned things aren't so scary once you get through them; in fact, it just makes you stronger. The sad loneliness that used to creep into my soul has gone, leaving it filled with happiness and hope. Nothing can stop us now because together we're the Devil's

Dust, and we take what we want.

THE END

COMING SOON

ACKNOWLEDGEMENTS

Breathe Devil Dust lovers.... Just breathe. This is not the end of the Devil's Dust series. I am doing a spin off into another series, it will be Zeek in the Sin City Outlaws! I can't wait to get in his twisted mind!

Writing this book was so much fun! Talk about a roller coaster of emotions, huh? I want to thank my husband (PA) he has helped me so much! He has stayed up at night discussing plots twists, and cooking dinner almost every night.

Thank you, my reader! Without you, this book never would have been written. You are my biggest support, and I fucking love every one of you!

My betas, you deserve hugs and chocolate. Stephanie, Brie, Rebecca, and Andrea you helped me shape this story up to its finest. THANK YOU!

I also want to thank every blog that signed up for the tour, and cover reveal. You guys do a big thing for us authors, and I appreciate your time and effort in help get my work out there! Rock Stars Of Romance, you did awesome and I love you!

Oh man, can I get a HELL YEAH for Furious Fotog, and the models Chase Ketron, and Ryian Pettersen?! That cover is FUCKING HOT!

Little Devil's, thank you for your continuous support and love! You have been there since day one, and have stuck by my side.

XOXO

ALSO BY M.N. FORGY

What Doesn't Destroy Us
(The Devil's Dust #1)

The Scars That Define Us
(The Devil's Dust #2)

The Broken Pieces Of Us
(A Devil's Dust Novella)

The Fear That Divides Us
(The Devil's Dust #3)

Love That Defies Us
(A Devil's Dust Novella)

ABOUT THE AUTHOR

M.N. Forgy was raised in Missouri where she still lives with her family. She's a soccer mom by day and a saucy writer by night.

M.N. Forgy started writing at a young age but never took it seriously until years later, as a stay-at-home mom, she opened her laptop and started writing again. As a role model for her children, she felt she couldn't live with the "what if" anymore and finally took a chance on her character's story.

So, with her glass of wine in hand and a stray Barbie sharing her seat, she continues to create and please her fans.

STALK HER

Website:

www.mnforgy.com

Goodreads:

www.goodreads.com/author/show/8110729.M_N_Forgy

Facebook:

www.facebook.com/pages/M-N-Forgy/625362330873655

Twitter:

http://twitter.com/M_N_FORGY

Newsletter:

www.mnforgy.com/newsletter/

M.N. Forgy's Reader Addicts Group:

www.facebook.com/groups/480379925434507/

Made in the USA
San Bernardino, CA
27 November 2015